THE LYING GAME

BY

SARA SHEPARD

An Imprint of HarperCollinsPublishers

HarperTeen is an imprint of HarperCollins Publishers.

The Lying Game

alloyentertainment
Produced by Alloy Entertainment
151 West 26th Street, New York, NY 10001

Library of Congress Cataloging-in-Publication Data
Shepard, Sara, 1977–
    The Lying Game / by Sara Shepard. — 1st ed.
        p.   cm.
    Summary: Seventeen-year-old Emma Paxton steps into the life
of her long-lost twin Sutton to solve her murder, while Sutton looks
on from her afterlife.
    ISBN 978-0-06-209154-3 (int. ed.)
    ISBN 978-0-06-186971-6 (pbk.)
    [1. Twins—Fiction.   2. Sisters—Fiction.   3. Murder—Fiction.
4. Dead—Fiction.   5. Mystery and detective stories.]   I. Title.
PZ7.S54324Ly   2010   2010040332
[Fic]—dc22   CIP
                                                              AC

Design by Liz Dresner

12 13 14 15   LP/BV   10 9 8 7 6 5 4 3

First paperback edition, 2011

We are what we pretend to be, so we must be careful about what we pretend to be.

—KURT VONNEGUT

PROLOGUE

I woke up in a dingy claw-foot bathtub in an unfamiliar pink-tiled bathroom. A stack of *Maxim*s sat next to the toilet, green toothpaste globbed in the sink, and white drips streaked the mirror. The window showed a dark sky and a full moon. What day of the week was it? Where was I? A frat house at the U of A? Someone's apartment? I could barely remember that my name was Sutton Mercer, or that I lived in the foothills of Tucson, Arizona. I had no idea where my purse was, and I didn't have a clue where I'd parked my car. Actually, what kind of car did I drive? Had someone slipped me something?

"Emma?" a guy's voice called from another room. "You home?"

"I'm busy!" called a voice close by.

A tall, thin girl opened the bathroom door, her tangled dark hair hanging in her face. "Hey!" I leapt to my feet. "Someone's in here already!" My body felt tingly, as if it had fallen asleep. When I looked down, it seemed like I was flickering on and off, like I was under a strobe light. *Freaky. Someone definitely slipped me something.*

The girl didn't seem to hear me. She stumbled forward, her face covered in shadows.

"Hel*lo*?" I cried, climbing out of the tub. She didn't look over. "Are you deaf?" Nothing. She pumped a bottle of lavender-scented lotion and rubbed it on her arms.

The door flung open again, and a snub-nosed, unshaven teenage guy burst in. "Oh." His gaze flew to the girl's tight-fitting T-shirt, which said NEW YORK NEW YORK ROLLER COASTER on the front. "I didn't know you were in here, Emma."

"That's maybe why the door was *closed*?" Emma pushed him out and slammed it shut. She turned back to the mirror. I stood right behind her. "Hey!" I cried again.

Finally, she looked up. My eyes darted to the mirror to meet her gaze. But when I looked into the glass, I screamed.

Because Emma looked exactly like me.

And I wasn't there.

Emma turned and walked out of the bathroom, and I followed as if something was yanking me along behind her. Who was this girl? Why did we look the same? Why was I invisible? And why couldn't I remember, well, *anything*? The wrong memories snapped into aching, nostalgic focus—the glittering sunset over the Catalinas, the smell of the lemon trees in my backyard in the morning, the feel of cashmere slippers on my toes. But other things, the most important things, had become muffled and fuzzy, as if I'd lived my whole life underwater. I saw vague shapes, but I couldn't make out what they were. I couldn't remember what I'd done for any summer vacations, who my first kiss had been with, or what it felt like to feel the sun on my face or dance to my favorite song. What *was* my favorite song? And even worse, every second that passed, things got fuzzier and fuzzier. Like they were disappearing.

Like *I* was disappearing.

But then I concentrated really hard and I heard a muffled scream. And suddenly it was like I was somewhere else. I felt pain shooting through my body, before a final, sleepy sensation of my muscles surrendering. As my eyes slowly closed, I saw a blurry, shadowy figure standing over me.

"Oh my God," I whispered.

No wonder Emma didn't see me. No wonder I wasn't in the mirror. I wasn't really here.

I was dead.

❧ 1 ❧

THE DEAD RINGER

Emma Paxton carried her canvas tote and a glass of iced tea out the back door of her new foster family's home on the outskirts of Las Vegas. Cars swished and grumbled on the nearby expressway, and the air smelled heavily of exhaust and the local water treatment plant. The only decorations in the backyard were dusty free weights, a rusted bug zapper, and kitschy terra-cotta statues.

It was a far cry from my backyard in Tucson, which was desert-landscaped to perfection and had a wooden swing set I used to pretend was a castle. Like I said, it was weird and random which details I still remembered and which ones had evaporated away. For the last hour, I'd been following Emma trying to make sense of her life and willing myself to remember my own. Not like I had a choice. Everywhere she went, I went. I wasn't entirely sure how I knew these things about Emma, either—they just appeared in my head as I watched her, like a text message popping up in an inbox. I knew the details of her life better than I did my own.

Emma dropped the tote on the faux wrought-iron patio table, plopped down in a plastic lawn chair, and craned her neck upward. The only nice thing about this patio was that it faced away from the casinos, offering a large swath of clear, uninterrupted sky. The moon dangled halfway up the horizon, a bloated alabaster wafer. Emma's gaze drifted to two bright, familiar stars to the east. At nine years old, Emma had wistfully named the star on the right the Mom Star, the star on the left the Dad Star, and the smaller, brightly twinkling spot just below them the Emma Star. She'd made up all kinds of fairy tales about these stars, pretending that they were her real family and that one day they'd all be reunited on earth like they were in the sky.

Emma had been in foster care for most of her life. She'd never met her dad, but she remembered her mother, with whom she had lived until she was five years old. Her mom's name was Becky. She was a slender woman who loved shouting out the answers to *Wheel of Fortune*, dancing around the living room to Michael Jackson songs, and reading tabloids that ran stories like BABY BORN FROM PUMPKIN! and BAT BOY LIVES! Becky used to send Emma on scavenger hunts around their apartment complex, the prize always being a tube of used lipstick or a mini Snickers. She bought Emma frilly tutus and lacy dresses from Goodwill for dress-up. She read Emma *Harry Potter* before bed, making up different voices for every character.

But Becky was like a scratch-off lottery ticket—Emma never quite knew what she was going to get with her. Sometimes Becky spent the whole day crying on the couch, her face contorted and her cheeks streaked with tears. Other times she would drag Emma to the nearest department store and buy her two of everything. "Why do I need two pairs of the same shoes?" Emma would ask. A faraway look would come over Becky's face. "In case the first pair gets dirty, Emmy."

Becky could be very forgetful, too—like the time she left Emma at a Circle K. Suddenly unable to breathe, Emma had watched her mother's car vanish down the shimmering highway. The clerk on duty gave Emma an orange Popsicle and let her sit on the ice freezer at the front of the store while he made some phone calls. When Becky finally returned, she scooped up Emma and gave her a huge hug. For once, she didn't even complain when Emma dripped sticky orange Popsicle goo on her dress.

One summer night not long after that, Emma slept

over with Sasha Morgan, a friend from kindergarten. She woke up in the morning to Mrs. Morgan standing in the doorway, a sick look on her face. Apparently, Becky had left a note under the Morgans' front door, saying she'd "gone on a little trip." Some trip *that* was—it had lasted almost thirteen years and counting.

When no one could track down Becky, Sasha's parents turned Emma over to an orphanage in Reno. Prospective adopters had no interest in a five-year-old—they all wanted babies they could mold into mini versions of themselves—so Emma lived in group homes, then foster homes. Though Emma would always love her mom, she couldn't say she missed her—at least not Miserable Becky, Manic Becky, or the Lunatic Becky who'd forgotten her at the Circle K. She did miss the *idea* of a mom though: someone stable and constant who knew her past, looked forward to her future, and loved her unconditionally. Emma had invented the Mom, Dad, and Emma stars in the sky not based on anything she'd ever known, but instead on what she wished she'd had.

The sliding glass door opened, and Emma wheeled around. Travis, her new foster mom's eighteen-year-old son, strutted out and settled on top of the patio table. "Sorry about bursting in on you in the bathroom," he said.

"It's okay," Emma muttered bitterly, slowly inching

away from Travis's outstretched legs. She was pretty sure Travis *wasn't* sorry. He practically made a sport of trying to see her naked. Today, Travis wore a blue ball cap pulled low over his eyes, a ratty, oversized plaid shirt, and baggy jean shorts with the crotch sagging almost to his knees. There was patchy stubble on his pointy-nosed, thin-lipped, pea-eyed face; he wasn't man enough to actually grow facial hair. His bloodshot brown eyes narrowed lasciviously. Emma could feel his gaze on her, canvassing her tight-fitting NEW YORK NEW YORK camisole, bare, tanned arms, and long legs.

With a grunt, Travis reached into his shirt pocket, pulled out a joint, and lit up. As he blew a plume of smoke in her direction, the bug zapper glowed to life. With a crisp snap and a fizzle of blue light, it annihilated yet another mosquito. If only it could do that to Travis, too.

Back off, pot breath, Emma wanted to say. *It's no wonder no girl will get near you.* But she bit her tongue; the comment would have to go into her Comebacks I Should've Said file, a list she'd compiled in a black cloth notebook hidden in her top drawer. The Comebacks list, CISS for short, was filled with pithy, snarky remarks Emma had longed to say to foster moms, creepy neighbors, bitchy girls at school, and a whole host of others. For the most part, Emma held her tongue—it was easier to keep quiet, not make trouble, and become whatever type of girl a situation needed her to be. Along the way, Emma had picked up some pretty impressive coping skills: At age ten, she honed her reflexes when Mr. Smythe, a tempestuous foster parent, got into one of his object-throwing moods. When Emma lived in Henderson with Ursula and Steve, the two hippies who grew their own food but were clueless about how to cook it, Emma had begrudgingly taken over kitchen duties, whipping up zucchini bread, veggie gratins, and some awesome stir-fries.

It had been just two months since Emma had moved in with Clarice, a single mom who worked as a bartender for VIP gamblers at The M Resort. Since then, Emma had spent the summer taking pictures, playing marathon games of Minesweeper on the banged-up BlackBerry her friend Alex had given her before she'd left her last foster home in Henderson, and working part-time operating the roller coaster at the New York New York casino. And, oh yeah, avoiding Travis as much as she could.

It hadn't started out that way, though. At first, Emma had tried to make nice with her new foster brother, hoping they could be friends. It wasn't like every foster family sucked and she'd never made friends with the other kids; it just sometimes took a lot of effort on her part. She'd feigned interest in all of the YouTube videos Travis watched about how to be a small-time thug: how to unlock a car with a cell phone, how to hack soda machines, how to open a padlock with a beer can. She'd suffered through a couple of Ultimate Fighting Championship matches on TV, even attempting to learn the wrestling-move vocabulary. But the nicety had ended for Emma a week later, when Travis tried to feel her up while she was standing in front of the open fridge. "You've been so friendly," he'd murmured in her ear, before Emma had "accidentally" kicked him in the crotch.

All Emma wanted to do was get through her senior year here. It was the end of August, and school started on Wednesday. She had the option of leaving Clarice's when she turned eighteen in two weeks, but that would mean quitting school, finding an apartment, and getting a full-time job to pay rent. Clarice had told Emma's social worker that Emma could stay here until she got her diploma. *Nine more months*, Emma chanted to herself like a mantra. She could hold on until then, couldn't she?

Travis took another hit off the joint. "You want some?" he asked in a choked voice, holding the smoke in his lungs.

"No thanks," Emma said stiffly.

Travis finally exhaled. "Sweet little Emma," he said in a syrupy voice. "But you aren't always this good, are you?"

Emma craned her neck up at the sky and paused on the Mom, Dad, and Emma stars again. Farther down the horizon was a star she'd recently named the Boyfriend Star. It seemed to be hovering closer than usual to the Emma Star tonight—maybe it was a sign. Perhaps this would be the year she'd meet her perfect boyfriend, someone she was destined to be with.

"Shit," Travis whispered suddenly, noticing something inside the house. He quickly stubbed out the joint and threw it under Emma's chair just as Clarice appeared on the back deck. Emma scowled at the joint's smoldering tip—nice of Travis to try to pin it on her—and covered it with her shoe.

Clarice still had on her work uniform: a tuxedo jacket, silky white shirt, and black bow tie. Her dyed blond hair was slicked into an impeccable French twist, and her mouth was smeared with bright fuchsia lipstick that didn't flatter anyone's skin tone. She held a white envelope in her hands.

"I'm missing two hundred and fifty dollars," Clarice announced flatly. The empty envelope crinkled. "It was a personal tip from Bruce Willis. He signed one of the bills. I was going to put it in my scrapbook."

Emma sighed sympathetically. The only thing she'd gleaned about Clarice was that she was absolutely obsessed with celebrities. She kept a scrapbook describing every celeb interaction she'd ever had, and glossy signed head shots lined the wall space in the breakfast nook. Occasionally, Clarice and Emma ran into each other in the kitchen around noon, which was the crack of dawn for Clarice after a bar shift. The only thing Clarice ever wanted to talk about was how she'd had a long conversation with the latest winner of *American Idol* the night before, or how a certain action film starlet's boobs were definitely fake, or how the host of a dating reality show was kind of a bitch. Emma was always intrigued. She didn't care much about celebrity dirt but dreamed of someday being an investigative journalist. Not that she ever told Clarice that. Not that Clarice had ever asked anything personal about her.

"The money was in this envelope in my bedroom when I left for work this afternoon." Clarice stared straight at Emma, her eyes squinting. "Now it's not. Is there something you want to tell me?"

Emma sneaked a peek at Travis, but he was fiddling with his BlackBerry. As he scrolled through his photos, Emma noticed a blurry shot of her at the bathroom mirror. Her hair was wet, and she'd knotted a towel under her arms.

Cheeks burning, Emma turned to Clarice. "I don't know anything about it," she said in the most diplomatic voice she could muster. "But maybe you should ask Travis. He might know."

"Ex*cuse* me?" Travis's voice cracked. "*I* didn't take any money."

Emma made an incredulous noise at the back of her throat.

"You know I wouldn't do that, Mom," Travis went on. He stood and pulled up his shorts around his waist. "I know how hard you work. I *did* see Emma go into your room today though."

"What?" Emma whirled around to face him. "I did not!"

"Did too," Travis shot back. As soon as he turned his back on his mom, his expression morphed from a fake smile to a wrinkled-nose, narrowed-eyes glower.

Emma gaped. It was amazing how calmly he lied. "I've seen you go through your mom's purse," she announced.

Clarice leaned against the table, twisting her mouth to the right. "*Travis* did that?"

"No, I didn't." Travis pointed accusingly at Emma. "Why would you believe her? You don't even *know* this girl."

"I don't need money!" Emma pressed her hands to her chest. "I have a job! I'm fine!" She'd been working for years. Before the roller coaster, she'd had a job as Head Goat Girl at a local petting zoo, she'd dressed up as a toga-robed Statue of Liberty and stood on the street corner to advertise a local credit union, and she'd even sold knives door-to-door. She'd saved more than two grand and stashed it in a half-empty Tampax box in her bedroom. Travis hadn't found the money yet, probably because the tampons were a better security system against creepy boys than a rabid pack of Rottweilers.

Clarice gazed at Travis, who was giving her a sickening, pouty smile. As she creased the empty envelope back and forth in her hands, a suspicious look crossed her face. It looked as if she momentarily saw through Travis's facade.

"Look." Travis walked over to his mom and put his arm on her shoulder. "I think you need to know what Emma's really all about." He pulled his BlackBerry from his pocket again and began to fiddle with the click wheel.

"What do you mean?" Emma walked over to them.

Travis gave her a sanctimonious look, hiding the BlackBerry screen from view. "I was going to talk to you about this in private. But it's too late for that now."

"Talk to me about *what*?" Emma lunged forward, making the citronella candle in the center of the table wobble.

"*You* know what." Travis tapped away on the keyboard with his thumbs. A mosquito buzzed around his head, but he didn't bother to flick it away. "You're a sick freak."

"What do you mean, Travis?" Clarice's fuchsia-lined lips pursed worriedly.

Finally, Travis lowered the BlackBerry so everyone could see. "This," he announced.

A stiff, hot wind blew against Emma's cheek, the dusty air irritating her eyes. The blue-black evening sky seemed to darken a few shades. Travis breathed heavily next to her, reeking of pot smoke, and pulled up a generic video uploading site. With a flourish, he typed in the keyword *SuttonInAZ* and hit PLAY.

A video slowly loaded. A handheld camera panned over a clearing. No sound escaped from the speakers, as if the microphone had been muted. The camera whipped around to show a figure sitting in a chair with a black blindfold covering half her face. A round silver locket on a thick chain clung to a bony, feminine collarbone.

The girl thrashed her head frantically back and forth, the locket bouncing wildly. The picture went dark for a moment, and suddenly someone slipped behind her and pulled the necklace chain back so that it pressed up against the girl's throat. The girl's head arched back. She flailed her arms and kicked her legs.

"Oh my God." Clarice's hand flew to her mouth.

"What *is* this?" Emma whispered.

The strangler pulled the chain harder and harder. Whoever it was had a mask over his head, so Emma couldn't see his face. After about thirty seconds, the girl in the video stopped struggling and went limp.

Emma backed away from the screen. Had they just watched someone *die*? What the hell? And what did this have to do with her?

The camera remained fixed on the blindfolded girl. She wasn't moving. Then the picture went momentarily dark again. When an image snapped back on the screen, the camera was tilted over, fallen on the ground. Emma could still see a sideways shot of the figure in the chair. Someone walked up to the girl and pulled the blindfold off her head. After a long pause, the girl coughed. Tears dotted her eyes. The corners of her mouth pulled down. She blinked slowly. For a split second before the screen went dark, she stared half consciously into the lens.

Emma's jaw dropped to her worn Converse sneakers.

Clarice gasped loudly.

"Ha," Travis said triumphantly. "I *told* you."

Emma stared at the girl's huge, blue eyes, slightly upturned nose, and round face. She looked *exactly* like her.

That was because the girl in the video was me.

2

THAT'S RIGHT, BLAME THE FOSTER KID

Emma grabbed the phone from Travis's hands and started the clip over, staring hard at the image. As the person reached out and began to choke the blindfolded girl, fear streaked through Emma's stomach. When the anonymous hand pulled off the blindfold, Emma's identical face appeared on the screen. Emma had the same thick, wavy, chestnut-brown hair as the girl in the movie. The same round chin. The same pink lips kids used to tease Emma about, saying they were puffy as though she'd had an allergic reaction. She shuddered.

I watched the video again in horror, too. The locket glinting in the light caused a tiny shard of a memory to surface: I remembered lifting the lid of my baby box, pulling out the locket from under a half-chewed teething giraffe, a lacy receiving blanket, and a pair of knit booties, and putting it around my neck. The video itself brought back nothing though. I didn't know if it had happened in my backyard . . . or three states away. I wished I could slap my post-death memory across the face.

But the video had to be how I died, right? Especially from that quick flashback I'd had when I'd awakened in Emma's bathroom: that face close to mine, my heart beating hard, my murderer standing above me. But I had no idea how this whole death thing worked: Had I popped into Emma's world the moment after I'd taken my last breath, or was it days—*months*—later? And how did the video get posted online? Had my family seen it? My friends? Was this some kind of twisted ransom note?

Emma finally glanced up from the screen. "Where did you find this?" she asked Travis.

"Guess someone didn't know she was a star on the Internet, huh?" Travis snatched the phone from her hands.

Clarice raked her fingers through her hair. She kept glancing from the video screen to Emma's face. "Is this what you do for fun?" she asked Emma in a hoarse voice.

"She probably does it to get high." Travis paced around the patio like a prowling lion. "I knew some girls at school last year who were, like, obsessed with it. One of them almost died."

Clarice clapped her hand over her mouth. "What's wrong with you?"

Emma's eyes darted from Travis to Clarice. "Wait, no. That's not *me*. The girl in this video is someone else."

Travis rolled his eyes. "Someone who looks exactly like you?" he deadpanned. "Let me guess. A long-lost sister? An evil twin?"

There was a low rumbling of thunder in the distance. The breeze smelled like wet pavement, a telltale sign that a storm was close. *A long-lost sister.* The idea ignited in Emma's mind like a Fourth of July sparkler. It was possible. She'd asked Social Services once if Becky had had any other kids she'd abandoned along the way, but they said they didn't know.

A thought burned in my mind, too: I was adopted. That much I remembered. It was common knowledge in my family; my parents had never tried to hide it. They'd told me my adoption had been a last-minute scramble and they'd never met my birth mother. *Could* it be possible? It explained why I was literally stuck to this girl who looked just like me, following her around as if our souls had been tethered together.

Clarice tapped her long nails on the table. "I don't tolerate lying or stealing in this house, Emma."

Emma felt like she'd just been kicked in the stomach. "That's not me in the video," she protested. "And I didn't steal from you. I swear."

Emma reached for her canvas bag on the patio table. All she had to do was call Eddie, her manager at the roller coaster. He'd vouch for her hours today. But Travis got to her bag first, knocking it over so all of its contents spilled out onto the pavement.

"Oops!" he cried gleefully.

Emma watched helplessly as her tattered copy of *The Sun Also Rises* landed on a dusty anthill. A crumpled ticket for a free all-you-can-eat BBQ buffet at MGM Grand got caught in the breeze and drifted toward Travis's free weights. Her BlackBerry and a tube of cherry-flavored ChapStick skittered to a stop next to a terra-cotta turtle. Last but not least, there was a suspicious-looking wad of bills held together with a thick purple rubber band. The wad thudded to the patio, bounced once, and landed in front of Clarice's chunky heels.

Emma was too stunned to speak. Clarice snatched the money and licked her pointer finger to count it. "Two hundred," she said when she was finished. She held up a twenty with blue scribble in the upper left-hand corner. Even in the fading light, Emma could see a big looped *B*, presumably for *Bruce Willis*. "What did you do with the other fifty?"

A neighbor's wind chimes tinkled in the distance. Emma's insides were frozen. "I-I have no idea how that got in my bag."

Behind her, Travis snickered. *"Busted."* He was leaning casually against the stucco wall, just to the left of the big round thermometer. He crossed his arms over his chest, and his top lip was curled in a sneer.

The hair on the back of Emma's neck rose. All at once, she understood what was going on. Her lips started to twitch, just like they always did when she was about to lose it. *"You* did this!" She pointed a finger at Travis. "You set me up!"

Travis smirked. Something inside Emma broke loose. Screw keeping the peace. Screw adapting to whatever the foster family needed her to be. She shot for him, grabbing Travis by his meaty neck.

"Emma!" Clarice shrieked, pulling her off her son. Emma staggered backward, bumping against one of the patio chairs.

Clarice spun Emma around so that they were face-to-face. "What's gotten into you?"

Emma didn't answer. She glowered at Travis again. He had flattened himself against the wall, his arms in front of him protectively, but there was a thrilled glow in his eyes.

Clarice turned away from Emma, sank down in the chair, and rubbed her eyes. Mascara smudged on her fingertips. "This isn't working," she said softly after a moment. She raised her head and gazed soberly at Emma. "I thought you were a sweet, nice girl who wouldn't cause any trouble, Emma, but this is too much for us."

"I didn't *do* anything," Emma whispered. "I swear."

Clarice pulled out a nail file and started nervously sawing on her pinkie. "You can stay until your birthday, but after that you're on your own."

Emma blinked. "You're kicking me *out?*"

Clarice stopped filing. Her face softened. "I'm sorry," she said gently. "But this is the best choice for all of us."

Emma turned away and stared hard at the ugly block wall at the back of the property.

"I wish things were different." Clarice pulled the sliding door open and padded back into the house. As soon as she was out of view, Travis peeled himself off the wall and straightened up to full height.

He sauntered casually around Emma, scooped up the tiny nub of the joint that was still under the chair, blew off the bits of dried grass that had stuck to the tip, and dropped it into his enormous pants pocket. "You're lucky she didn't press charges," he said in a slimy voice.

Emma said nothing as he swaggered back into the house. She wanted to leap up and claw his eyes out, but her legs felt like they had been filled with heavy wet clay. Her eyes blurred with tears. *This* again. Every time a foster family told Emma she had to move on, she invariably thought back to the cold, lonely moment when she'd realized Becky had ditched her for good. Emma had stayed a week at Sasha Morgan's house while the police tried to track down her mom. She'd put on a brave face, playing Candy Land, watching *Dora the Explorer*, and making scavenger hunts for Sasha like the ones Becky had masterminded for her. But every night in the glow of Sasha's Cinderella night-light, Emma struggled to read the parts of *Harry Potter* she could understand—which weren't many. She'd barely mastered *The Cat in the Hat*. She needed her mom to read the big words. She needed her mom to do the voices. Even now, it still hurt.

The patio was silent. The wind blew the hanging spider plants and palm trees sideways. Emma stared blankly at the terra-cotta sculpture of a shapely woman that Travis and his friends liked to dry-hump. So that was that. No more staying here until the end of high school. No more applying to a photojournalism program at USC . . . or even community college. She had nowhere to go. No one to turn to. Unless . . .

Suddenly, the image from the video fluttered through her mind once more. *A long-lost sister.* Her heart lifted. She had to find her.

If only I could have told her it was too late.

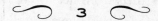

3

YOU KNOW IT'S TRUE IF YOU
READ IT ON FACEBOOK

An hour later, Emma stood in her little bedroom, her Army-Navy bags splayed open on the floor. Why wait to pack? She also held her phone to her ear, talking to Alexandra Stokes, her best friend from back in Henderson.

"You could always stay with me," Alex offered after Emma finished telling her that Clarice had just kicked her out. "I can talk to my mom. She might be cool with it."

Emma shut her eyes. She and Alex had been on the cross-country team together last year. They'd both wiped out on a downhill part of a trail run on the first day of practice, and they'd become fast friends while the nurse cleaned their wounds with ultra-stingy hydrogen per-oxide. She and Emma had spent their entire junior year sneaking into the casinos and taking pictures of celebrities and lookalikes with Alex's Canon SLR, trolling the pawn shops but never buying anything, and sunning themselves at Lake Mead on weekends.

"That's a lot to ask of your family." Emma removed a pile of vintage T-shirts from her top drawer and plopped them into the duffel. She'd stayed with the Stokeses for a couple of weeks after Ursula and Steve relocated to the Florida Keys. Emma had had a great time, but Ms. Stokes was a single mom with enough to manage already.

"It's crazy for Clarice to kick you out," Alex said. Soft smacking sounds filled the receiver; she was probably chomping on a piece of chocolate Twizzlers, her favorite candy. "She can't honestly think you stole that money."

"Actually, it wasn't just that." Emma scooped up a stack of jeans and tossed them in the bag, too.

"Was there something else?" Alex asked.

Emma picked at a loose military patch on the old duf-fel. "I can't get into it right now." She didn't want to tell Alex about the video she'd seen. She wanted to keep it to herself for a little while longer, just in case it wasn't real. "But I'll explain soon, okay? I promise."

After Emma hung up, she sat on the carpet and looked around. She'd pulled all her photography prints by Margaret Bourke-White and Annie Leibovitz off the walls and her collection of classic novels and sci-fi thrillers off the shelves; the place now looked like a pay-by-the-hour motel room. She stared into the open bureau drawer, which contained her favorite things, the stuff she carried to every foster home. There was the hand-knitted monster toy Mrs. Hewes, a piano teacher, had given her the day she'd mastered "Für Elise" despite not actually having a piano at home to practice on. She'd saved a couple of scavenger hunt clues from Becky, the creases soft and the paper nearly disintegrating. And there was Socktopus, the threadbare stuffed octopus Becky had bought for Emma during a road trip to Four Corners. Nestled at the bottom of the drawer were her five cloth-bound journals, stuffed with poetry, the Comebacks I Should've Said list, the Ways to Flirt (WTF) list, the Stuff I Love and Hate list, and a thorough review of every secondhand store in the area. Emma had mastered the thrift store circuit. She knew exactly which days new shipments hit the floor, how to haggle for better prices, and to always paw through the bottom of the shoe bin—she'd once scored a barely scuffed pair of Kate Spade flats that way.

Finally, Emma lifted the battered Polaroid camera and a large stack of Polaroid photos from the corner of the drawer. The camera had been Becky's, but Emma had brought it with her to Sasha's house the night her mom had taken off. Not long after that, Emma had begun to write fake news captions to match the photos about her life and the goings-on of her foster families: "Foster Mom Gets Sick of Kids, Locks Self in Bedroom to Watch *Leave It to Beaver.*" "Hippies Leave for Florida Unannounced." "Semi-decent Foster Mom Gets Job in Hong Kong; Foster Kid Not Invited." She was the one and only reporter on the Emma beat. If she were in the right mind-set, she'd craft a new top story for today: "Evil Foster Brother Ruins Girl's Life." Or maybe "Girl Discovers Doppelgänger on Internet. Perhaps a Long-Lost Sister?"

Emma paused at the thought. She glanced at the tattered Dell laptop on the floor, which she'd bought from a pawn shop. Taking a deep breath, she set it on the bed and opened the lid. The screen glowed to life, and Emma quickly called up the video site where Travis had found the fake strangling film. The familiar video was the very first item on the list. It had been posted earlier that evening.

Emma pressed PLAY, and the grainy image appeared. The blindfolded girl bucked and scratched. The dark figure pulled the necklace taut around her neck. Then the camera fell, and someone emerged and whipped off the blindfold. The girl's face was ashen and dazed. She looked around frantically, her eyes rolling around in her head like loose marbles. Then she looked at the camera. Her blue-green eyes were glassy and her pink lips glowed. It was

Emma's exact face. Everything about it was the same.

"*Who are you?*" Emma whispered, a shiver running up her spine.

I wished I could answer her. I wished I could do something useful instead of just dangling over her silently like a creepy ghost-stalker. It was like watching a movie, except I couldn't even call out or throw popcorn at the screen.

The clip ended, and the site asked Emma if she wanted to replay it. The bed springs squeaked as she shifted her weight, thinking. After a moment, she typed *SuttonInAz* into a Google search. A few sites popped up instantly, including a Facebook page by the same name. SUTTON MERCER, it said. TUCSON, ARIZONA.

Screeching tires out the window sounded like a cackle. The Facebook page loaded, and Emma gasped. There was Sutton Mercer, standing in a foyer of a house with a bunch of girls by her side. She wore a black halter-style dress, a sparkly headband, and silver high heels. Emma blinked at her face, feeling queasy. She leaned in closer, certain she would see a difference that would set Sutton apart from herself, but everything, down to Sutton's petite ears and the same perfectly square, perfectly straight teeth, was identical.

The more Emma thought about it, the more she could believe she had a long-lost twin. For one thing, there were certain times in life where she felt accompanied, as if someone was watching her. Sometimes she woke up in the morning after having crazy dreams about a girl who looked like her . . . but she knew it *wasn't* her. The dreams were always vivid: riding on a sun-dappled Appaloosa at someone's farm, dragging a dark-haired doll across a patio. Besides, if Becky was irresponsible enough to forget Emma at the Circle K, maybe she'd done the same thing with another baby. Perhaps all those duplicate pairs of shoes Manic Becky bought weren't for Emma at all, but for Emma's twin sister, a girl Becky had already abandoned.

Perhaps Emma was right, I thought. Perhaps they'd been for me.

Emma moved the mouse over the girls standing next to Sutton in the photo. MADELINE VEGA, said a small pop-up tag. Madeline had sleek black hair, huge brown eyes, a willowy build, and a gap between her front teeth, just like Madonna. Her head tilted suggestively to one side. There was a fake—or perhaps real?—tattoo of a rose on the inside of her wrist, and her bloodred dress plunged provocatively to her breast bone.

The girl next to Madeline was a redhead named Charlotte Chamberlain. She had pink, pale skin and pretty green eyes, and wore a black silk dress that tugged over her broad shoulders. Two blondes with similar wide eyes and upturned noses stood on either end of the group.

Their names were Lilianna and Gabriella Fiorello; in the caption Sutton had nicknamed them THE TWITTER TWINS.

I looked over Emma's shoulder. I recognized the girls in the photos. I understood we used to be close. But they were like books I'd read two summers ago; I knew I'd liked them, but I couldn't tell you now what they'd been about.

Emma scrolled down the page. Most of the Facebook profile was public. Sutton Mercer was going to be a senior this year, just like Emma. She attended a school called Hollier High. Her interests were tennis, shopping at La Encantada Mall, and the Papaya Quench full body wrap at Canyon Ranch. Under LIKES AND DISLIKES, she'd written, *I love Gucci more than Pucci, but not as much as Juicy.* Emma frowned at the line.

Yeah, I had no idea what it meant, either.

Next, Emma clicked on the photo page and peered at a picture of a bunch of girls in tennis polos, skirts, and sneakers. A plaque that said HOLLIER TENNIS TEAM rested at their feet. Emma rolled the mouse over the girls' names until she found Sutton's. She stood third from the left, her hair pulled back tautly into a smooth ponytail. Emma moved the mouse to the dark-haired Indian girl to the right. A tag over her head said NISHA BANERJEE. There was a saccharine, kiss-ass smile on her face.

I stared hard at her, a spotty, snapping sensation coursing

through my weightless body. I knew I didn't like Nisha, but I didn't know why.

Next Emma looked at a shot of Sutton and Charlotte standing on the tennis courts next to a tall, handsome, graying man. There was no tag over his face, but the caption said, *Me, C, and Mr. Chamberlain at Arizona Tennis Classic.* After that was a shot of Sutton with her arms around a handsome, sweet-looking, blond-haired guy wearing a Hollier soccer jersey. *Love ya, G!* she'd written. Someone named Garrett had replied in the comments window: *I love u too, Sutton.*

Aw, Emma thought.

My heart warmed, too.

The last picture Emma clicked on was a shot of Sutton sitting around a patio table with two attractive, older adults and a dirty-blond, square-jawed girl named Laurel Mercer. Sutton's adoptive sister, presumably. Everyone was grinning and holding slushy drinks in a toast. *I heart the fam*, the caption proclaimed.

Emma lingered on the photo for a long time, her chest aching. All of her daydreams about a Mom Star, Dad Star, and Emma Star family looked pretty much like this: an attractive, happy family, a nice house, a good life. If she cut her own head out of a snapshot and pasted it on Sutton's body, the picture would look no different. Yet her story was as opposite from this as could be.

There were a few YouTube clips on the Facebook page, and Emma clicked on the first one. Sutton stood on what looked like a lush green golf course with Madeline and Charlotte. Everyone knelt down and vigorously shook canisters in their hands. Slowly, silently, they spray-painted designs on a large rock. WE MISS YOU, T, Madeline's message said. Sutton's message said NISHA WAS HERE.

"Where's Laurel?" Charlotte asked.

"A thousand bucks says she's too scared," Sutton murmured on the screen. Her voice was so familiar it made Emma's throat catch.

Emma clicked on the other videos. There was one of Sutton and her friends skydiving, another of them bungee jumping. A whole bunch of videos showed one of the girls walking around the corner unaware, and the rest of them ambushing her and making her scream. The last video was titled "Cross my heart, hope to die." It opened with Madeline pirouetting into a pool at night. As soon as she hit the water, she started to flail. "Help!" she screamed, her dark hair plastered against her face. "I think I broke my leg! I . . . can't . . . move!"

The camera wobbled. "Mads?" Charlotte cried out.

"*Shit,*" someone else said.

"Help!" Madeline continued to flail.

"Wait a minute," Sutton's voice called haltingly. "Did she say it?"

The camera zinged to Charlotte, frozen midstep. She held a red-and-white life preserver in her hands. "What?" she asked dazedly.

"Did she say it?" Sutton said again.

"I-I don't think so," Charlotte squeaked. She clamped her lips together and dropped the life preserver on the deck. "Very funny. We know you're faking, Mads," she yelled, annoyed. "*Such* a bad actress," she said under her breath.

Madeline stopped splashing. "*Fine,*" she panted, paddling for the ladder. "But I had you going for a minute. Char looked like she was going to pee her pants." Everyone cackled.

Whoa, Emma thought. So this was what they did for fun?

I was a little freaked, too.

Emma searched the rest of the Facebook profile for any references to the weird strangling video Travis had found, but there wasn't a single mention. The only semi-spooky thing she found was a scan of a black-and-white flyer that said MISSING SINCE JUNE 17, a boy's face grinning back at her. THAYER VEGA, it said in block letters under the photo. Emma clicked back to the names on Sutton's profile picture. Madeline's last name was Vega, too.

Finally, she clicked on Sutton's Wall. Sutton had written a post just a few hours before: *Ever wish you could run away? Sometimes I do.* Emma frowned. Why would Sutton want to run away? It looked like she had everything.

I had no idea, but that post told me tons. If I'd written it only a few hours before, it meant I hadn't been dead for long. Did anyone even know I'd been killed? I looked at the rest of my Wall that was visible on the screen. No *RIP, Sutton* notes or plans for a Sutton Mercer memorial. Maybe no one knew then. Maybe no one had found me? Was I lying in a field somewhere, my necklace still at my throat? I gazed down at my shimmering body. Even though no one else could see me, every so often I could just make out a tiny flicker of myself—a hand here, an elbow there, a pair of terry-cloth shorts and yellow FitFlops. I didn't see any blood. My skin wasn't blue.

Just as Emma was about to close up the computer, some more posts on Sutton's Wall caught her eye. *Can't wait for your b-day party!* Charlotte had written. *It's going to be sick!* Emma's birthday was coming up, too. She checked Sutton's Info tab. The birthday listed was September 10, the same as Emma's.

Her heart pounded. That was some coincidence.

I felt scared and hopeful and confused, too. Maybe it was real. Maybe we *were* twins.

After a moment, Emma opened a new window and logged into her own Facebook page. It looked paltry and pathetic next to Sutton's—her profile picture was a blurry close-up of herself and Socktopus, and she only had five friends: Alex, an old foster sister named Tracy, Ben & Jerry's Chunky Monkey, and two of the cast members from *CSI*. Then she found Sutton's page again and clicked on the button that said SEND SUTTON A MESSAGE. When the window appeared, she typed: *This will sound crazy, but I think we're related. We look exactly the same, and we have the same birthday. I live in Nevada, not too far from you. You're not by any chance adopted, are you? Write back or call if you want to talk.*

MESSAGE SENT! the screen announced. Emma stared around the quiet room, the small fan on the desk blowing warmish air in her face. After the possibly life-altering thing that had just happened, she expected the world to have miraculously and drastically transformed—a leprechaun to dance through the open window, Clarice's kitschy terra-cotta patio sculptures to come to life and start a conga line, *something*. But there was still the long, jagged crack in the plaster in the ceiling and the blotchy, M-shaped stain on the carpet near the closet.

The little clock in the corner of the laptop screen clicked from 10:12 to 10:13 P.M. She refreshed her Facebook page. She peeked out a slit in the dusty blinds at the night sky and found the Mom, Dad, and Emma stars. Her heart rollicked in her chest. What had she *done*? She reached for her phone and dialed Alex's number, but Alex didn't pick up. YOU THERE? she texted Alex, but there was no response.

The traffic on the highway grew sparse and whispery. Emma let out a long sigh, thinking of what came next. Maybe she could move back to Henderson, live in Alex's spare room, and pay rent to Alex's mom. She'd work full-time—perhaps night shifts at the twenty-four-hour Target near Alex's house—and somehow finish high school, too. Maybe she could even intern at the local newspaper on the weekends. . . .

Bzzzzzzz.

Emma's eyes popped open. Out the window, the moon had climbed high in the sky. The clock on the side table said 12:56 A.M. She'd dozed off.

Bzzzzzzz.

Her phone was flashing. She stared at it for a long moment, as if she was afraid it might leap up and bite her.

There was an envelope icon on the screen. Her heart churned faster and faster. Trembling, she clicked OPEN. Emma had to read the Facebook message four times before the words really sunk in.

OMG. I can't believe this. Yes, I was totally adopted. But I never knew you existed until now. Can u meet me at the hiking base of Sabino Canyon in Tucson 2morro at 6 PM? Attached is my cell number. Don't tell anyone who you are until we talk—it's dangerous! See you soon!

Love, Sutton (your twin)

Of course, there was one problem with that note: I didn't write it.

4

REUNION INTERRUPTED

Late the following afternoon, Emma staggered off a
Greyhound bus, her green duffel in tow. Heat radiated
off the parking lot in waves; the air was so stifling that
she felt like she'd just stepped into the barrel of a giant
hair dryer. To her right were small adobe homes and a
purple-stucco yoga studio for men called hOMbre. To
her left was a large, crumbling building called the Hotel
Congress, which looked haunted. Posters for upcoming
concerts plastered the front windows. A couple of hip-
sters loitered on the street, smoking cigarettes. Beyond
that was what looked like a shop for dominatrix hookers;
whip-wielding mannequins in catsuits, fishnet stockings,

and thigh-high boots filled the front windows.

Emma spun around again and faced the Greyhound bus station. TUCSON DOWNTOWN, said a low-slung sign out front. After hours of sitting on a bus next to a guy with a devil beard and a serious addiction to jalapeño-flavored Doritos, she was finally here. She was tempted to run up to the large Greyhound on the sign and give it a big, wet kiss, but then her phone vibrated in her pocket and she scrambled to answer it. Alex's photo appeared on the screen.

"Hey!" Emma clutched the old BlackBerry to her ear. "Guess where I am?"

"You *didn't*," Alex gasped on the other end.

"I did." Emma dragged her duffel to a bench under the awning and sat down to rest. Alex had finally written back to Emma's YOU THERE? text last night. Emma had called her immediately, blurting out the whole story in one long, breathless sentence.

"I left Clarice a note," Emma said, moving her long legs out of the way as an older couple pulling wheeled suitcases passed. "Social Services won't check up on me, either—I'm too close to turning eighteen."

"So what are you going to say to this Sutton girl? I mean, if she's really your sister, do you think you'll be able to move in with her?" Alex sighed wistfully. "It's like Cinderella, except without the lame prince!"

Emma leaned back on the bench and gazed at the purplish mountains in the distance. "I don't want to get too far ahead of things," she said. "Let's just see if we even get along."

It was all an act. The entire bus ride, Emma imagined how meeting Sutton might just change her life. Maybe she could move to Tucson and go to Sutton's school. She could get to know Sutton's adoptive parents, too. *Maybe they'll even let me move in with them*, she dared to consider. Goose bumps rose on her arms. Okay, that was a long shot, but who knew? It *was* like a cooler version of Cinderella.

But first things first: the meeting today. Emma spotted a single neon-green cab on the other side of the bus station and waved it over. "Please don't tell anyone, okay?" she said to Alex.

"I promise," Alex agreed. "Good luck."

"Thanks."

Emma hung up, climbed into the backseat of the cab, and gave Sabino Canyon as her destination, barely able to temper the giddiness in her voice. The cabbie pulled away and wove through Tucson's streets. Emma stared out the grimy window, grinning at the various college buildings of the University of Arizona, including one that had PHOTOGRAPHY INSTITUTE on a big sign out front. Emma couldn't wait to go inside and check out the exhibit. Next they passed the college green. Students loitered in the sun.

A running group pranced by like a herd of deer. There was a girl dressed up as a marijuana plant in the middle of the courtyard holding a sign that said HONK 4 WEED! The cabbie honked.

Next they pulled onto Highway 10 and drove north. The houses grew larger and the streets were speckled with fancy gyms, cute bistros, gourmet markets, and upscale boutiques. Emma passed the entrance to La Encantada Mall, and then the lush Elizabeth Arden Red Door spa. *Maybe Sutton and I can have a pedicure day*, she thought.

Actually, that made her a little nervous. She'd never gotten a professional pedicure before. Whenever someone touched her feet, she let out a hitchy laugh like Ernie on *Sesame Street*.

As for me, all I felt was numbness as the car whipped past these landmarks. Certain emotions and senses flashed deep beneath the surface—vague blips of elation and thrill as we passed a restaurant called NoRTH, the smell of jasmine perfume as the cab swept past the shops at La Encantada—but nothing solid emerged. Questions buzzed in my head like a swarm of bees. Who had written back to Emma? Had anyone else discovered I was dead? I was desperate to get another look at my Facebook page, but Emma hadn't clicked on it again. A whole day had passed since my death—maybe more; where did everyone think I was? And why hadn't someone found my body? Then again, if someone had murdered me, I could be chopped up in a zillion pieces by now.

I wanted to cry out. I wanted to wail. But all I could do was follow Emma in a state of mute shock and panic. It was like those terrible dreams where I was falling down, down, down from the top of a tall building. I always tried to call out for someone to catch me, but no one ever answered.

The cab took a left, and a mountain rose up before Emma's eyes. A pitted, wooden sign said SABINO CANYON. "Here you are," the driver said, pulling to the curb.

This was it. Emma handed the cabbie a twenty and crunched across the gravel to a bench. She inhaled the jumbled scents of sunscreen, dust, and sun-baked rock. Evening hikers stretched their calves against a parking barrier a few feet away. The shimmering mountain range interrupted the blue sky. Little pinpricks of pink, yellow, and purple wildflowers dotted the trail.

It's perfect, Emma thought. On instinct, she pulled her old Polaroid camera from the duffel. She hadn't brought that much with her to Tucson—just her wallet, Socktopus, a change of clothes, the camera, and her journal, because she was afraid to go anywhere without it. She'd left most everything else, including her savings, in a storage locker at the Vegas bus station. The device made a churning noise as she snapped a photo. Emma watched the picture slowly develop. *Long-Lost Sisters Meet for the First Time*, she mentally captioned.

It was six on the dot. She sat down on a bench, pulled out a Maybelline compact, and took stock of her reflection. She wore a striped jersey Gap dress that she'd found at Cinnamon's, a secondhand shop near Clarice's house, and she'd smeared a lot of shiny gloss over her lips. She covertly sniffed her skin, hoping she didn't smell like bus exhaust or jalapeño Doritos. Meeting Sutton reminded her of walking into a new foster home for the first time. The parents always gave her a long, discerning look, instantly deciding whether she passed or failed. *Please like me*, she always thought as she stood in countless kitchens or on interchangeable front porches. *Please make this bearable. Please don't let me have a booger hanging out of my nose.*

More people emerged from the canyon trail. Emma checked the clock on her phone. It was 6:10. What if Sutton was late to everything? People like that drove Emma crazy. And what were they going to say to each other, anyway? "Hi, Sutton," Emma mouthed, practicing a smile. "So Becky lost you, too?" She pantomimed reaching out her hand, and then shook her head and pulled back. They'd hug, wouldn't they? What if they just stood there awkwardly, staring into space?

The strange film fluttered through her mind again.

Who agreed to be strangled for fun, anyway? She thought about the girls Travis had mentioned yesterday.

"Oh!" cried someone behind her.

Emma jumped and turned around, looking at the unfamiliar man in shorts and a polo shirt standing a few feet away. With his salt-and-pepper hair and slightly round physique, he reminded Emma of Dr. Lowry, the only social worker she'd ever liked, mostly because he'd spoken to Emma like a human being and not a foster child freak. But then the photo on Facebook of Charlotte and Sutton standing on a tennis court with this guy popped into her head. *Me, C, and Mr. Chamberlain at Arizona Tennis Classic.* This was someone from Sutton's world, not hers.

Not that I had much recollection of him.

There was a troubled look on the man's face. "W-What are you doing out *here*, Sutton?"

Emma blinked hard, realizing what he'd called her. She gave him a wobbly smile. Her tongue felt bloated and heavy in her mouth. *Don't tell anyone who you are*, the email had said. *It's dangerous.*

"Um, just hanging out," Emma answered, feeling ridiculously foolish. Her palms itched, too, just like they always did when she lied to adults.

"Are you going for a hike?" Charlotte's dad pressed. "Is this where kids meet these days?"

Emma glanced toward the road, hoping she'd see a girl

who looked just like her pulling up to the curb to clear this up. A few cars passed without stopping. A couple of kids on Schwinn cruiser bikes rode past, laughing. "Um, not exactly."

A dog across the path let out a bark. Emma stiffened—a Chow had bitten her when she was nine, and she'd been wary of dogs ever since. But the dog was straining at a rabbit that had suddenly emerged from around the bend. Charlotte's dad pushed his hands in his pockets. "Well, see ya. Have a nice night." He quickly walk-jogged away.

Emma slumped on the bench. *Awkward.* The clock on her phone now said 6:20. She clicked onto her NEW MESSAGES folder, but there was no text saying I'M LATE, BE THERE SOON! Uneasiness began to filter through her body, poisoning everything. Her stomach felt like it was eating itself. All of a sudden, the surroundings didn't seem quite so magical anymore. The hikers making their way back down the mountain looked like twisted, dark monsters. There was an acrid odor in the air. Something felt very, very wrong.

Crack. Emma's head whipped around at the sound. Before she could see what it was, a small hand covered her eyes and yanked her to standing. "Wha?" Emma called out. A second hand pressed against her mouth. Emma tried to wrench away, but a hard, cold object pressed between her shoulder blades. She instantly froze. She'd never felt a gun at her back before, but this couldn't be anything else.

"Don't move, bitch," whispered a husky voice. Emma felt hot breath on her neck, but all she could see was the inside of someone's palm. "You're coming with us."

I wished I could see who "us" was, but that was a little wrinkle in this being-dead thing: When Emma couldn't see, neither could I.

5

SHE IS ME

Emma's feet tripped beneath her, dragging on the ground. The gun dug into her skin. Dark, blurry shapes fluttered through the blindfold someone had quickly tied around her eyes, and the sound of traffic roared in her ears. She let out a panicked whimper. The freaky strangling film flashed through her mind like whirling ambulance lights. *Those hands pulling that necklace taut. Sutton slumping over lifelessly.*

I thought of the same thing. Terror filled me.

Someone pushed Emma across the road. A horn blared, but then Emma's foot hit the curb on the other side. As she staggered across the sidewalk, the sound of cars yielded to loud, throbbing bass. The aroma of grilled hamburgers and hot dogs and cigarettes drifted into Emma's nostrils. There was a loud splash. Someone giggled. Someone else cried, "Love it!" Emma's hands twitched. Where was she?

"What the hell?"

Suddenly the scarf was ripped from Emma's eyes. The world lit up for me again at exactly the same time. A familiar girl with long, reddish hair, pale skin, broad shoulders and a thick waist hovered in front of Emma. She wore a short blue dress with lace around the neck. *Charlotte*—the name came to Emma. "She's learned her lesson already, don't you think?" Charlotte snapped, throwing the blindfold behind a potted cactus.

Someone freed Emma's hands from their confines behind her back. She no longer felt the gun pressed between her shoulder blades either. Emma whipped around. Three pretty girls in party dresses and sparkly makeup stood before her.

The tallest one had dark hair, jutting collarbones, a deconstructed ballerina bun, and a tattoo of a rose on the inside of her wrist. Madeline Vega, the girl in Sutton's Facebook profile photo. Next to Madeline stood two girls with Crayola-maize hair and pale blue eyes. Both girls held iPhones. One was preppy, in a polo dress, a white headband, and wedge sandals with grosgrain ties. The other looked like she'd stepped off a Green Day video—she wore lots of eye makeup, a plaid dress, high boots, and a stack of black jelly bracelets around her wrists. They had to be Gabriella and Lilianna Fiorello, the Twitter Twins.

"Gotcha!" Madeline gave Emma a weak smile. The Twitter Twins grinned, too.

"Since when did we get all eco?" Charlotte sighed loudly behind them. "*Recycling* is not part of our rules."

Madeline pulled the short, white A-line dress she was wearing down her thighs. "It wasn't technically a repeat, Char. Sutton knew it was us the whole time." She raised a tube of lipstick into the air, then pressed it between Emma's shoulder blades again. "My mom's Chihuahua would've known this wasn't a gun."

Emma wrenched away. The tube of lipstick had definitely fooled *her*. Then, she realized something else— Madeline had called her Sutton, just like Charlotte's dad had. "Wait a minute," she blurted, struggling to find her voice. "I'm not—"

Charlotte cut her off, her gaze still on Madeline. "Even if Sutton knew it was you, it's still poor form. And you know it." She had a sarcastic voice and a penetrating stare. Although Charlotte wasn't the prettiest in the crowd, she was clearly the alpha. "Besides, since when do we do things like that with *them*?" She pointed at Gabriella and Lilianna, who lowered their eyes sheepishly.

Madeline fiddled with the leather strap of her oversized

watch. "Don't be such a hater. It was spontaneous. I saw Sutton and just . . . went for it."

Charlotte stepped a tiny bit closer to Madeline and puffed up her chest. "We made up the rules together, remember? Or do those tight buns you wear to ballet class cut off the circulation to your brain?"

Madeline's chin wobbled for a moment. Her big eyes, high cheekbones, and bow-shaped lips reminded Emma of a figurehead on a ship. But Emma noticed Madeline slowly massaging a hot-pink rabbit's foot on the key ring of her bag, as if all the beauty in the world hadn't brought her luck. "It's better than your too-tight jeans cutting off the circulation to your butt," Madeline shot back.

I reached out to Madeline, but my fingers slipped through her skin. "Mads?" I called out. I touched Charlotte on the shoulder. "Char?" She didn't even flinch. Nothing new about them came back to me. I knew I loved them, but I really didn't know why. But how could they stand there and think Emma was me? How could they not know their BFF was dead?

"Um, guys," Emma tried again, staring across the wide avenue. The entrance to Sabino Canyon glowed beckoningly in the sunset. "There's somewhere I need to be."

Madeline gave her a *duh* look. "Uh, yeah? Nisha's party?" She looped her arm around Emma's elbow and yanked her toward the small wrought-iron gate that led to the backyard of the house whose driveway they stood in. "Look, I know you and Nisha have issues, but this is the last party before school tomorrow. It's not like you have to talk to her. Where have you been anyway? We've been calling you all day. And what were you doing sitting in front of Sabino? You looked like a zombie."

"It was freaky," Lilianna piped up.

"Super freaky," Gabriella agreed in an identical voice. Then she reached into her pocket and pulled out a small prescription bottle. Popping off the cap, she shook two pills into her hand and pushed them into her mouth, washing them down with a swig from a Diet Coke bottle. *Party girl*, Emma thought warily.

She stared at the four girls. Should she tell them who she really was? What if it really *was* dangerous? Suddenly she felt her shoulder and realized that she'd lost her duffel bag in the fake kidnapping. When she looked across the street, it was still there. She'd slip away and get it as soon as she could. And if Sutton showed up, maybe she'd see it and know Emma had been there.

"Hang on a second." Emma stopped short next to a large flowering barrel cactus. She wriggled her arm from Madeline's grasp and pulled her phone out of her pocket—at least *it* wasn't in the duffel, too. *No new messages*. She shaded the screen with one hand and composed several new texts to the cell number Sutton had given Emma in her Facebook reply last night: *Your friends found me. I'm at a party across the street. They think I'm you. I didn't know what to tell them. Txt me with further instructions, K?*

Emma typed quickly—she knew the third-place finish in the speed-texting contest in Vegas two years ago would come in handy someday—and pressed SEND. There. Sutton could meet her here and straighten out who was who . . . or Emma could meet her later and just pretend she was Sutton for the duration of the party.

"Who are you writing to?" Madeline leaned over Emma's phone, trying to get a look at the screen. "And why are you using a BlackBerry? I thought you got rid of that thing."

Emma slipped her phone back into her pocket before Madeline could see. Sutton's Facebook posts flitted into Emma's mind. She straightened up and gave Madeline the same coy look she'd seen her sister make in the YouTube videos. "Wouldn't *you* love to know, bitch."

As soon as she'd finished saying the words, Emma clamped her mouth shut and sucked in her stomach. She wouldn't have been more surprised if a bouquet of daisies had popped out of her mouth. Comments like that ended up on her CISS list, not in her day-to-day conversation.

Madeline let out a haughty sniff. "Fine, ho beast." Then she whipped out her iPhone. A big sticker of a ballet dancer on the back said SWAN LAKE MAFIA. "Smush in!"

Everyone pressed together and smiled. Madeline held the phone outstretched. Emma stood on the end, grinning weakly.

And then they started down the driveway. The night air had cooled significantly, and the jumbled aromas of the charcoal grill, citronella candles, and cigarettes wafted into Emma's nostrils. Gabriella and Lilianna walked and tweeted at the same time. As they bypassed the front door to cut around the stone path on the side of the house, Charlotte pulled Emma back so they were walking alone.

"Are you okay?" Charlotte straightened her flutter-sleeved dress so that her thick bra strap didn't show. Her arms were dotted with thousands of freckles.

"I'm fine," Emma said breezily, even though her fingers still trembled, and her heart banged madly against her ribs.

"So where's Laurel?" Charlotte pulled a tube of lip gloss from her purse and smeared it over her lips. "I thought you said you were going to drive her here."

Emma's eyes darted back and forth. *Laurel.* That was Sutton's sister, right? She wished she had a Wiki-Sutton application on her BlackBerry or something. "Uh . . ."

Charlotte widened her eyes. "You ditched her again, didn't you?" She wagged her finger playfully in Emma's face. "You're a bad, bad sister."

Before Emma could reply, they stepped into the backyard. Someone had strung a banner that said GOODBYE, SUMMER! across a salmon-colored storage shed. Girls in long, flowing maxi dresses and boys in Lacoste polos filled the patio. Two muscled guys in drenched HOLLIER WATER POLO shirts stood in the pool with two skinny girls in bikinis on their shoulders, poised for a chicken fight. A girl with curly hair and long feather earrings laughed way too loudly with a younger, hotter version of Tiger Woods. There was a long table filled with Mexican hot dogs, vegetarian burritos, sushi rolls, and chocolate-covered strawberries. Another table held a bunch of bottles of soda, fruit punch, and ginger ale, and two big jugs of Beefeater and Cuervo.

"Whoa," Emma couldn't help but blurt when she saw the liquor. She wasn't much of a drinker—she and Alex had once drank too much playing a *Twilight* drinking game and took turns puking in Alex's mom's Zen rock garden. And she never knew what to do at parties either. She always felt shy and reserved, the freak foster kid with no home.

"Right?" Madeline murmured, sidling up to Emma. Her gaze was on the table, too. "Casa Banerjee has gone downhill since Nisha's mom died. Her dad's so oblivious these days, Nisha could probably have crack pipes as door prizes and he wouldn't notice."

Someone touched her arm. "Hey, Sutton," called a tall, buff, captain-of-a-sports-team type. Emma smiled broadly. A petite dark-haired girl waved at Emma from the drinks table by the French doors. "Your dress is so pretty!" she cooed. "Is it BCBG?"

Emma couldn't help but feel a tiny twinge of jealousy. Not only did Sutton have a family, but she was wildly popular, too. How come Emma had gotten such a crappy life and Sutton had gotten the great one?

I wasn't sure about that, considering Emma was alive and I wasn't.

More kids passed by, brightening when they saw her. Emma grinned and waved and laughed, feeling like a princess greeting her loyal subjects. It felt freeing and almost . . . *fun.* She understood why sometimes the shyest kids could climb onstage in school plays and completely lose their inhibitions.

"There you are," growled a sexy voice in Emma's ear. Emma whirled around to see a handsome blond guy in a gray fitted polo and long khaki-green shorts. A familiar Facebook photo shimmered into her mind: Garrett, Sutton's boyfriend.

"I haven't heard from you all day." Garrett handed Emma a red plastic cup filled with liquid. "I called, I texted . . . where have you been?"

"I'm right here!" I wanted to scream. Brief flashes of

kisses, hand-holding, and prom slow dances with Garrett flitted in and out of my brain. I distinctly heard the words *I love you*. A longing feeling struck me hard.

"Oh, around," Emma answered vaguely. "But someone's got to cut the cord a little, don't you think?" she added, poking Garrett lightly in the ribs. It was something Emma had always been dying to tell every overprotective boyfriend she'd had in the past, the kind who texted her nonstop and freaked if she didn't immediately reply. Plus it sounded like something Sutton might say.

Garrett pulled her close and stroked her hair. "Good thing I found you." His hand moved from her hair to her shoulder, then dangerously close to her boob.

"Um . . ." Emma jerked away.

I was so happy she did.

Garrett raised his palms in surrender. "Sorry, sorry."

Then her BlackBerry vibrated against her hip. Her heart leapt. *Sutton.*

"Be right back," she said to Garrett. He nodded, and Emma wove through the crowds of people toward the house. When Garrett turned to talk to a tall Asian guy in a World Cup jersey, Emma crouched low and darted to the side gate.

She turned to glance at the party once more and noticed someone staring at her from the large teak table across the patio. It was a dark-skinned girl with big eyes and a tightly drawn mouth. She wore a yellow wrap dress and a gold cuff on her bicep. It was Nisha, from Sutton's tennis team photo. This was her party. She stared at Emma as though she wanted to hoist her by the scruff of her neck and throw her out on her butt.

Even though every ounce of Emma's be-nice-and-don't-make-trouble being wanted to wave and smile, she steeled herself, thought of Sutton, and shot Nisha a bitchy look. Outrage flashed across Nisha's face. After a moment, she whipped her head around, her ponytail smacking the face of the girl behind her.

A cautious feeling flitted through me. Nisha and I clearly had issues—big issues.

Not that I had a clue what they were.

6

WHO CAN RESIST A BROODER?

Nisha's driveway was quiet and peaceful. Crickets chirped in the bushes, and the air was cool against Emma's bare skin. Bluish light from a TV flickered in the window of a house a few doors down. A dog barked behind a block-wall fence. Emma's pulse began to slow, and her shoulders slowly fell from their crunched position by her ears. She pulled out the BlackBerry and stared at the screen. The message was from Clarice: GOT YOUR NOTE. EVERYTHING OKAY? LET ME KNOW IF YOU NEED ANYTHING.

Emma deleted the message, then refreshed her inbox again. *No new messages.* Then she looked across the broad highway. A big floodlight shone across the Sabino parking lot. Emma gulped. The park bench was now empty. Had someone taken her stuff? Where was Sutton? And what was she supposed to do when this party ended? Her wallet had been in her bag. Now she had no cash. No ID.

Swish. Emma turned around and faced Nisha's house. No one was in the driveway. Then, a stiff *thwock* echoed through the air, a soda can opening. Emma pivoted again. A figure stood on the front porch of the house next door. There was a large telescope by his side, but he was staring straight into Emma's eyes.

Emma backed away. "Oh. Sorry."

The guy stepped forward, his prominent cheekbones catching the light. Emma took in his round eyes, thick eyebrows, and closely shorn hair. His mouth was drawn into a straight, tense line that seemed to say *back off.* He was dressed more casually than the boys at the party, wearing frayed hiking shorts and a threadbare gray T-shirt that showed every contour of his well-muscled chest.

I recognized him, but of course—I should've been getting used to this by now—I didn't know why.

Giggles emerged from Nisha's backyard. Emma glanced over her shoulder, then back at the boy. She was intrigued by his sullen slouch, and by the fact that he didn't seem to care that a party was raging next door. She'd always been a sucker for the brooding type. "Why aren't you at the party?" she asked.

The guy just stared at her, his eyes two huge moons.

Emma walked down the sidewalk until she was right in front of his house. "What are you looking at?" She gestured to the telescope.

He didn't blink. "Venus?" Emma guessed. "The Big Dipper?"

A small noise escaped from his throat. He ran his hand against the back of his neck and turned away. Finally Emma pivoted on her heel. "Fine," she said, trying to sound as breezy as possible. "Hang out by yourself. I don't care."

"The Perseids, Sutton."

Emma turned back to him. So he knew Sutton, too. "What are the Perseids?" she asked.

He curled his hands around the porch railing. "It's a meteor shower."

Emma crossed toward him. "Can I see?"

The guy stood motionless as Emma walked through the yard. His house was a small, sand-colored bungalow with a carport instead of a garage. A few cacti lined the curb. Up close, he smelled like root beer. The porch light shone down on his face, revealing striking blue eyes. A plate containing a half-eaten sandwich was on the porch swing, and two leather-bound books were on the ground. The tattered cover of the first book said *The Collected Poetry of William Carlos Williams*. Emma had never met a cute guy who read poetry—not one who'd admit it, anyway.

Finally he looked down, adjusted the telescope lens to Emma's height, and stepped out of the way. Emma stooped to the eyepiece. "Since when did you become an astronomer?" he asked.

"Since never." Emma tilted the telescope to the big, full moon. "I usually just give the stars names of my own."

"Oh yeah? Like what?"

Emma flicked the little lens cap, which hung from a black string off the eyepiece. "Well, like the Bitch Star. There." She pointed to a small twinkler just over the rooftops. A few years ago, she'd named it for Maria Rowan, a girl in seventh grade who'd spilled a puddle of lemonade under Emma's desk in Spanish and then told everyone Emma was incontinent. She'd even translated it into Spanish, *incontinencia*. Emma had fantasized about rocketing Maria into the sky, just like the Greek gods used to banish their children to the underworld for all of eternity.

The guy let out a cough-like laugh. "Actually, I think your Bitch Star is part of Orion's belt."

Emma pressed her hand to her chest, like an offended southern belle. "Do you talk to all the girls like that?"

He moved a little closer to her, their arms nearly touching. Emma's heart jumped to her throat at the effortlessness of it all. For a second, she thought about Carter Hayes, the captain of the Henderson High School basketball team, whom she'd adored from afar. She'd crafted tons of adorable things to say to Carter in her Ways to Flirt list, but whenever they were alone together, she'd always somehow found herself talking about *American Idol*. She didn't even like *American Idol*.

The guy tilted his head up to the sky again. "Maybe the other stars Orion carries around could be the Liar Star and the Cheater Star. Three naughty girls who were dragged by their hair to Orion's cave." He looked at her meaningfully.

Emma leaned against the railing, feeling the words carried some special connotation she couldn't possibly decipher. "It sounds like you've done a lot of thinking about this."

"Maybe." He had the longest lashes Emma had ever seen. But suddenly his gaze felt less flirty and more . . . curious, maybe.

And suddenly a flash about him came to me. It wasn't a memory exactly, just an odd mix of gratitude and humiliation. It disappeared almost immediately, nothing more than a glimmer.

The guy broke his gaze away and vigorously rubbed the top of his head. "Sorry. It's just . . . we haven't really talked since . . . you know. A while."

"Well, there's no time like the present," Emma said.

A whisper of a smile appeared on his lips. "Yeah."

They looked at each other again. Fireflies danced around their heads. The air suddenly smelled like wildflowers.

"Sutton?" a girl's voice called through the darkness.

Emma turned. The guy's shoulders stiffened.

"Where did she go?" someone else asked.

Emma smoothed her hair behind her ears. She peered across the front yard and saw two figures in Nisha's driveway. Lilianna's black Doc Martens clonked as she walked. Gabriella held her iPhone outstretched, using a flashlight app to lead the way.

"Be right there!" Emma yelled back. She glanced at the guy. "Why don't you come over to the party?"

He made an indignant scoff. "No thanks."

"Come on." She kept smiling. "I'll tell you all about the Slutty Star, the Nerd Star . . ."

The girls reached the end of the guy's driveway. "Sutton?" Lilianna yelled, squinting in the porch light.

"Who is that?" Gabriella called.

Slam. Emma whipped around. The guy was gone. The dried wreath that hung on the front door shook back and forth, the lock closed with a click, and the blinds on the big bay window to the right quickly twisted shut. *Okaaaay.*

Emma walked slowly off the porch and across the yard.

"Was that Ethan Landry?" Gabriella demanded.

"Were you talking?" Lilianna asked at the same time. Her voice rippled with intrigue. "What did he *say*?"

Charlotte appeared behind the Twitter Twins. Her cheeks were flushed, and her forehead looked shiny. "What's going on?"

Gabriella paused from texting. "Sutton was talking to Ethan."

"Ethan Landry?" Charlotte's eyebrows shot up. "Mr. Rebel Without a Cause actually *spoke*?"

Ethan. At least I could now put a name to his face.

And so could Emma. But then she took in the girls' confused looks. Leave it to her to instantly bond with a guy who wasn't one of Sutton's preapproved friends. At that, she pulled out her phone again. There still weren't any new messages or texts.

Charlotte's gaze felt like a piercing-hot laser; Emma had a feeling she had to come up with an explanation— fast. "I think I've had too much to drink," she blurted.

Charlotte clucked her tongue. "Oh, sweetie." She grabbed Emma by the arm and steered her toward the long line of parked cars. "I'll take you home."

Emma straightened up, relieved Charlotte had bought her story. Then she realized what Charlotte was offering. She was going to take her to *Sutton's* home. "Yes, *please*," she said, and followed Charlotte to her car.

It was a relief to me, too. Back at my house, maybe we'd finally get some answers.

7

THE BEDROOM EMMA NEVER HAD

Charlotte pulled her big black Jeep Cherokee alongside the curb and shifted it into PARK. "Here we are, Madam," she said in a fake British accent.

She had driven Emma to a two-story stucco house with big arched windows. Palms, cacti, and a couple of beautifully maintained flower beds covered the gravel front yard. Flowers in big stone pots lined the archway to the front door, wind chimes dangled over the front porch, and a terra-cotta sun sculpture hung over the three-car garage. Etched into the side of the mailbox at the curb was a simple letter *M*. Two cars sat in the driveway, a Volkswagen Jetta and a big Nissan SUV.

I could only come up with one word for it: *home.*

"Someone sure got the short end of the twin stick," Emma muttered under her breath. If only Becky had ditched *her* first.

"What was that?" Charlotte asked.

Emma picked at a loose thread on her dress. "Nothing."

Charlotte touched Emma's bare arm. "Did Mads freak you out?"

Emma regarded Charlotte's red hair and blue dress, wishing she could tell her what was going on. "I knew it was them the whole time," she said instead.

"Okay." Charlotte turned up the radio. "See you tomorrow then, drunky. Remember to take lots of vitamins before you pass out. And, hey, sleepover at my house on Friday? I promise it'll be good. My dad's still out of town, and my mom won't bother us."

Emma frowned. "Your dad's out of town?" The man she'd seen at Sabino Canyon popped into her head.

A worried look crossed Charlotte's face, the first crack in her armor Emma had seen all night. "He's been in Tokyo for the past month. Why?"

Emma ran her hand along the back of her neck. "No reason." The guy on the trail must have been someone else.

She slammed the car door and walked up the driveway. The air smelled citrusy from the orange and lemon trees in the front yard. A silver windsock flapped on the eaves of the front porch. The swirling patterns in the stucco reminded Emma of icing on a cake. She peeked through the foyer window and saw a crystal chandelier and a grand piano. Small reflective stickers on an upstairs bedroom window said, CHILD INSIDE. IN CASE OF FIRE, PLEASE RESCUE FIRST. No foster family had ever bothered to put those stickers on Emma's windows.

She wished she could take a photo, but then she heard an engine rev behind her. Emma turned and saw Charlotte watching her from the curb, one eyebrow raised. *Just leave*, Emma silently willed. *I'm fine.*

The Jeep didn't budge. Emma scanned the sidewalk, crouched down, and overturned a large rock near to the porch. To her astonishment, a silver key glimmered underneath. She almost burst out laughing. Hiding keys under rocks was something she'd seen on TV; she didn't think people actually *did* it.

Emma climbed the porch stairs and stuck the key into the lock. It turned easily. She stepped across the threshold and gave Charlotte another wave. Satisfied, Charlotte pulled away from the curb. The engine snarled, and the red taillights vanished into the night. And then Emma took a deep breath and pushed open the door to the house.

My house, not that I could recall much of it. The creak of the porch swing I used to sit on and read magazines.

The smell of the lavender room spray my mom drenched the place with. I could distinctly remember the sound of our doorbell, two high-pitched, tweet-like dings, and that the front door would sometimes stick a bit before opening. But other than that . . .

The foyer was cool and silent. Long shadows dripped down the wall, and the tall wooden grandfather clock ticked in the corner. The floorboards creaked beneath Emma's feet as she took a tentative step onto the striped carpet runner that led straight to the staircase. She reached out to flip on a nearby light switch, then hesitated and pulled back. She kept expecting alarms to sound, a cage to drop over her head, and people to jump out and shout, "Intruder!"

Grasping the banister, Emma tiptoed up the stairs in the darkness. Maybe Sutton was upstairs. Maybe she just fell asleep, and this was all a big misunderstanding. This night could be salvaged. She could still have the fairy-tale reunion she'd imagined.

A brown wicker hamper stuffed with dirty towels sat just outside a white-tiled bathroom at the top of the landing. Two night-lights glowed near the baseboard, casting yellowish columns of light up the wall. Dog tags jingled from behind a closed door at the end of the hall.

Emma turned and gazed at a bedroom door. Pictures of supermodels on a Parisian catwalk and James Blake and

Andy Roddick playing at Wimbledon hung at eye level, and a pink-glitter placard that said SUTTON swung from the knob. *Bingo.* Emma pushed gently at the door. It gave way easily and soundlessly.

The room was fragrant with notes of mint, lily of the valley, and fabric softener. Moonlight streamed through the window and spilled across a perfectly made four-poster bed. A giraffe-print rug sat to its left, and an egg chair in the corner was strewn with T-shirts, bikini tops, and a few balled-up pairs of sports socks. On the windowsills were candles in big glass jars, blue, green, and brown wine bottles with flowers protruding from their mouths, and a bunch of empty Valrhona French chocolate wrappers. Every available surface was covered with pillows—there were at least ten on the bed, three on the chair, and even a couple of others strewn around on the floor. A long, white-wood desk held a sleeping MacBook Air laptop and a printer. A single card that said SUTTON'S EIGHTEENTH BIRTHDAY BASH! FABULOUSNESS REQUIRED! was propped up next to the mouse. A filing cabinet beneath the desk had a big pink padlock on the handle and a sticker that said THE L GAME. Was that like *The L Word*?

But there was one crucial thing missing, Emma thought. Sutton.

Of *course* I was missing. I gazed around the quiet room along with Emma, hoping it might spark a memory—or a clue. Was there a reason the window that faced the back-yard was halfway open? Had I deliberately left a copy of *Teen Vogue* open to an article about Fashion Week in London? I couldn't remember reading that issue, let alone why I'd stopped at that page. I couldn't remember any of the items in this room, all the things that used to be mine.

Emma checked her phone again. *No new messages.* She wanted to look around the house, but what if she bumped into something . . . or someone? She reached for her phone and composed a new text to Sutton's number: I'M IN YOUR BEDROOM NOW. WHEREVER YOU ARE, TEXT ME BACK TO LET ME KNOW YOU'RE OKAY. I'M WORRIED.

She pressed SEND. A split second later, a muffled ding-dong emanated from across the room, which made Emma jump. She moved in the direction of the sound, a silver clutch bag next to the computer. She unzipped it. Inside was an iPhone in a pink case and a blue Kate Spade wallet. Emma pulled out the phone and gasped. The text she'd just written glowed on the screen.

She immediately began to scroll through the day's texts. There was the last one Emma had sent. Above that, at 8:20, was a text from Laurel Mercer, Sutton's sister: THANKS FOR NOTHING, BITCH.

Emma dropped the phone and backed away from the desk, as if it was suddenly covered in toxic mold. *I can't look through her phone,* she scolded herself silently. Sutton might walk in any minute and see. That wouldn't be the greatest way to start off the sisterly relationship.

She picked up her BlackBerry again and sent Sutton a private message on Facebook saying the same thing—maybe Sutton was just downstairs on a different computer and had forgotten her phone? Then she surveyed the rest of the room. Behind the desk was a bulletin board plastered with pictures of Sutton and her friends, the girls Emma had met just hours ago. Some of them looked recent: In a picture of Sutton, Charlotte, Madeline, and Laurel at the monkey house at the Tucson Zoo, Charlotte wore the same blue dress she'd had on at the party tonight. There was one of Sutton, Madeline, Laurel, and a familiar dark-haired boy standing at the edge of a canyon waterfall. Laurel and the guy splashed each other while Sutton and Madeline struck aloof, blasé poses. Other photos looked much older, maybe from junior high. There was a picture of the trio of friends standing over a bowl of cookie dough in someone's kitchen, trying to shove goopy spoons in one another's faces. Madeline wore a ballet leotard and was, er, *flatter* than she was now. Charlotte had braces and rounder cheeks. Emma stared at Sutton; it was her identical face, just four years younger.

Tiptoeing to Sutton's closet in the corner, Emma wrapped her hand around the knob. Was snooping in Sutton's closet just as bad as looking through her texts?

Deciding it wasn't, she pulled open the door to reveal a big square room filled with wooden hangers and organized shelves. Sighing wistfully, she reached out and touched all the dresses, blouses, blazers, sweaters, and skirts, pressing some of the soft fabrics to her cheek.

A couple of games were piled in the back of the closet: Clue and Scattergories and Monopoly. On top of that was a box that said JUNIOR BIRDWATCHER'S KIT. It included a bird book and a pair of binoculars. A tag on the front read: TO SUTTON, LOVE DAD. The box looked unopened; Emma figured Sutton hadn't much liked the gift. She touched a file folder stuffed with what looked like old tests and papers. A spelling quiz from fifth grade had an A-plus on top of it, but a ninth-grade book report on *Fahrenheit 451* had earned a C, accompanied by a note in red pen that said *Clearly did not read the book.* Then she noticed a paper titled "My Family History." *I don't know my real family history,* Sutton had typed. *I was adopted when I was a baby. My parents told me when I was a little girl. I've never met my birth mother, and I know nothing about her.*

Emma felt ashamed for smiling, but she couldn't help it.

Emma spotted a jewelry case toward the back of the closet; she opened the lid and sifted through Sutton's chunky bracelets, delicate gold necklaces, and dangling silver earrings. She didn't see the locket Sutton had worn in the snuff video though. Maybe she was wearing it now?

I looked down at my shimmering body. I didn't have it on. Perhaps it was with my *real* body. My dead body. Wherever *that* was.

In the three-way mirror at the back of Sutton's closet, Emma blinked at multiple versions of her stupefied reflection. *Where are you, Sutton?* she implored in her head. *Why did you make me come all this way and then not show up?*

She exited the closet. When she sat down on Sutton's bed, exhaustion flattened her like a bullet train. Her head throbbed. Every muscle felt like a wrung-out sponge. She leaned back on the mattress. It was as soft as a cloud, way better than the Kmart blue light specials foster families always stuck her with. She kicked off her wedges and heard them thud to the floor. She might as well wait here for Sutton. Surely she'd show up sooner or later.

Her breathing slowed. Fake news items swirled through her mind. *Girl Impersonates Sister at Party. Sister Is Kind of a Flake.* Surely tomorrow would be a better day. *Twin Sisters Finally Meet*, maybe.

Emma turned over on her side and snuggled into the Tide-scented pillow. The shapes and shadows in the big bedroom became blurrier and blurrier.

And with another few breaths, everything faded away for both of us.

8

COFFEE, MUFFINS, MISTAKEN IDENTITY . . .

"Sutton. *Sutton.*"

Emma awoke to someone shaking her shoulders. She was in a bright room. Green-and-white striped curtains fluttered at the window. The ceiling was smooth and unlined. A low bureau and a large LCD-screen TV sat in the place where Clarice's ratty dresser used to be.

Wait a minute. She wasn't *at* Clarice's anymore. Emma sat up.

"Sutton," the voice said again. A blond woman hovered over her. There were tiny streaks of gray at her temples and minute lines around her eyes. She wore a blue suit, high heels, and a lot of makeup. The photo of

Sutton's family raising slushy drinks into the air flickered in Emma's mind. This was Sutton's *mom*.

Emma leapt out of bed, staring crazily around the room. "What time is it?" she exclaimed.

"You have exactly ten minutes to get to school." Mrs. Mercer shoved a dress on a hanger and pair of T-strap heels at her. She paused on Emma for a moment. "I hope you didn't walk in front of the open window like that."

Emma looked down at herself. At some point in the night, she'd sleep-stripped off the striped dress she'd worn to the party and now wore only a bra and a pair of boy shorts. She quickly crossed her arms over her chest.

Then she stared at the wedges she'd kicked to the floor last night. They lay in the exact same spot she'd left them. Sutton's silver clutch and pink-cased iPhone still sat on her desk. Reality snapped into nauseating focus. *Sutton didn't come back last night*, Emma realized. *She never found me.*

"Wait a minute." Emma grabbed Mrs. Mercer's arm. This had gone too far. Something was really wrong. "This is a mistake."

"Of course it's a mistake." Mrs. Mercer rushed across the room and threw a pair of Champion mesh shorts, a racer-back tank top, sneakers, and a Wilson tennis racket into a big red tennis bag with the name SUTTON stitched across the side. "Didn't you set an alarm?" Then she paused and smacked herself lightly on the forehead. "What am I thinking? Of course you didn't. It's *you*."

I watched my mom as she dropped the tennis bag on the bed and zipped it up tight. Even my own mother couldn't tell that Emma wasn't me.

Mrs. Mercer pointed Emma toward the dress she'd laid flat on the bed. When Emma didn't move, she sighed, yanked the dress from the hanger, and dragged it over Emma's head.

"I can trust you to put your shoes on by yourself, can't I?" Mrs. Mercer said tightly, holding up a shoe by its T-strap. The label said MARC BY MARC JACOBS. "Be down for breakfast in two minutes."

"Wait!" Emma protested, but Mrs. Mercer had already marched out of the room and slammed the door so hard that a snapshot of Sutton, Laurel, Charlotte, and Madeline fell from the bulletin board and landed facedown on the floor.

Emma stared around the silent room in panic. She darted to the ottoman where she'd left her cell phone. *No new messages,* said the screen. She raced to Sutton's iPhone on the desk. There was one new text since she'd last checked, but it was only from Garrett: YOU VANISHED LAST NIGHT! SEE YOU IN FIRST PERIOD? XX!

"This is insane," Emma whispered. The post she'd seen on Sutton's Facebook Wall before she left Vegas popped into her head. *Ever think about running away? I do.* Could Sutton have run away thinking Emma could take her place long enough for her to get a head start? She strode barefoot out of Sutton's bedroom and down the stairs.

The downstairs hallway was decorated with huge framed family photographs: school pictures, shots from family vacations to Paris and San Diego, and a portrait of the Mercer family at what looked like a fancy wedding in Palm Springs. Emma followed the sound of the morning news and the smell of coffee to the kitchen. It was a huge room with sparkling, floor-to-ceiling windows that looked out onto a brick patio and the mountains beyond. The counters were dark, the cabinets white, and there was a bunch of pineapple paraphernalia all over the room— wooden pineapples atop the cabinets, a ceramic pineapple cylinder that held spatulas and slotted spoons, a pineapple-shaped placard near the back door that said WELCOME!

Mrs. Mercer poured coffee at the sink. Sutton's sister, Laurel, dissected a croissant at the kitchen table, dressed in a flowing printed top that looked identical to a shirt Emma had seen in Sutton's closet last night. Mr. Mercer stepped in through the door, carrying plastic-wrapped copies of the *Wall Street Journal* and the *Tucson Daily Star.* Emma noticed his doctor's coat, which said J MERCER, ORTHOPEDIC SURGERY. Like Mrs. Mercer, he was also a little older than most of the foster parents Emma had known, possibly a well-preserved fiftysomething. Emma wondered if they'd tried to have kids on their own before adopting Sutton. And what about Laurel? She had the same square jaw as Mrs. Mercer and the same round blue eyes as Mr. Mercer. Perhaps she was their biological daughter. Maybe the Mercers had finally conceived as soon as the adoption had gone through—Emma had read about that phenomenon somewhere.

Everyone looked up when Emma appeared in the doorway, including an enormous Great Dane. He rose from a striped doggie bed by the door and trotted over. He sniffed her hand, his big jowls grazing her skin. DRAKE, glinted a bone-shaped tag on his collar. Emma stood absolutely still. In seconds, Drake would probably start barking his head off, knowing Emma wasn't who everyone thought she was. But then Drake snorted, turned, and trotted back to his bed.

A flash about Drake suddenly bubbled to the surface for me. His loud panting. The feel of his tongue on my face. How he'd howl goofily whenever an ambulance roared by. I felt an achy longing to wrap my arms around his big neck and kiss his cold, wet nose.

Mrs. Mercer set down a bottle of vitamins and walked over to Emma. "Drink." She shoved a glass of orange juice toward Emma. "Do you have cash for lunch?"

"I need to tell you something," Emma said loudly and

sharply. Everyone stopped and stared at her. She cleared her throat. "I'm not Sutton. Your daughter is missing. She might have run away."

A spoon clattered against a plate, and Mrs. Mercer's eyebrows arched. Emma braced herself for something awful to happen—alarms to go off, fireworks to erupt, ninjas to emerge from the laundry room and take her down, anything that might indicate what she'd just revealed was very, very dangerous. But then Mr. Mercer just shook his head and took a sip of coffee from an ALOHA FROM HAWAII! pineapple mug. "And who, pray tell, might you be?" he asked.

"I'm her . . . long-lost twin sister, Emma. I was supposed to meet Sutton yesterday. But she's . . . gone."

Mrs. Mercer blinked rapidly. Mr. Mercer exchanged an incredulous look with Laurel.

"Save the creativity for English class." Mrs. Mercer plucked a croissant from a platter on the island and pushed it toward Emma.

"I'm serious. My name is Emma," she told them.

"Emma, hmm? And what's your last name?"

"Pa—" Emma started, but Laurel slammed her coffee cup to the table. "You seriously don't believe her, do you, Mom? She's just trying to get out of school."

"Of course I don't believe her." Mrs. Mercer pushed a folded piece of paper into Emma's hand. "Here's your schedule. Laurel, can you get Sleeping Beauty's shoes and tennis bag from upstairs?"

"Why do *I* have to do it?" Laurel whined.

"Because I don't trust your sister." Mrs. Mercer grabbed a set of keys from a pineapple-shaped holder by the cordless phone. "She might fall back to sleep."

"Fine." Laurel groaned and scraped back her chair.

Emma stared blankly at the shiny brass buttons on Mrs. Mercer's business suit, then at the new-agey crystal necklace at her throat. How could this be happening? Why didn't they believe her? Was it *that* crazy?

Maybe. Even though I wanted my parents to believe what Emma was saying, it *did* kind of sound insane.

Laurel walked across the room toward the stairs. "Thanks a lot for last night, jerk," she hissed at Emma as she passed.

Emma stepped back as if Laurel had just slapped her. Then she remembered Charlotte's remark at the party. *Did you ditch Laurel again? You're a bad, bad sister.* There was also the text from Laurel on Sutton's phone: THANKS FOR NOTHING, BITCH.

"*I* didn't ditch you." Emma spun around and stared at Laurel's receding back. "I was waiting for Sutton when Madeline dragged me to the party. I had no control."

Laurel backtracked and stopped right in front of Emma. "*Sure*, Sutton. Just blow off the one thing I asked you weeks ago to do. I was basically stranded at Red Door. I bet you rigged it so you knew my phone was about to die, too, huh?" She had natural highlights and tiny freckles across her nose. Her wide jaw worked a fresh piece of Juicy Fruit gum. "Where's your locket?"

Emma's hand fluttered to her collarbone and she shrugged helplessly.

Laurel's lips parted. She let out a low scoff. "But I thought it was so *special* to you," she said icily. "Something *no one* else has. 'The only way someone's getting this from me is if they chop off my head!'" Her voice took on a singsong quality as she mimicked Sutton's.

"Girls, don't fight," Mr. Mercer warned, reaching across the kitchen island to grab his leather briefcase and car keys.

"Yes, don't fight," Mrs. Mercer urged. "Just get those bags, okay? You have thirty seconds." Laurel whirled around and started up the stairs. "Whose car are you taking? Sutton, is yours still at Madeline's?"

Mrs. Mercer turned to Emma, waiting. "Uh, yes?" Emma guessed.

"We'll take mine," Laurel yelled from the floor above.

Mrs. Mercer ushered Emma out into the foyer. Emma's nose twitched with the smell of Fracas perfume. She looked deep into the woman's eyes, trying to convey exactly who she was . . . and exactly who she *wasn't*. Surely she'd recognize her own daughter, right?

But Mrs. Mercer just pressed her hands on Emma's shoulders. A tendon stood out in her neck. "Can you please go easy on us today?" She shut her eyes and let out a huge sigh. "We're throwing you a huge birthday party in two weeks. Just once can you actually earn it?"

Emma flinched, then quickly nodded. Apparently they really *didn't* believe her.

Laurel thundered back down the stairs with a bunch of sports bags and purses in her arms. She pushed the T-straps Mrs. Mercer had picked out, the tennis duffel, and a buttery-leather beige purse Emma didn't recognize into Emma's arms. Emma peeked inside the handbag. Sutton's blue Kate Spade wallet and pink-cased iPhone were nestled into the inside pockets. At the bottom of the bag were pens, pencils, Dior mascara, and a spanking-new iPad. Emma raised her eyebrows. At least she'd finally find out what an iPad was like.

Mrs. Mercer opened the front door wide. "Get out of here." Laurel strode to the porch, her car keys jingling in her hands. A silver RETURN TO TIFFANY & CO. keychain dangled from the ring. After shoving on her shoes, Emma followed. She had a feeling that if she didn't, Mrs. Mercer would jab her out the door with the decorative rowing oar that stood in the corner of the foyer.

As soon as Emma stepped outside, sweat beaded at her

forehead. Sprinklers hissed on the lawn across the street, and little kids in plaid school uniforms waited at the corner for the bus. Laurel glared at Emma over her shoulder as she walked across the driveway, her high heels making staccato clacks. "That was a lame way to try to get out of school." She hit a button on the keychain remote. After two short *bleeps*, a black VW Jetta under the basketball hoop unlocked. "Your long-lost twin sister? Where'd you come up with *that*?"

Emma peered across the street again. She kept hoping to see Sutton saunter down the sidewalk, ready with an apology and an explanation. Bees swarmed impassively around the flowering bushes. A landscaping truck trundled past. The mountain range glowed in the rising sun, Sabino Canyon somewhere among it.

"Hello, space cadet?"

Emma flinched. Laurel walked toward her again, a small white envelope in her hands. SUTTON, it said on the front in tall capital letters. "It was under my wiper." Laurel's voice was tinged with bitterness. "Do you have *another* secret admirer?"

Emma considered the note for a moment. A few buds of pollen had stained the upper right corner. Should she open something that wasn't hers? But Laurel kept staring, waiting, snapping her gum in Emma's ear.

Finally Emma gave Laurel a look. "Do you mind giving

me a little space?" It sounded like something Sutton might say.

Laurel sniffed and took one step away. Emma slid her finger under the flap on the envelope and pulled out a sheet of lined paper.

Sutton's dead. Tell no one. Keep playing along . . . or you're next.

Emma whipped around the yard, but the morning was eerily still. The school bus grumbled to the corner and picked up the little kids. As it pulled away, its squeaky brakes sounded like screams.

"What's it say?" Laurel leaned over.

Emma quickly crumpled the note in her hand. "Nothing." Her voice was barely audible.

Laurel's lip curled in a snarl. Then she opened the passenger door and pointed to the seat. "Just get in."

Emma did as she was told, dazedly slumping into the seat and staring straight ahead. Her heart pounded so hard she was afraid it might explode.

"You're being so weird," Laurel said, starting the car. "What's wrong with you?"

As I watched, spots began to cloud my vision. A rushing sound whooshed in my ears. *What's wrong with you?* I heard Laurel say again and again. The words rippled out in waves, growing louder and louder. Suddenly I saw Laurel sitting in a dark grotto. Light danced across her face. The corners of her mouth turned down. Tears dotted her eyes. *What's wrong with you? What's wrong with you?* The words clanged in my head like a clapper in a bell.

A tiny flare erupted in the darkness of my mind. And then another flare, and then another. It was like a line of falling dominoes, cascading until I had a fully formed scene from my past. A *memory*.

All at once, I could distinctly remember where and when Laurel had asked, "What's wrong with you?" before. And that wasn't the only thing I saw. . . .

9

IMITATION IS THE HIGHEST FORM OF FLATTERY

"The party has officially started," I call, strutting out from behind a big boulder where I changed into a silver bikini. My legs are freshly waxed, my face is blemish-free, and my hair glows softly in the lights from the resort. All eyes are on me.

Garrett whistles. "You put the hot in hot springs."

I grin. "You know it."

Garrett beckons me closer. He's submerged in the warm, swirling water of the hot springs at the Clayton resort, a secret spa in the shadows of the mountains. We aren't technically allowed to be here—the spring is strictly for the wealthiest visitors—but that wasn't about to stop my friends and me. We always find ways of getting what we want.

"*Come on in, dahling,*" Madeline calls. *She's already in the hot spring, too. Her hair is swept up on the top of her head in a sloppy bun, her arms are lithe from her million-hours-a-week of Pilates and ballet, and the heat from the water gives her skin a sexy sheen. Mads always looks a little bit better than I do, which always pisses me off. And she's sitting close to Garrett—a little too close. Not that I'm really worried about anything happening— both Madeline and Garrett know I'd kill them if it did—but I like to have Garrett all to myself.*

We've only been dating for two months. Everyone thinks I'm dating him because he's one of the school's star soccer players, or because he looks devastatingly gorgeous on top of the lifeguard stand at the W Resort pool, or because his family has a beach house in Cabo San Lucas that they visit every spring. But the truth is, I like Garrett because he's a little . . . damaged. He isn't like all the other cocky guys around here, living their charmed, uneventful, hermetically sealed suburban lives.

I wedge myself between the two of them, shooting Madeline a cool smile. "You weren't feeling my boyfriend up under the water, were you, Mads? I know you have some trouble telling guys apart."

Madeline's face flushes. Not long ago, shortly after Mads's brother, Thayer, took off, Mads made out with a dark-haired guy from Ventana Prep at a party in the desert. After a while, she excused herself to refresh her drink, returned to the designated make-out area, and resumed kissing again . . . except this new guy was blond. Madeline didn't even notice for at least a couple of minutes; I was the only one who'd seen. Sometimes I wonder if Mads is trying really hard to do the Lindsay Lohan thing: pretty girl goes rogue, gets wild, and screws up life.

I pat Madeline's shoulder, which is warm from the steam. "Don't worry. Your secret is safe with me." I pantomime locking my lips and throwing away the key.

Then I sink down into the hot water. Some girls get into the springs slowly, making little squeals as they expose an inch of flesh to the heat at a time. I like to plunge in all at once. The eye-watering burn gives me a rush.

Charlotte is the next one to emerge from behind the rocks. She's still wearing a pink terry-cloth cover-up, her hands shielding her pale, pudgy legs. We all cheer hello. Laurel follows right behind Charlotte, giggling hysterically. I sigh and curl my toes under the water. What is Laurel doing here? I didn't invite her.

Garrett's cell phone rings. MOM, says the Caller ID. "I'd better get that," he murmurs. He pushes out of the spring, water plopping onto the rocks. "Hello?" he says in a gentle voice, disappearing into the trees.

Madeline rolls her eyes good-naturedly. "Garrett's such a mama's boy."

"It's not like he doesn't have a good reason," Charlotte says in a know-it-all voice. She perches on a rock close to the springs. "I mean, when we were togeth—"

"Why don't you get in with us this time, Char?" I interrupt, *wanting to cut Charlotte off before she starts in on another one of her I-know-what's-best-since-I-dated-your-boyfriend-before-you monologues.*

Charlotte pulls her legs away from the water. "I'm fine," *she says prissily.*

I giggle. "C'mon. What's a little lobster-splotchy skin among friends? I bet some guys find heat hives sexy."

Charlotte twists her mouth and moves her bare foot farther away from the water. "I'm fine right here, Sutton."

"Suit yourself." *I grab Madeline's iPhone from a nearby rock.* "Picture time! Everyone gather around!"

All of us squeeze into the frame and I snap the flash. "Good, but not great," *I say when I check the result.* "Mads, you're doing your beauty-queen face again." *I frame my face with my hands and give them an all-I-want-is-world-peace smile.*

Laurel looks over my shoulder. "I'm not in it at all." *She points out her arm, the only part of her body that made it in the photo.*

"I know," *I say.* "I planned it that way."

A heartbroken look crosses Laurel's face. Madeline and Charlotte shift uncomfortably. After a moment, Charlotte pokes Laurel's shoulder. "Love the necklace, Laur."

Laurel brightens a little. "Thanks! I got it today."

"Very pretty," *Madeline chimes in.*

I lean over to see what all the fuss is about. A large silver circle dangles from Laurel's neck. "Can I see that?" *I ask Laurel in the sweetest voice I can muster.*

Laurel looks at me nervously, then leans closer.

*"Pretty." I trace my finger over the locket. "Pretty familiar."
I narrow my eyes, lift my hair from my neck, and show her the
same necklace around my throat. I'd had it forever, but I'd only
started wearing it recently. I'd announced to the group that it was
going to be my signature necklace, like how Nicole Richie always
wears drapey boho dresses or how Kate Moss does the blazer and
micro-denim-shorts thing. Laurel was there when I said it, too.
She was also there when I'd added that from then on I was never
going to take it off. The only way someone was going to get it from
me was if they chopped off my head.*

*Laurel fiddles with the strap on her bikini top. She's wearing
what I call her slut-kini; the top's straps are so thin and the trian-
gles so small that she's practically giving all of us a free peepshow.
"It's not quite the same," she argues. "Your locket is bigger, see?
And mine isn't even a locket. It doesn't open."*

*Charlotte squints at my neck, then at Laurel's. "She's right,
Sutton."*

"Yeah, they're different enough," Madeline agrees.

*I want to fling molten-hot water into their faces. How dare
my friends fuss over my sister's complete lack of originality? It's
bad enough Laurel tagged along with us. It's bad enough that
my friends let her into our club just because they feel sorry for her
after Thayer's disappearance. And it's really bad enough that my
parents—especially my dad—dote on her at home, meanwhile
treating me like I'm a bomb about to detonate.*

Before I know what I'm doing, my hand wraps around the locket and I yank the chain from Laurel's neck. Then I fling it into the woods. There's a tiny plink of metal bouncing off one of the rocks, and then a nearly inaudible rustling sound as the necklace lands in the thick brush.

Laurel blinks hard. "W-Why did you do that?"

"That's what you get for copying me."

Tears fill her eyes. "What's wrong with you?" She lets out a tortured wail, climbs out of the hot springs, catapults over the rocks, and runs into the woods.

No one moves for a few long beats. Steam swirls around my friends' faces, but it suddenly seems foreboding instead of sexy. I groan and climb out of the water, too, feeling a stab of guilt.

"Laurel!" I call into the woods. No answer. I jam my feet into my flip-flops, pull on a T-shirt and a pair of terry-cloth shorts, and start in the direction she went.

The solar lights that line the path end a few yards past the springs, giving way to eerie darkness. I take a few tentative steps into a thicket of mesquite trees, my arms outstretched in front of me. "Laurel?" I hear a flutter close by, then a snap. "Laurel?" I take another few steps, pushing through tall desert grass. Tiny cactus spines prick my skin.

More footsteps. A sob. "Laurel, come on," I say through clenched teeth. "I'm sorry, okay? I'll buy you a new necklace." One that doesn't look exactly like mine, I want to add.

After passing a few more trees, I emerge into an empty

clearing—a long-dried-out creek bed. Hot, stale air hangs heavily around my face. Twisted shadows spill across the cracked earth. Cicadas croak noisily in the bushes. "Laurel?" I cry. I can't see the resort lights through the trees anymore. I'm not even sure where the resort is. Then, I hear a footstep. "Hello?" I call out, suddenly alert. Something blinks at me from the savanna grass. I hear a whisper, followed by a faraway giggle. And then I feel a hand on my shoulder. Something cold and sharp presses up against my neck.

My whole body stiffens. Strong hands grab me and pin my arms back. Something presses against my throat, cutting off my breathing, digging into my skin. Pain shoots through me. It's a knife. "Scream and you die," a voice rasps in my ear.

And then . . . darkness.

10

EVERY GUY LOVES A FELON

I snapped back to Laurel's car, where Emma sat stiffly in the passenger seat as she backed out of the driveway.

Sutton's dead, she thought. *Sutton's DEAD.* It was impossible to comprehend. *Dead . . . where? How? Did it have to do with that snuff video? Had someone actually strangled her?*

A tight ball filled her stomach. Her eyes watered with tears. Even though she'd never met her sister, even though she'd found out about her existence only two days earlier, it was an earth-shattering loss. Discovering she had a twin was like hitting the jackpot, something Emma had never dared to dream of. All the hope she'd bottled up for years had reached a crescendo these past two days. And now . . .

Think about how *I* felt. I'd stared hard at the note when Emma opened it. Actually seeing SUTTON'S DEAD written there on the paper in black and white made it undeniable. I was really dead. *Gone.* And I *had* been murdered—my jumbled memories had been right. The darkness. The flailing. The knife at my throat. Now whoever had done this wanted a sister I'd never met to take my place so no one else would ever find out the truth. As if it was that easy! If only I had a say in this. I didn't want to hand my life over to someone else.

And Emma didn't want to step into it either. She sniffed loudly and Laurel turned. "What?" The corners of her mouth turned down.

Emma pressed her fingertips against the note. *Sutton's dead.* Laurel deserved to see this, didn't she? Sutton's very own sister should know she was dead, right? Yet, Emma couldn't show her. What if Laurel didn't believe her, figuring it was just another attempt to skip school? And what if the second part of the threat was true? *Keep playing along, or you're next.* If Emma told someone, something terrible could happen.

"Nothing," she finally answered.

Laurel shrugged and rolled down the neighborhood street, turning right at a big park with a dog run, a huge playground, and three outdoor tennis courts. When she made another turn, a line of organic markets, high-end nail salons, and funky boutiques flanked one side, and a UPS store, a stucco police station, and the stone entrance for Hollier High School were on the other. Cars jammed the left-turn lane, waiting to enter the school lot. Blond girls in Ray-Bans lazed in convertibles. The bass throbbed inside a big Escalade with a HOLLIER VARSITY FOOTBALL bumper sticker. A dark-haired girl on a sea-green Vespa wove through the waiting cars, sometimes with just a few inches to spare.

Emma stared at the police station as they made the turn into the school. Six squad cars sat in the parking lot. A cop in a uniform stubbed out a cigarette on the front walk.

Laurel gunned the car up a small slope and passed a large red sign that said JUNIOR PARKING LOT. She glanced at Emma out of the corner of her eye. "You can't lie to Mom forever about where your car is. And I don't really want to be your chauffeur for the rest of the year."

Just then, something occurred to Emma. She turned to Sutton's sister. "Why didn't you just drive your car to Nisha's party last night?"

Laurel blew air out of her cheeks. "*Duh*. Because Dad took it into the shop. You *knew* that."

They drove past the line of parked cars. The mood was like a tailgate party before a football game. Kids lounged on the bumpers, sipping Jamba Juice smoothies. Guys played soccer in the dusty square to the right of the lot. Three pretty girls wearing sherbet-colored Havaiana flip-flops watched a slide show of vacation photos on a laptop propped up inside a Mini hatchback.

Sutton's dead, Emma thought once more. The realization kept sweeping over her like a series of crashing waves. She had to do something. She couldn't keep this to herself any longer. No matter what the note said. Emma's heart started to pound.

Laurel pulled into a space near a large trash can already filled to the brim with water bottles and Starbucks cups. As soon as she cut the engine, Emma yanked at the door handle, leapt out of the car, and took off through the field toward the police station.

"Hey!" Laurel screamed behind her. "Sutton? What the hell?"

Emma didn't answer. She picked her way across the hardscrabble vegetation that separated the school from the police-station parking lot. Brambles scratched her arms, but she barely noticed. She emerged on a narrow strip of lawn and burst through the station doors.

It was cool and dark inside. The big room, arranged into a series of cubicles and desks, smelled like Kung Pao chicken and sweat. Phones rang, walkie-talkies buzzed, and a sports radio droned in the background. The Venetian blinds had dust on the slats, and there was a crumpled Fanta can full of cigarette butts on the floor near the door. On the far wall was a big bulletin board tacked with IF YOU SEE SOMETHING, SAY SOMETHING posters and Most Wanted lists. A black-and-white photo of a young guy with dark hair and familiar soulful eyes caught Emma's eye. MISSING SINCE JUNE 17. THAYER VEGA. It was the same eerie poster Emma had seen on Sutton's Facebook.

A wild-haired older man in a trench coat took up most of the only bench. There were handcuffs around his wrists. When he saw Emma, he brightened and gave her a big I'm-the-kind-of-guy-who-shows-my-naughty-parts-to-little-girls smile.

"Can I help you?"

Emma turned. A young cop with white-blond buzz-cut hair eyed her from behind a big desk. A small oscillating fan on his desk blew stale air into her face. The screen saver on his monitor showed pictures of two bug-eyed children in baseball and gymnastic uniforms. Emma eyed the handcuffs linked to his belt and the gun in his holster. She licked her lips and took a few steps toward him.

"I want to report a . . . a missing person. Possibly a murder."

Blondie's pale, almost nonexistent eyebrows shot up. "Who's missing?"

"My twin sister." And then, everything that had happened spewed out of her, spurting like blood from a wound. "Last night, I thought it was just a miscommunication, and Sutton was fine," she finished. "But this morning, I got this." She unfolded the note and smoothed it out on the cop's desk. SUTTON'S DEAD. TELL NO ONE. KEEP PLAYING ALONG . . . OR YOU'RE NEXT. It looked so real and scary under the harsh fluorescent lights.

Blondie's lips moved silently as he read it. "*Sutton*," he whispered emphatically. It was as though a light bulb had illuminated over his head. He picked up the receiver on his phone and pressed a button. "Quinlan? You free?"

He hung up the phone and patted the orange chair next to his desk. "Stay here," he told Emma. Then he grabbed the note, strode to the back of the station, and disappeared into a small office marked DETECTIVE QUINLAN. Emma stared at the officer's profile in silhouette against the large, bright back window. His hands moved quickly as he spoke.

The door to the detective's office swung open again, and the blond cop strode out. Quinlan, a taller, older, dark-haired guy with a manila folder under his arm and a University of Arizona coffee mug in his hand, followed. When he saw Emma at the front desk, he grimaced. "How many times are we going to go down this road?" he demanded, waving Emma's note in the air.

Emma looked around. *Was he talking to someone else?* Besides Mr. Indecent Exposure on the bench, she was the only person in the room. "Excuse me?"

Quinlan leaned his forearms on the back of the chair. "Although a fake murder threat is a new one even for you, Sutton."

Sutton's name was a punch to Emma's gut. "No. I'm *not* Sutton. I'm her twin sister, Emma. Didn't he tell you?" She jutted a thumb at the blond cop. "Something awful happened to Sutton, and now whoever did it is threatening me! I'm telling the truth!"

"Just like you were telling the truth about that dead body near Mount Lemmon last year?" The muscles around Quinlan's mouth grew tight. "Or about how your neighbor was raising ninety Chihuahuas in her guest house? Or how you *swore*, up and down, you heard a baby crying in a Dumpster behind Trader Joe's?" He tapped the folder. "You don't think I keep a record of your stunts?"

Emma stared at the folder. The name SUTTON MERCER was written on the tab in thick black ink. It made her think of her foster brother, David, in Carson City. David used to call the cops every few weeks to tell them the Port-a-Potties on a nearby worksite were on fire, mostly so he could watch fire trucks drive around. The 911 dispatchers finally caught on to his tricks, and they didn't believe David the day he called screaming about the brush fire that raged in their backyard. Flames had swallowed half the family's house before they finally sent out a rescue truck. David had officially become the Boy Who Cried Port-a-Potty. Did the cops really think Sutton was the Girl Who Cried Baby in the Dumpster?

Emma rummaged through Sutton's bag until she found her pink iPhone. With trembling fingers, she called up the video site Travis had shown her. "There's a video of someone strangling her. Maybe you can figure out where this is."

The site's main page finally loaded. Emma typed *SuttonInAZ* in the Search Window. After a moment, a new page appeared: NO MATCHES FOUND. "What?" Emma squeaked. She stared pleadingly at the cops. "This is a mistake. The video was here two days ago, I swear!"

Quinlan grunted. Before Emma knew what was happening, he reached out and grabbed the beige bag from her shoulder. He pulled out Sutton's blue Kate Spade wallet, undid the snap, and unveiled the license in the clear windowpane slot in the front. ARIZONA, the license said at the top in blue letters. Sutton had grinned for the camera, her makeup perfectly done and not a hair out of place. Emma fleetingly thought of her own driver's license photo, which had been taken in a badly lit DMV without air conditioning the day after she'd had emergency wisdom teeth extractions. Her hair stuck to her forehead, her makeup had begun to leak down her face, and her cheeks puffed out like a chipmunk's. She sort of looked like a greasy Shrek.

Quinlan tick-tocked the wallet back and forth in front of Emma's face. "Says here you're Sutton Mercer. Not some girl named Emma."

"That's not mine," Emma said weakly. She felt like the bird that had gotten trapped in Clarice's closed garage a few weeks earlier—frantic and helpless. How was she going to make anyone believe she wasn't Sutton . . . when she looked *exactly* like her? A realization struck Emma: The killer was watching her while she waited for Sutton. Maybe it was the killer who had lured her here? How long had Sutton been dead? After all, if there was no missing girl, there was no crime.

She gestured to the note. "Can't you at least dust it for fingerprints?"

He stood back, crossed his arms over his chest, and gave her an are-you-kidding-me? look. "I would think a girl who's had her car impounded wouldn't be making trouble for herself. We can add to those fines, you know."

"But . . ." Emma trailed off helplessly. She had no idea how to reply. The blond cop's phone rang, and he lunged to answer it. A cop wearing a brown cowboy hat burst through the front doors and marched to one of the interrogation rooms.

"Here." Detective Quinlan tossed the note and Sutton's wallet into Emma's lap with a look of disgust. Then he brought his face close to Emma's. "I'm taking you back to school now. If I catch you in here again, I'm going to lock you up for a night. See how you like it *then*. Got it?"

Emma nodded.

Quinlan guided Emma out the door and across the parking lot. To Emma's horror, he unlocked the back of the squad car and gestured to the backseat. "In you go."

Emma gaped at him. "Seriously?"

"Uh-huh."

She balled up her fists. *Unbelievable.* After a moment, she climbed into the back of the cop car, where the criminals sat. It smelled like a mix of puke and evergreen air freshener. Someone had written ASSHOLE on the faux-leather seat.

Quinlan swung into the front seat and turned the key in the ignition. "I'm running over to Hollier," he said into the CB radio attached to the center console. "Be back in a sec." Emma slumped down in the seat. At least he didn't turn on the siren.

As Quinlan made a left out of the lot, Emma's new reality slowly began to take shape. It had been easy—even fun—playing Sutton at a party. But she wanted to *meet* Sutton, not take over her life. And although she'd always wanted to investigate a crime, she'd never imagined she'd be part of something like this. But if no one would believe her—and if Sutton's family and the police didn't, who would?—Emma didn't have much of a choice. It was up to her alone to figure out what exactly was going on.

But she wasn't actually alone. I considered once again why I was here with Emma, watching her every move, hovering behind her as she took over my life, hung out with my friends, and kissed my boyfriend. Old Mrs. Hunt, our spooky neighbor with too many cats, once told me that ghosts lingered in our world when they had unfinished business that prevented them from moving on to the next. Maybe that's why I was here, too—to solve my own murder.

11

WATCH OUT FOR DEVIL CHILD!

Ten minutes later, Emma stood in the girls' bathroom on the first floor of Hollier High. The pink-tiled room smelled like Ajax and stale cigarettes. Thankfully, there were no feet underneath the stall doors or other girls crowded at the sink.

She stared at her tearstained face in the streaky mirror. There were circles under her eyes, worried wrinkles in her forehead, and red blotches on her cheeks and chin, which always appeared when she cried. She tried to smile, but her mouth just snapped right back into a frown. "Pull yourself together," she scolded her reflection. "You can do this. You can be Sutton."

She had to, at least until she figured out a way to get someone to believe her, anyway. She'd pulled it off the night before, sure, but that had been before she'd known what was going on.

Grief coursed through her again, sending a new flood of tears down her cheeks. She grabbed a paper towel from the dispenser. How many times had Sutton used this bathroom? How many times did she peer into this mirror? How would she feel about Emma taking her place?

I wasn't sure, to be honest. How could Emma figure out who killed me . . . *as* me? It seemed impossible. And yet . . . Emma was the only one apart from my killer who knew I was dead. She was the only chance I had.

The bell rang. Emma dabbed a bit of concealer she'd found in the bottom of Sutton's bag under her eyes, gave her dark hair a final fluff, and strode out the door as confidently as she could, even though her stomach was roiling. The hallway was packed with people at their lockers, girls hugging and squealing about their summer vacations, and guys in football and basketball jerseys shoving one another into the water fountains.

"Hi, Sutton!" a girl called as she passed. Emma forced the corners of her lips into a smile. "Can't wait for your party next Friday!" a guy yelled to Emma from the other end of the hall. Inside a classroom, two dark-haired girls whispered and pointed right at her. The note flashed back to Emma's mind again. *Anyone could've written it . . . even someone at school.*

She pulled out the schedule Mrs. Mercer had given her at breakfast. Luckily, she was close to Sutton's first class of the day, something simply abbreviated as G–103 in Room 114. As Emma crossed through the doorway, she saw a big black, red, and yellow flag hanging from the post by the blackboard. A placard that said RESPECT THE MIGHTY UMLAUT! stood on the teacher's desk. Along the far wall was a poster of a pudgy-faced boy in lederhosen. A speech bubble by his mouth contained the words EINS, ZWEI, DREI!

Emma scowled. The *G* on the schedule stood for *German*. *Eins, zwei,* and *drei* were the only German words she knew. *Perfect.* She willed herself not to start crying all over again.

More kids smiled at Emma as she walked down the aisle and fell into a seat at the back. Then she noticed a familiar dark-haired guy sitting by the window, staring out at the red running track: It was Ethan, the stargazing guy Emma had met last night. Mr. Rebel Without a Cause.

Ethan turned and looked over his shoulder, as if he sensed Emma was watching. His eyes seemed to come alive when he saw her. Emma lobbed him a tiny smile hello. He smiled back. But when another girl walked up the aisle and purred "Hey, Ethan," Ethan only gave her a terse nod.

"Psst!" a voice called from the other side of the room. Emma swiveled around and saw Garrett's spiky blond head a few rows over. He waved at her and winked. Emma waved back, but she felt like such an impostor. What would Sutton's boyfriend think if he knew she was really dead? And now she couldn't even tell him.

The bell rang again, and everyone scrambled to find their desks. An Asian woman with man-short hair and wearing a long blue dress that looked way too stifling for the Arizona heat marched stiffly into the room. *Frau Fenstermacher*, she wrote on the board in spiky handwriting, drawing a sharp line underneath. Emma wondered if she'd changed her last name for authenticity.

Frau Fenstermacher pushed her clear, Lucite-framed glasses farther down her nose as she examined the class list. "Paul Anders?" she barked.

"Here," a guy in dark-framed glasses and a Grizzly Bear band T-shirt mumbled.

"Answer in German!" The teacher was barely over five feet tall, but there was something solid and menacing about her that made it look like she could kick someone's ass.

"Oh." Paul blushed. *"Ja."* It sounded like *yah*.

"Garrett Austin?"

"Ja, ja." Garrett said it like the Swedish Chef. Everyone giggled.

Frau Fenstermacher called more names. Emma ran her fingers nervously over an anarchy symbol someone had carved into the top of the desk. *Say ja when she calls for Sutton Mercer,* she silently chanted over and over. She was sure she was going to forget.

Nine *ja*s later, Frau Fenstermacher blanched at the roll sheet. "Sutton Mercer?" she called in the angriest voice of all.

Emma's mouth opened, but it was like someone had stuffed wiener schnitzel down her throat. Everyone turned to stare at her. The giggles started again.

Frau's eyebrows came to a point. "I see you there, *Fraulein* Mercer. I know who you are, too. You're a *Teufel Kind*. Devil Child. But not in my class, *ja?*" She spit as she spoke.

The whole class swiveled from Emma to Frau Fenstermacher to Emma again, as if they were watching a Ping-Pong match. Emma licked her dry lips. *"Ja,"* she said. Her voice cracked.

Everyone laughed again. "I heard she almost got arrested twice this summer," a girl in a long sweater vest and skinny jeans whispered to a wavy-haired girl across the aisle. "And I heard her car was impounded, too. She had so many traffic violations that they finally towed the thing away."

"The cops brought her to school this morning," the wavy-haired friend whispered back.

Sweater Vest shrugged. "Not surprised."

Emma sank down in her chair, thinking about the file at the police station with Sutton's name on it. What kind of crazy girl *was* she? She reached into the pocket and touched the edge of the note, desperately wanting someone to see it, to believe it. But then she loosened her grip, pulled out Sutton's iPad, and placed it on the desk. Now if only she could figure out how to turn it on.

Six more classes of circumspect teachers. Eight wrong turns. A lunch period with Madeline and Charlotte congratulating Emma on showing up to school in a police car—apparently, to them, it was a *good* thing. Finally, at the end of the day, Emma opened Sutton's locker. She'd broken down and looked through Sutton's wallet for money before lunch, realizing there was no way she could get through the day without eating something. Besides cash, Sutton's *America's Next Top Model*–worthy driver's license, an Amex Blue, and a wallet-sized Virgo horoscope for the month of August, Emma had found a tiny slip of paper that listed Sutton's locker number and combination. It was as though Sutton had put it there on purpose, hoping Emma would find it.

If only I'd put it there on purpose. If only I'd left Emma tons of clues about who'd done this to me—put a big bull's-eye on the killer's head, maybe. I admired her for carefully examining each scrap of paper in my wallet as though it held a vital clue, though. She'd compiled a list of kids in my classes, too, writing things like *Sienna, two desks up, history: smiled, seemed friendly, referenced "the egg-baby incident"* and *Geoff, catty-corner, trig: kept shooting me weird looks, made a joke(?) that I looked "different" today.* Would I have known to sleuth like this, had our roles been reversed? Would I have dove in to avenge a sister I didn't even know? There was something else I noticed about Emma, too: how she walked down the halls with her lips clamped together, like she was holding her breath. How she popped into the girls' room to stare at herself in the mirror, as if to work up the courage all over again. We were both keeping secrets. We were both so alone.

Emma opened the locker. It was empty, save for a moldy-looking notebook at the bottom and a couple of pictures of Sutton, Madeline, and Charlotte taped up on the inside door. Just as Emma was about to gather the books she'd received today and somehow wedge them into Sutton's leather purse—*what kind of moron didn't carry a real backpack to school?*—she felt a hand on her arm.

"Are you thinking about ditching tennis?"

Emma turned. Charlotte stood in front of a WHY DRUGS AREN'T COOL poster. She'd pulled her red hair into a high ponytail, and she'd changed into a white T-shirt, black Champion shorts, and a pair of gray Nike sneakers. A tennis bag similar to the one Sutton's mom had packed for Emma this morning swung from her shoulder.

Tennis. *Right.* "I was thinking about it," Emma mumbled.

"No, you're not." Charlotte looped her arm through Emma's elbow and pulled her down the hall. "C'mon. Laurel put your gear in the team locker room after you attempted your jailbreak this morning. Maggie will kill us if we're late."

Emma gazed at Charlotte as they walked, surprised she was on the tennis team, too. Physique-wise, Charlotte looked more like a wrestler. Then Emma bit her lip guiltily. *Was that mean?*

Not any meaner than I was, according to the one memory that had resurfaced. And I had a feeling, somehow, that was just the tip of the iceberg.

Emma and Charlotte strode down the yearbook hallway, which was decorated with snapshots of students from previous years. Emma spotted a photo of Sutton laughing with her friends in what looked like the front courtyard at school. Next to that photo was a candid of Laurel and a familiar dark-haired guy on the gym bleachers, engaged in a thumb war. Emma did a double take. It was the same guy she'd seen on Sutton's photo bulletin board the night before . . . and on the Missing poster in the police station this morning: Thayer, Madeline's brother. Emma wondered what had happened to him. Where and why he'd run away. If, like Sutton, he hadn't run away at all. "So how was your day?" Charlotte's ponytail bounced against her back.

"Um, all right." Emma darted around two girls walking in the other direction, both carrying *My Fair Lady* scripts. "All my teachers acted like they wanted to have my head, though."

Charlotte sniffed. "Like that's a surprise?"

Emma ran her fingers along the scratchy strap on Sutton's tennis bag. *Yes,* she wished she could admit. It wasn't every day a teacher called her a Devil Child, or made her sit in the very front row so she could "keep an eye on her," or glared at her and said, "All the desks in this room are bolted down, Sutton. Just so you know." Uh, *okay.*

But Charlotte had already moved on to whine about her gym teacher and something she called the Stink Vent. "And Mrs. Grady in history totally has it in for me," she moaned. "She called me to her desk after the bell rang and went, 'You're a smart girl, Charlotte. Don't hang around with that crowd I always see you with. Make something of your life!'" She rolled her eyes.

They turned down the biology wing. A human skeleton stood outside one of the classrooms, which made Emma shudder. *Sutton could look like that,* she thought.

Then Charlotte nudged Emma's side. "So enough about me. How are you?" She squinted at Emma's chest. "Where's your necklace?"

Emma felt her bare neck. "I don't know."

Charlotte raised her eyebrows. "*That's* a surprise." She hiked her tennis bag higher on her shoulder. "So how are things with you and Garrett?"

"Uh, he's fine," Emma answered slowly. She thought of the happy picture of Sutton and Garrett on Facebook. It was all she had to go by.

Charlotte shot her a lukewarm, closemouthed smile. "I heard he's getting you something pretty special for your birthday."

"Oh really?"

"Mm-hmm. Lucky." Charlotte's voice was strained. Emma sneaked a wary peek at her, but Charlotte was busy fiddling with a strap on her tennis bag.

A moment later, they entered the echoing locker room, which was abuzz with the sounds of slamming locker doors and cheerleaders warming up with a couple of *Be aggressive*s and hand claps. Emma quickly changed into the shorts and tank top Sutton's mom had packed, then followed Charlotte through a rabbit warren of hallways to join the rest of the tennis team. All the girls lay on the floor with their butts in the air doing piriformis stretches. Emma noticed Laurel in the second row; when Laurel saw them, she quickly looked away. A girl at the very front of the room glowered at Emma. *Nisha.*

"Sutton?" another voice called. A twentysomething woman marching up the side of the room smiled in Emma's direction. She had a strawberry-blond ponytail and wore a blue polo shirt with the words HOLLIER TENNIS COACH and the name MAGGIE stitched over one boob. "Go on up! Co-captains in the front!"

Co-captain? Emma almost burst out laughing. Most of her tennis experience was from playing Wii Tennis at Alex's house. She glanced at Charlotte helplessly, but Charlotte just shrugged.

"Chop-chop!" Coach Maggie said, making a rolling motion with her hands. Emma shifted her gaze to Nisha at the front once more. Nisha wore a heather-gray T-shirt that said HOLLIER VARSITY TENNIS CAPTAIN. Emma winced. The universe was definitely plotting against her.

She slowly wove through the maze of butt-up girls until she reached the front of the room. She gave Nisha a co-captainly, let's-be-friends smile, but Nisha shot her back a disgusted glare.

Maggie blew her whistle, and the rest of the team sat up. "As you know, it's tradition that on the first day of practice every year, we wear our Hollier uniforms as a show of team spirit." A couple of girls let out *whoo*s and whistles. "Nisha Banerjee and Sutton Mercer, our two new co-captains, will do the honors of passing out your uniforms."

Maggie gestured to a stuffed blue plastic tub in front of Nisha. Emma peered inside and saw carefully folded tennis dresses in neat, even piles. She tried to pull one out, but Nisha slapped her away. "*I've* got it."

Nisha turned to the team and began calling out names. One by one each girl marched up to the front of the room. Nisha handed them their uniforms, like a principal handing graduates their high school diplomas. After every girl had received an outfit, and after Maggie stepped into the coaches' office, Nisha pulled the final dress from the bin and handed it to Emma. "And here's yours, Sutton."

Emma unfolded the dress and held it in front of her. The sleeves were about an inch long. The shirt didn't cover her stomach. Either someone had really shrunk it in the dryer, or it had been specially designed for a Smurf. Several girls snickered.

Heat rose to Emma's cheeks. "Um . . . do we have something a little bigger?"

Nisha tossed her ponytail over her shoulder. "I already assigned the rest, Sutton. That's what you get for not helping me do uniforms yesterday afternoon!"

"But . . . I wasn't *here* yesterday!" Emma protested. Technically, she'd been on the smelly bus to Tucson.

Nisha let out a sharp sniff. "So I suppose that was

someone else who looked *exactly like you* at my party then?" She pointed at the Mini-Me uniform. "Hurry up and get dressed, co-captain! You want to show your team spirit, don't you?" With a roll of her hips, she sauntered out of the gym toward the tennis courts, several younger players in her wake. The giggling grew louder and louder, bouncing off the gym's high walls.

Emma balled up the uniform in her hands. No one had ever been so blatantly mean to her before. Nisha really had it out for Sutton.

I was thinking the same thing, too. And it actually kind of made me nervous.

Charlotte approached Emma, her mouth a tight line. "We can't let her do this to you," she hissed in Emma's ear. "Are you thinking what I'm thinking?"

Emma stared at her blankly.

"Let's get her," Charlotte finished. "Soon."

Get her? An uncertain shudder rumbled deep within Emma's core. But before she could say a word, Charlotte pulled her toward the doorway, leading her into the punishing Arizona sunshine, and leaving us both to wonder what she meant.

12

EMMA'S FIRST FAMILY DINNER DYSFUNCTION

As soon as Emma stepped through the door from tennis practice, the smell of steak, baked potatoes, and crescent rolls swarmed her nostrils. Mrs. Mercer stuck her head through the kitchen doorway. "There you are. Dinner's ready."

Emma pulled a hand through her wet hair. *Right now?* She'd hoped she'd get a couple minutes to herself before dinner. Maybe go upstairs, curl up in a ball, mourn the dead sister she'd never met, figure out what to do next . . .

She dropped Sutton's tennis bag in the foyer and stepped into the kitchen. Mrs. Mercer carried tumblers of water to the table while Mr. Mercer uncorked a bottle of wine and poured two glasses. Laurel was already sitting down, fiddling with her fork. She'd taken off after tennis practice without offering Emma a ride.

Emma slid in next to Laurel. There was a tiny folded paper crane near her water glass. Laurel cleared her throat and nudged her chin toward it. "You should open that."

Emma stared at the crane, and then looked cautiously around the room. She'd rather *not* open it, thanks, especially if it was going to be another creepy note. But Laurel kept staring. The shiny origami paper crinkled as Emma slowly deconstructed the bird. On the plain white underside it read: I FORGIVE YOU. —L

"I heard Nisha's party sucked." Laurel twisted a cloth napkin in her hands. "And I finally asked Char after tennis. She told me they kidnapped you."

Emma folded the origami paper back into a bird and touched Laurel's arm. "Thanks." It wasn't much, but at least someone finally believed *something* she'd said.

"You're welcome," Laurel said, shooting Emma a tiny hopeful look.

Suddenly, a blurry flash about Laurel appeared before my eyes. I saw the two of us standing at a gate with a sign on it that said LA PALOMA SPA POOL—GUESTS ONLY! We both wore terry-cloth shorts and oversized sunglasses. "Just pretend like you belong here," I instructed, taking

Laurel's hand. She gave me that same eager, loyal, you're-the-big-sister-and-I-want-to-be-just-like-you look as she was giving to Emma now.

So we'd been friends . . . once upon a time, anyway. It certainly hadn't seemed that way from my memory of the hot springs.

"Still, maybe you can make it up to me," Laurel said to Emma, crossing her arms over her chest. "Manicures at Mr. Pinky next week before your birthday party? Maybe Thursday?"

"Okay," Emma said, although Thursday might as well have been in the next millennium. Would she even be here next week?

Mrs. Mercer pulled a dish out of the oven with a loud clang. Mr. Mercer gathered shiny steak knives out of the drawer. Laurel leaned forward. The front of her blouse gaped so that Emma could see the top of her pink scalloped-edge bra. "Why did you run off this morning?" she whispered. "Mads told me she saw you getting out of a cop car during homeroom."

Emma stiffened. "I was trying to ditch," she whispered back. "A cop driving by saw me. He said if I didn't go back to school with him, he'd raise the impound fee on my car."

"That sucks." A honey-blond lock of hair fell into Laurel's eyes.

They were interrupted by Mrs. Mercer rushing to the table with steaming plates. She dished out portions of steak, spinach, and baked potatoes to everyone. Mr. Mercer sneaked Drake a piece of roll, which the dog swallowed without chewing. When everyone had been served, Mrs. Mercer sat and unfolded a napkin on her lap. "I just got a call from Coach Maggie, Sutton. She said you were off your game today."

"Oh." Emma sliced the baked potato with her fork. Tennis hadn't exactly been successful, though at least she hadn't had to wear the Smurf Dress—Maggie had told Emma they'd straighten out the uniform problem tomorrow. During practice, she'd returned a few shots—thanks, Wii!—but serves whipped past her head, and when she was playing doubles with Charlotte, she ran for a shot and slammed right into Charlotte's side. "Yeah, I guess I'm a little rusty," she said. Not to mention she was slightly distracted the whole time.

Mr. Mercer clucked his tongue. "It's probably because you didn't practice all summer."

"You should put in some time at the courts tonight." Mrs. Mercer wiped her mouth with a pineapple-printed napkin.

"Maybe Sutton was off her game because Nisha Banerjee was a total bully today," Laurel jumped in. Emma shot Laurel a grateful look. It was nice that she was sticking up for her.

Sticking up for *me*, Emma meant. But I agreed with her. It was nice that Laurel had my back.

A softened, wistful look appeared on Mrs. Mercer's face. "How is Nisha? I ran into her dad at the club this weekend. Apparently she went to tennis camp this summer. *And* did a precollege program at Stanford. She's been so strong, especially after what happened with her mom."

Emma sniffed. If strong was a synonym for *bitchy*, then Mrs. Mercer was exactly right. "Nisha's kind of diabolical."

"Totally," Laurel added.

"And Madeline and Charlotte aren't?" Mrs. Mercer bit into a piece of steak.

"Madeline and Charlotte are awesome," Laurel piped up. "*And* nice."

Mrs. Mercer sipped her wine. "You know how I feel about you girls hanging out with them. They're always getting in so much trouble."

Emma swallowed a mouthful of steak, thinking about the manila file Detective Quinlan had trotted out at the police station today. Madeline and Charlotte weren't the only ones getting in trouble.

"Even their parents are . . . odd," Mrs. Mercer continued, chewing a bite of spinach. When she swallowed, she added, "I've always found Mrs. Vega too pushy. The way she's always so crazed about Madeline and dance. And Mr. Vega is so . . . intense. Those fights he used to have with

Thayer, right out in public . . ." She trailed off and glanced shiftily at Laurel. Laurel slathered an even coat of butter on a roll.

Emma leaned forward, hoping she would elaborate on Thayer Vega. "And what's with Charlotte's mother?" Mrs. Mercer said instead, wrinkling her nose. "Every time I open the paper, she's in another dress, christening a boat on Lake Havasu with a bottle of champagne."

Mr. Mercer stabbed a bite of steak. "Mrs. Chamberlain's dresses are very . . . interesting."

"You mean inappropriate?" Mrs. Mercer pressed her hand to her mouth. "Sorry, girls. It's not nice to talk about people. Right, James?"

"Indeed," Mr. Mercer murmured. Then his gaze settled laser beam–like on Emma. An alarmed expression flashed across his face. Emma tilted her head nervously. Her heart began to pound. He was suddenly staring at her like he *knew*.

Then he looked away. Emma sliced the baked potato open and mashed the starchy insides, just as she'd done since she was a little kid. "Maybe Madeline and Charlotte get in trouble because their parents are, like, preoccupied with other things."

Mrs. Mercer leaned back in her chair. "Well! How astute of you, Oprah."

Emma shrugged nonchalantly. It was practically the

first lesson in Foster Children Psychology 101—most kids acted out when they weren't getting enough attention or nurturing. They had no parents to help them with home-work or attend their sports games or encourage them to enter science fairs. No one read them bedtime stories, or gave them kisses every night, or sat down with them at nice family dinners.

Something suddenly occurred to her. In a way, this was the first real family dinner she'd had in, well, *ever*. Even with Becky, most meals were either in the car after hitting the drive-through or on trays in front of the TV. Or else Emma ate a bowl of cereal alone while Becky delivered an hour-long soliloquy to an empty apartment courtyard.

Jealousy rippled through her once more, but she quickly brushed it aside and thought again of the note. *Sutton's dead*. Emma would never have a family dinner with her sister.

Everyone was silent for a while, forks clanking against plates, spoons scraping against serving dishes. Mr. Mercer's beeper went off; he checked it and slid it back in its holster. Emma caught him staring at her a few more times. Finally he pressed his palms to the table. "Okay, this is driving me nuts. When did you get that scar on your chin?"

Emma's heart shot to her throat. Everyone turned and looked at her. "Uh, what scar?"

"There." He pointed across the table. "I've never seen that before."

Laurel squinted. "Oh yeah. Weird!"

Mrs. Mercer frowned.

Emma touched her chin. She'd gotten the scar when she'd fallen off the Hamburglar at McDonald's Playland. She'd blacked out for a couple of seconds, and when she came to, she'd expected to see Becky standing over her comfortingly. Instead Becky was nowhere in sight. Emma finally found her on the other side of Playland, crying her eyes out while rocking back and forth on a Fry Guy ride, her knees jackknifed up so that her feet fit in the little stirrups. When Becky saw the blood gushing from Emma's chin, it just made her cry harder.

Emma couldn't very well tell Mr. Mercer *that*. She lifted her water glass to her lips. "It's been there for a while. I guess you don't know me as well as you think you do."

"Is that because you're some girl named Emma?" Sutton's mom quipped.

Emma nearly choked on her water. There was a wry, almost devious smile on Sutton's mom's face. "And how *is* Emma today, by the way?" Mr. Mercer added with a wink.

Mrs. Mercer gazed at Emma, waiting for her answer. *She* was *kidding, wasn't she?* Emma was no longer sure. She wasn't sure about *anything.* "Uh, Emma's a little disoriented," she said quietly.

Little did my family know how true that answer really was.

13

THE BODY ON THE GROUND

An hour and a half later, Emma walked down the front path from Sutton's house and made a right turn toward the big park at the end of the development. After some thought, she'd decided to take Mrs. Mercer's advice and practice her tennis swing. Maybe she'd miraculously improve and kick Nisha's perky, tennis-skirted ass tomorrow—or, at the very least, she wouldn't do a face-plant while trying for a drop shot.

Her BlackBerry, nestled in the tennis bag along with Sutton's iPhone, beeped. ALEX, said the Caller ID.

"So you *are* alive!" Alex cried when Emma answered. "You were supposed to check in with me last night! I thought you fell into the canyon!"

Emma laughed grimly. "No, I'm still here."

"So?" Alex said. "How is it? Is your sister awesome? Have you bonded?"

"Uh . . ." Emma sidestepped a Razor Scooter a kid had abandoned on the sidewalk. It was hard to believe she'd only been here for a day. "She's great. We're having a great time." She hoped her voice didn't sound forced. On instinct she looked behind her, sure someone was listening.

"So are you going to stay there for a while? Are you going to move in with her? Are you just *dying*?"

Emma swallowed hard, the menacing SUTTON'S DEAD note flashing through her mind for the billionth time. *Something like that.* "We'll see."

"I'm so thrilled for you!" The phone cut out for a second. "Ugh, I've got another call," Alex said. "I'll talk to you later, okay? You'll have to tell me everything!"

And then she hung up. Emma held the warm phone to her ear for a few seconds more, the guilt gushing inside her like a broken fire hydrant. She'd never lied to Alex before, especially about something so momentous. Not that she really had a choice.

A snapping noise made Emma freeze. Was that . . . a footstep? She slowly turned around, the silence ringing in her ears. The night had grown dark and still. A red security system light blinked from the dash of an SUV at the curb. Something moved by the front wheel, and Emma leapt back. A sand-colored lizard skittered from underneath the car and raced around a large wheeled trash bin.

She ran her hands down the length of her face, trying to calm down. The park loomed at the end of the street, a large expanse of well-manicured grass, playgrounds, and ball fields. She jogged the rest of the way, the tennis bag jostling against her hip. A couple of sweaty, shirtless guys were packing up their gear on the basketball court. Two joggers stretched by a large green trash receptacle.

A silver parking meter–style machine stood outside the chain-link entrance to the tennis courts. SEVENTY-FIVE CENTS FOR THIRTY MINUTES, said a small sign on the post. Emma glanced around nervously. The basketball players had left abruptly, taking most of the noise with them. Wind swished in her ears. There was another tiny sound to her left, like someone swallowing. "Hello?" Emma called softly. No answer.

Get a grip, she told herself. Squaring her shoulders, she shoved a couple of quarters into the narrow slots of the meter. Floodlights snapped on overhead, so blinding that Emma winced and shielded her eyes. She opened the chain-link door and looked out onto the blue-green courts. And then . . . she saw it. A guy splayed face-up in the middle of the court, his arms and legs stretched out in an X.

Emma screamed. The guy shot up, which made Emma scream even louder and toss the racket toward his head. It clanged against the court and landed near the net. The guy squinted hard at her face.

"*Sutton?*" he said after a moment.

"Oh!" Emma said. *Ethan.*

Ethan scooped up the tennis racket and walked over to her. He wore a black T-shirt, blue gym shorts, and gray New Balance sneakers. "I am *so* glad it's you," Emma said.

Ethan wrinkled his nose. "Do you always hurl tennis rackets at people you're happy to see?"

Emma took the racket from him. "Sorry. You scared me. I thought you were . . ." She trailed off. *My sister's killer. An evil note-writing stalker.*

"The bogeyman?" Ethan filled in.

Emma nodded. "Something like that."

The jogging couple ran past. A low-rider car trundled by on the street, letting out a honk to the tune of *The Godfather* theme. Emma looked at Ethan again. "What were you doing lying in the dark?"

"Stargazing." Ethan gestured toward the sky. "I come here almost every night. It's a great place for it because it's so dark here. Until you came along, that is." He leaned against a stone-covered water fountain just outside the courts. "What are *you* doing here? Spying on me?"

Emma blushed. "*No.* I wanted to practice tennis. My

game has gone from an A to a D-minus over the summer."

"Hoping to show Nisha who's boss?"

Emma jolted up. *How did he know that?*

Ethan grinned, as if reading her mind. "Your rivalry is legendary. Even I've heard about it."

Emma inspected Ethan's sharp cheekbones, deep-set eyes, and muscular shoulders. In German class, Ethan had stared out the window the whole time, not speaking to anyone. He was the only person Frau Fenstermacher hadn't picked on. In the hall, he'd walked by himself, big Bose headphones clapped over his ears. Girls shot him appreciative glances as he passed, but he gave each of them shy shrugs and continued on.

"So do you want a practice partner?" Ethan interrupted her thoughts.

Emma cocked her head. "You mean . . . tennis?"

"No, croquet." He smiled and gestured toward the parking lot. "I have a racket in my car. But if you don't want to . . ."

"I'd love to." Emma smiled. Nerves snapped and danced beneath her skin. "Thanks."

"Okay." Ethan's expression was sheepish, maybe even a little nervous. They turned and both tried to walk through the chain-link exit at the same time. They collided into each other, Emma's side hitting Ethan's hip.

"Oops," Emma laughed. They both stepped back at the

same time. Then Emma moved forward through the exit once more. So did Ethan. They bumped again. Emma stepped on Ethan's foot. "Sorry," Emma said, quickly jerking away.

"I was just . . ." Ethan stepped out of the way once more, extending his arm in an after-you gesture. Emma's cheeks burned.

Finally they each managed to step through the gate, and Ethan retrieved his tennis racket from the car. They hit the ball back and forth for a while. After a half hour had passed, Emma could feel her swing getting stronger and her footwork no longer resembling that of a headless chicken. "Wanna take a break?" Ethan called from the other side of the court.

Emma nodded. They collapsed on the bench at the sidelines. Ethan removed a bottle of Fiji water and a package of dark chocolate M&Ms from his messenger bag. "You don't seem so rusty."

Emma took a long drink from the water bottle, careful not to let water dribble messily down her chin. "Yeah, I do. But thanks for helping me out. It was really sweet."

"No problem." Ethan shrugged.

The fluorescent lights buzzed above their heads. Ethan rolled a tennis ball under his foot. "So why didn't you want to come to the party with me yesterday?" she asked after a moment.

Ethan turned away from her to face the large wooden sandbox on the other side of the fence. A couple of shovels and castle molds lay abandoned in the sand. Emma bet the whole thing smelled like pee. "Your crowd isn't really my thing."

Emma shrugged. She wasn't sure if she was into Sutton's crowd, either. "You wouldn't have had to talk to them. *I* was the one who invited you."

He picked at a scab on his knee. "Honestly? I kind of thought it was a setup. I was afraid I'd go to that party and . . . I don't know. Someone would drop pig blood on my head or whatever, horror-film style."

"I wouldn't set you up!"

Ethan sniffed. "Sutton Mercer wouldn't set someone up?" He looked at her doubtfully.

Emma stared at the glowing net in the middle of the court. She had no idea what Sutton would or wouldn't do. All those comments from teachers, the manila file from the police. She was starting to feel personally responsible for all of it, even though she didn't have the slightest idea what any of it was.

Emma reached into the open bag of M&M'S and grabbed a handful. Absently, she arranged a few on her thigh in the shape of a smiley face: two blue M&M eyes, a green nose, and a red and brown M&M smile.

"You do that, too?" Ethan asked.

Emma looked up. "Do what?"

"Make faces with your food." Ethan pointed at Emma's creation.

Emma ducked her head. "I've done it since I was little." She'd sculpted smiley faces in ice cream sundaes with chocolate chips, or with extra ketchup on a plate after she'd eaten all her fries. A counselor once caught her making a happy face with Cheerios during a session and told Emma that she probably did it because she was lonely. But Emma just thought everything she ate deserved some personality.

Ethan popped an M&M into his mouth. "When I was little, my dad made me a Belgian waffle we called Bob. Bob was a regular waffle with two big blueberries for eyes, a whipped cream nose—"

"—and let me guess," Emma interrupted drolly. "A bacon smile?"

"Wrong." Ethan pointed at her. "A piece of honeydew!"

"Melon on a waffle?" Emma stuck out her tongue. *"Blegh."*

Ethan grinned at her and shook his head. "I can't imagine Sutton Mercer playing with her food."

"There are lots of things you don't know about me," Emma teased. "I'm a huge mystery." *More than you know,* she silently added.

Ethan nodded approvingly. "Mystery is cool." He leaned

toward her a little more, his hand bumping Emma's shoulder. He didn't immediately pull away. Emma didn't either. For a moment, it felt like he was smiling at *her*, not the girl he thought was Sutton Mercer.

Click. The overhead lights faded, flooding the court in darkness. Emma stiffened and let out a little yelp. "It's okay," Ethan said. "The meter for the lights just ran out."

Ethan helped Emma up, and together they fumbled for the door. After climbing into his car and starting the engine, Ethan poked his head out the window and gave her a long, curious look. "Thanks, Sutton," he finally said.

"For what?" Emma asked.

He gestured out the window to the court and sky. "This."

Emma grinned in question, hoping he'd say more. He pulled out of the lot and headed for the exit. "Fireflies" by Owl City wafted from the stereo speakers. The song was one of Emma's favorites. As he turned toward the street, Emma slid down the chain-link fence to the warm asphalt. At least someone here was normal. Too bad it was the one person who seemed to want nothing to do with Sutton's life.

But watching from above, I wasn't so sure about that. There was something about Ethan that made me think he had more to do with my life than he let on.

14

VINTAGE EMMA

Ominous thunderclouds opened up on Thursday afternoon, and Coach Maggie made an announcement over the loud-speaker after seventh period that tennis practice was canceled. Emma was so relieved she contemplated throwing her arms around her Arizona History teacher. Her legs ached from practice yesterday and hitting with Ethan last night.

At the end of the day, as Emma entered the combination to Sutton's locker, a hand slithered around her waist and pulled her tight. Emma whirled around to see Garrett shoving a bouquet of tulips in her face. "Happy first-week-of-school–almost–birthday!" he proclaimed brightly, leaning in for a kiss.

Emma tensed as his lips touched hers. He smelled like turpentine from art class.

"Get your hands off him!" I wailed. But—you guessed it—nobody heard me. I mean, I got it that Emma had to pretend like everything was normal. I really did. But seeing Garrett affectionately touch someone else filled me with both jealousy and sadness. Garrett wasn't mine anymore. He would never be mine again. I kept waiting for the moment Garrett would stand back, cross his arms over his chest, and say, *Oh my God. You're someone else.* I kept hoping for it. But it didn't come.

"You've been such a stranger lately." Garrett shifted his backpack on his shoulder.

Yes! I thought. *Someone noticed!*

Emma had the same response, immediately working up a defense. But then Garrett added, "I feel like I haven't seen you in weeks. Want to go to Blanco for nachos?"

Emma peered inside the locker. "What, right now?"

Garrett crossed his arms over his chest. "Yeah, right now. You don't have tennis, right? I don't have soccer, either. And don't freak—one plate of nachos isn't going to make you gain five pounds. And anyway I'd still love you even if you *did* gain five pounds."

Emma scoffed. She wasn't balking because of *that*—she'd gotten honorable mention in a hot dog–eating contest in Vegas the year before. A tiny Japanese girl with an apparently hollow leg had edged her out. It was more that she felt strange going out with Garrett . . . alone. *I'd still love you*, he'd just said. If he really loved Sutton, wouldn't he have realized Emma wasn't her?

"I'm kind of busy," she murmured.

Garrett took Emma's hands in his. "We really need to talk. I've done some thinking about . . ." He trailed off. "You know, what we talked about this summer? I think you're right."

"Uh-huh," Emma said warily, suddenly feeling like the conversation was taking place in a language she didn't speak. It was exhausting to pretend she understood what everyone was talking about all day.

Last night, after tennis with Ethan, she'd logged onto Facebook on Sutton's computer, desperate to find out anything she could about Sutton—who she was, what she liked to do . . . who might have wanted to kill her. Thanks to autofill, the site had loaded Sutton's profile, her screen name, and her password. Emma had read Sutton's Facebook posts again, trying to glean as much intel as she could about her personality, her past, and her friends, but there hadn't been much she hadn't already seen before. The only new thing Emma had learned about Garrett, for instance, was that Sutton cheered him on at his varsity soccer games, hung out with him and his younger sister, Louisa, and made all his fashion decisions for him. Sutton had even written posts like "Love the new shirt I picked out for my BF? He's like my little doll!"

At first, I felt like I needed to defend myself. Who was she to judge *my* life? But then I wondered—why did I care so much about what Garrett wore? Was it because I just wanted someone besides myself whom I could dress up . . . or was it because I was actually really controlling?

Emma had also started to use Sutton's phone—it had rung a zillion times since she'd come into possession of it, and it would probably be weird *not* to answer it. She'd checked the past texts to see if they shed light on anything about Sutton, but all of them were either vague instructions on where to meet (MI NIDITO AT SEVEN) or timing issues (RUNNING LATE, C U IN 10) or insults shot back and forth—LOSER, she'd written to Charlotte, and Charlotte had shot back with BEE-YOTCH.

As for the night Sutton had written back to Emma's Facebook note summoning her to Tucson, there was an answered call from Lilianna at 4:23, a missed call from Laurel at 8:39, and then three missed calls from Madeline at 10:32, 10:45, and 10:59. There were no voice mails, though.

And then there was the file cabinet underneath Sutton's desk, the one that had the big pink padlock on it and the sign that said THE L GAME. Emma had searched everywhere for the key. She'd even taken a shoe to the handle, slamming it down hard on the lock, but all that had done was bring Laurel to her doorway to ask what in the world she was doing. She had to open it—but how?

"What are you two crazy kids up to?" Madeline appeared from around the corner and inserted herself between Emma and Garrett. Emma hadn't seen her since the day before when they'd eaten lunch together. Today she wore a green dress that was so short it surely broke the school's dress code, black fishnet stockings, and black boots. The corners of her ruby-red lips spread into a smile.

"I was trying to convince Sutton to grab nachos with me," Garrett said.

Madeline made a face. "Nachos give you cellulite." She clamped her hand around Emma's wrist. "Anyway, she can't. She's coming shopping with me. It's an emergency. I'm badly in need of a new everything."

"But—" Garrett crossed his muscular arms over his chest.

"Sorry," Emma said, gratefully taking Madeline's arm.

"We're still on for this Saturday though, right?" Garrett called after her. "Dinner?"

"Uh, sure!" Emma yelled back.

She and Madeline turned the corner into the science hall. All the doors stood open, revealing blocky lab tables, cabinets full of shiny glass flasks, and giant posters of the periodic table of elements. "You don't mind me stealing you away, do you?" Madeline said. "Hos before bros, right?"

"Totally," Emma agreed. "Garrett is kinda smothering me, anyway."

"Well, that *is* his MO." Madeline bumped her hip. "Race you!" She took off down the hall, and Emma ran after her. They darted out into the rain and through the parking lot until they reached Madeline's car, an old Acura with a dancing ballerina sticker on the back that said SWAN LAKE MAFIA. "Get in!" Madeline cried, hurtling into the car and slamming the door. Emma followed, giggling.

Rain pelted the windshield and the roof. "Whew!" Madeline threw her studded leather bag in the backseat and jammed her keys into the ignition. "La Encantada?"

"Sure," Emma answered.

Madeline gunned the engine and whipped out of the parking lot without checking for oncoming cars. A Katy Perry song came on the radio, and she cranked up the volume and belted out the refrain in perfect pitch. Emma's jaw dropped.

"What?" Madeline asked sharply.

"You have such a nice voice, that's all," Emma blurted. And then, in case that wasn't a very Sutton-like thing to say, she added: "Sing, bitch!"

Madeline tucked her dyed-black locks behind her ear and sang another verse. Halfway down the winding stretch of Campbell Avenue, Madeline's cell phone bleeped. She pulled it out of her pocket and checked the screen, one eye on the road. Her face settled into a scowl.

"Everything okay?" Emma asked.

Madeline stared straight ahead, as if the traffic light they'd stopped at was infinitely interesting. "Just more Thayer crap. Whatever." She threw the phone into the backseat. It hit the cushion hard.

"Do you want to talk about it?" Emma asked.

Madeline let out a little exclamation point of a breath. "With *you*?"

"Why not?" That *was* what good friends did, wasn't it?

I'm sure it was. But I had a feeling my friends and I weren't exactly the touchy-feely kind.

The traffic light turned green, and Madeline hit the gas. Her eyes were glassy, as though she was about to cry. "It's just, the cops told my parents they aren't searching for him anymore," she said in monotone. "He's, like, officially a runaway. There's nothing more they can do."

"I'm really sorry," Emma said. She'd hunted around Facebook for information about why Madeline's brother had run away, too, but there were hardly any mentions of it. She'd found a page dedicated to the fact that he was missing, listing the details of what Thayer had last been wearing (an oversized polo shirt and camo cargo shorts), where he'd last been seen (the hiking trails near the Santa

Rita mountains in June), and recounting that there had been a search that had yielded nothing, not a missing shoe, not an empty water bottle, absolutely no trace of Thayer. There was an 800 number for people to call if they had any information. Sutton wasn't Facebook friends with Thayer, so Emma couldn't get to his private page and find out anything more. She did notice that Laurel interacted a lot with Thayer—there were shared pictures of them horsing around, YouTube posts on their Walls, and comments back and forth about upcoming rock shows at the U of A. But Laurel's page didn't tell her much else. In fact, Laurel didn't even comment on Thayer's disappearance— her only entry the day he went missing was a post that said, "I'm going to see Lady Gaga in November! Super psyched!"

The windshield wipers squeaked and groaned. The rain had cleared, stopping almost as quickly as it had started, and the pavement glittered. A rainbow appeared on the horizon. Emma pointed it out. "Look. That's good luck."

Madeline sniffed. "Luck is for dumb bitches."

Emma eyed the rabbit's foot swinging on Madeline's keychain, wondering if she really believed that. "You know, runaways usually do okay," she said gently. "Wherever Thayer is, he's probably found other kids like him. They're probably taking care of each other."

Madeline's eyes flashed. "Where did you hear *that*?"

Emma ran her fingers along the hem of the striped dress from Anthropologie she'd picked from Sutton's closet that morning. She knew tons of foster kids who'd run away to escape their crappy situations. In fact, she'd even run away once, escaping from the violent Mr. Smythe. After a particularly volatile night, she'd packed a bag and took off, hoping to get to Los Angeles or San Fran or somewhere far away. She'd run into a couple of other kids hanging out in an abandoned trailer park on the way there. They had set up a little campsite with several tents, blankets, and pots and pans. Somehow they found food, and they'd even foraged a couple of bikes, a skateboard, and a PSP whose battery they regularly recharged at the local Dunkin Donuts. Because Emma was barely eleven, the older runaways took her under their wing, always letting her sleep in a tent, always making sure she had enough to eat. In some ways, they'd taken better care of her than most foster parents had. The police had come on the fourth day, just when Emma was getting comfortable. Everyone got sent back to various foster homes or juvie.

"I guess I saw it on TV," Emma finally explained.

"Yeah, well, it doesn't matter." Madeline flicked a lock of long, shiny hair over her shoulder. Her face snapped back into its hard, beautiful expression. "It's nothing a little credit card damage can't fix. I want to wear something new to Charlotte's sleepover tomorrow night. Maybe one of those short shirt-dresses from BCBG. And didn't you want new J. Brands for your birthday party?"

They pulled into the big parking lot at the sprawling outdoor mall. Madeline found a space and shut off the engine. The two of them started toward the escalators to the upper level. The air felt fresh and clean after the rain. Muzak played softly over the mall speakers. As they emerged on the ground level, Emma spied a storefront in the very back of the mall: BELLISSIMO SECONDHAND. A butterfly flapped in her chest.

"Can we stop in there for a sec?" Emma pointed.

Madeline followed her finger and made a face. "Ew. Why?"

"Because you can find amazing things in secondhand stores."

Madeline narrowed her eyes. "But we *never* go in there."

Emma linked her arm in Madeline's. "Chloë Sevigny's really into vintage. So is Rachel Zoe." She pulled Madeline down the corridor. "Come on. We need to break out of our comfort zones." In truth, there was no way Emma was shopping for two-hundred-dollar skinny jeans. That was way out of *her* comfort zone—she'd feel terrible spending the Mercers' money on something so frivolous. Besides, she couldn't let *all* of her personality disappear just because she'd stepped into her sister's life.

The bells jingled as Emma pushed through the front door. The store smelled like all vintage shops did, a little like moth balls and cardboard boxes and old ladies. A bald, smooth-skinned black guy wearing what looked like a snow leopard–skin jacket sat behind the counter thumbing through *Cosmopolitan*. Clothes jam-packed the racks, and there was a large wall of heels and boots on the back wall.

Emma sifted through a rack of dresses. Madeline stood motionless near the door with her arms close to her sides, as if she were afraid of germs. "Look." Emma pulled a pair of gold-tone wraparound sunglasses of the rack on the wall. "Vintage Gucci."

Madeline took dainty ballerina steps until she was next to Emma. "Those are probably fakes."

"They aren't." She ran her hand over the interlocking Gs and pointed at the label that said MADE IN ITALY. "These are a total find. And a steal, too." She flicked the price tag hanging from the nose bridge. Forty dollars. "I bet they'd look awesome on you. And think of it this way—no one else has them. You'd be special."

She unfolded the arms of the glasses and placed them on Madeline's face. Madeline let out a little note of protest, then adjusted the glasses and stared into the mirror. Emma smiled. She'd been right—they accentuated Madeline's round chin and high cheekbones. As Mads pivoted to the right and left, she looked like a glamorous heiress on holiday.

Her expression softened. "They *are* kind of nice."

"I told you."

"Do you really think they're real?"

"They're real, okay?" the shopkeeper lisped exasperatedly, dropping his *Cosmo* to the counter. "Do I *look* like I carry fakes? Now either buy them or take them off your grimy little face."

Madeline lowered the sunglasses down her nose and gave the shopkeeper a cool, indifferent stare. "I *will* buy them, thanks."

The shopkeeper rang them up silently, his lips in a prissy pucker. As soon as Emma and Madeline got out of the shop, they both grabbed each other and exploded into giggles. "What was that coat he was wearing?" Madeline shook her head. "A dead cat?"

"'Now either buy them or take them off your grimy little face!'" Emma imitated.

"So unreal." As Madeline slung her arm around Emma's shoulders, there was a lift in Emma's chest. For a moment, she'd actually forgotten the situation she was in.

They cruised to the upper floor, arm in arm. At the top of the escalator, Emma spied the top of a familiar dark head on the level below and stopped cold. A girl stood outside Fetch, the high-end pet store, browsing a table of squeak toys and studded leashes. She craned her neck upward, as if she sensed someone staring at her. *Nisha.*

Madeline eyed Nisha, too. "I heard she's next," she whispered in Emma's ear. "We're going to get her tomorrow."

"Get her?" Emma frowned.

"Charlotte thought of something brilliant. We'll pick you up at seven-thirty tomorrow morning. Be ready."

Nisha gave the girls a final look, then tossed her hair over her shoulder and walked in the other direction. *Be ready?* Emma wondered. *For . . . what?* She gazed questioningly at Madeline, but Madeline's eyes were obscured behind her new Gucci sunglasses. All Emma could see was her own reflection staring back at her, looking more confused than ever.

She wasn't the only one. Something about Madeline's voice put me on edge. I had a feeling that whatever they were going to do to Nisha was going to be . . . *trouble.* But both Emma and I would have to wait until tomorrow to find out exactly what it was.

15

THE SCENE OF THE CRIME

The following morning, Charlotte's SUV roared to the curb in front of the Mercers' house, nearly taking out a trash can. Laurel scuttled into the backseat fast. Madeline handed her a giant Starbucks cup. "Thanks again for letting me in on this," Laurel gushed.

"You had some good ideas with this one," Charlotte murmured while typing on her BlackBerry. "You deserve some credit."

Emma climbed in behind Laurel. Madeline handed her a hot coffee, too, though Emma didn't remember giving her an order. She took a sip and winced. It was black with Splenda, *yechh*. Twins must not share the same taste buds. "What's this all about, anyway?" she asked.

Charlotte waved the little stirring straw that had come with her latte at Emma. "Don't you worry about a thing. It's *our* turn, Sutton. This is for you."

Charlotte turned out of Sutton's neighborhood, passing the park where Emma and Ethan had played tennis. "It's all timed perfectly," she said in a low voice. "I've been watching Nisha since Monday."

"And you set up everything last night?" Madeline was wearing her new Gucci sunglasses. The sunlight caught the gold frames and sent reflections around the inside of the car.

Charlotte nodded. "You girls are going to love it." She wheeled around and peered at Laurel. "And you talked to . . . you know?"

"Yep." Laurel giggled.

"Perfect."

Within minutes, they were pulling into a space in the school parking lot. School didn't start for another half hour, so the bus lanes were empty and the boys' soccer team, who practiced both before and after school, were still galloping on the field. The girls grabbed Emma's arms and pulled her through the courtyard and a side door. The hallways were deserted. Posters for student council elections flapped in the air-conditioned breeze. Big swirls from the janitor's mop gleamed on the floor.

The locker room was deserted, too, smelling like a mix of powdery deodorant and bleach. Each sports team got its own wide aisle. Girls kept the same sports locker from year to year—Emma had opened Sutton's designated tennis locker on the first day of practice and found a few things still inside, including a shiny nylon jacket that said HOLLIER TENNIS on the back.

As they rounded the corner to the tennis team's bank of lockers, Madeline stopped short. *"Whoa."* Laurel covered her mouth with her hand.

Emma peered around them and nearly cried out. Papers lay scattered over the floor and on the benches. Red liquid covered a couple of doors and lockers. There was a tape outline of a body on the floor, with a big splattering of red stuff—*blood?*—near the head. Yellow police tape strung around the outline said CRIME SCENE: DO NOT CROSS.

Emma's vision began to narrow. She took a big step back. Could it *be*? She thought of the note again. *Sutton's dead.* Maybe someone had found Sutton's body . . . *here*. Maybe the snuff film had taken place in a field nearby. The killer had dragged Sutton into the locker room and deposited her here for someone to find. And if they'd found Sutton, what would that mean for Emma?

I tried to imagine my body lying on the cold locker room floor, blood seeping out of my head, my eyes fluttering closed. Had this been it? Had someone dumped me here? But the locker room setting didn't match the flickers I'd already had about my death—the screams, the darkness, the knife at my throat. Something seemed off about the whole thing. Then I noticed Laurel's small, nervous smile behind her hand.

"Psst." Charlotte yanked them into the shower room. The floor was shiny and wet, and someone had left a big bottle of Aveda shampoo on a built-in shelf in one of the stalls. Charlotte peeked around the doorway and gestured for the girls to do the same. A few girls on various teams passed the tennis lockers, doing a triple take at the crime scene. An angular cross-country runner took a picture of it with her phone. An Asian girl saw it and immediately turned around and went the other direction. When Nisha appeared at the far end of the hall, Charlotte squeezed Emma's hand. "Let the games begin."

A cold, clammy feeling of understanding washed over Emma. But before she could say anything, Charlotte put her finger to her lips. *Shhh.*

Nisha's dark hair cascaded down her back. She carried a green tennis bag on her shoulder. When she turned the corner and noticed the crime scene, she stopped hard. She took a few tentative steps toward it, staring at the locker surrounded by police tape. A helpless look washed over her face.

"Miss?" A woman in a police uniform burst into the room, making everyone, including Emma, Charlotte, and

Madeline, jump. Nisha flinched and pressed her arm to her chest as if to say, *Who me?* "Can you tell me whose locker this is?"

Nisha's tawny skin turned ashen. She glanced at the cop's badge, then at her gun. "Um, that's my locker."

Laurel let out a tiny yelp of a laugh. Charlotte shot her a look.

The cop tapped the locker door with the antenna of her walkie-talkie. "Would you mind opening it for me? I need to search it."

Nisha's bag slipped from her shoulder to the floor. She didn't pick it back up. "W-Why?"

"I have a warrant right here." The cop unfolded a piece of paper and flashed it in Nisha's face. "I need to search this locker."

Charlotte covered her mouth with her hand. Madeline's whole body shook, making tiny I-don't-want-to-laugh squeaks. They both turned to Emma. Charlotte lifted her eyebrows in a silent look that seemed to ask, *Don't you love this?* Emma looked away.

More girls gathered in the locker room, nudging and staring. The cop paced the aisle. Nisha opened and closed her mouth a few times without speaking. Tears welled in her eyes. "Am I in trouble? I didn't do anything!"

"I'll be the judge of that," the cop said. The handcuffs on her belt jingled.

Madeline nudged Laurel in the ribs. "*Where* did you find her?"

"I put an ad on Craigslist." Laurel beamed. "She's a theater major at the U of A."

The cop nodded at Nisha again, this time more forcefully. Nisha's hands shook as she worked the combination. By now Charlotte was doubled over, her shoulders shaking. Madeline had her tongue wedged between her teeth to stave off giggles. When the locker opened, the cop plunged her hand inside and pulled out a kitchen knife. More red stuff smeared the pointed tip.

Nisha sank down to the bench in the middle of the aisle. "I-I don't know how that got there!"

Emma picked nervously at dry skin on her palm. *Sure, Nisha was a bitch, but was she* this *much of a bitch?*

I watched uncertainly, too. Maybe I'd been a prankster when I was alive, but from the other side, a staged murder definitely turned the proverbial stomach of a girl who'd just been killed. In fact, it seemed almost eerily coincidental. . . .

"I need to search the top part of the locker, too," the cop demanded. "And then you and I are going to take a little trip down to the station."

"But this is a mistake!" Nisha's eyes filled with tears.

Emma tugged Charlotte's sleeve. "Guys. Come on. That's enough."

Charlotte shot up and whirled around. *"What?"*

"Nisha seems kind of freaked out."

Madeline cocked her head. "That's why it's funny."

"We don't want her to have a heart attack," Emma argued.

"Like *you* haven't done worse, Sutton?" A water droplet from the shower nozzle plopped on Charlotte's head, but she ignored it. "Don't get all soft on us now. Anyway, we had to go big with her. She knows what we're about. We couldn't just fill her pool with frogs or put Nair in her shampoo or something dumb like that."

"I think it was a genius idea," Laurel whispered behind them.

"Thank you." Charlotte grinned. "I knew we needed something special to kick off a new year of the Lying Game!"

Emma chomped down on the inside of her cheek to keep from showing surprise. *The Lying Game?*

The words swirled in my head, too. Sensations bobbed to the surface. Screams and laughs, hands clapped over mouths, the hot stomach-pull of excitement. I strained to remember more, but it was just a cascade of feelings that rushed over me.

Out in the aisle, the cop pressed the latch to open the top compartment of Nisha's locker. Charlotte grabbed Emma's hand. "Get ready." As the door opened, something shot out of the space. Nisha screamed and covered her eyes. Emma braced herself, too . . . and then she saw a shiny Mylar balloon float lazily into the aisle and bob to the ceiling. It was in the shape of a banana with bug eyes and a deranged smile. "That's bananas!" a robotic voice rang out from the balloon as it bounced off the ceiling. "That's bananas! That's bananas!" A note dangled from the end of the string that said GOTCHA!

Emma couldn't help but explode with laughter. Now *that* was funny.

Nisha wiped her eyes, a tiny wrinkle forming between her eyebrows. She looked over her shoulder for the cop, but the University of Arizona drama student had run off, bloody knife and all. Nisha ripped the GOTCHA! note off the string, crumpled it up, and tossed it to the floor. "That's bananas!" the balloon bleated again and again in a robotic voice.

Charlotte emerged from their hiding place in the showers, her high-heeled boots clicking on the tile. Nisha turned and glared at her, her face puce. "You better not tell on us," Charlotte said in a chillingly even voice. She wagged her finger back and forth. "Or else we'll get you worse."

Madeline and Laurel formed a convoy behind Charlotte, shooting Nisha the same don't-mess-with-us looks, too. Emma ran past Nisha as fast as she could. Out in the hall, the girls leaned against the wall and laughed long and hard. Madeline grabbed Charlotte's hand. Tears rolled down Laurel's cheeks.

"Her face!" Charlotte said between breaths.

"Priceless!" Madeline cried.

Laurel poked Emma's side. "C'mon. You can admit it now. You loved it, right?"

They were all staring at Emma like she was the be-all and end-all, the final thumbs-up or thumbs-down. Emma stared blankly out the floor-to-ceiling windows that lined the hallway. A mini yellow school bus pulled away from the curb. A group of girls in field hockey uniforms passed, all giggling. Then Emma turned back and regarded each of Sutton's friends. Whatever this was, Sutton had clearly been the ringleader.

Charlotte waved her hand in front of Emma's face. "Well? A-plus or F-minus?"

Emma hefted her purse higher on her shoulder and mustered a devious smile. "A-plus," she managed to say, trying to channel her sister. "It was awesome."

The girls smiled with relief. "I knew it." Charlotte gave Emma a high five. The bell rang, and they linked elbows and started down the hall. Emma was pulled along with them, but all her body parts, down to the individual cells, were quivering.

The Lying Game. If this was something Sutton and her

friends did often, if this was something they'd done to a lot of people at school, they might've pushed someone too far. She thought of what Charlotte had said. *Like you haven't done worse, Sutton?* What if that was just it? What if Sutton had done worse—much worse—and someone had killed her for it?

I concentrated hard, but I still couldn't see what that horrible thing could have been. But even so, I had a sinking feeling Emma might be right.

16

LAST BUS TO VEGAS

Emma pushed through the congested halls to her locker. Her nose still stung with the smell of the fake blood. Over her shoulder, she noticed two girls glance at her with a mix of fear and reverence. She distinctly heard them whisper the words "Nisha" and "crime scene." A guy in a soccer jersey stood in the doorway of the student council room and chanted, "That's bananas! That's bananas!" *Had the details of the prank gotten out already? How could they all laugh about it?*

"Hi, Sutton!" a girl called to Emma as she passed, but her smile looked twisted and sinister. "What up, Sutton?" a tall guy in baggy pants and skate shoes called from inside a science classroom, but was it Emma's imagination or did his voice have a steely, hateful edge? Sutton could've pranked these people—*all* of them. Anyone could be her killer.

She whipped around the corner and nearly collided into a tall figure carrying a large cup of coffee. "Whoa," he said, protectively placing a hand on the lid. Emma backed up. Ethan stood before her, wearing a gray hoodie, long army-green surfer shorts, and faded Converse shoes. His unapproachable, surly expression softened when he saw it was her. "Oh. Hey."

"Hey," Emma answered, grateful to see a friendly face. She started down the hall. "H-How are you?" She tried to sound cheerful, but her voice trembled.

"I'm cool." Ethan kept pace with her. "You? You've got that the-bogeyman's-after-me look again."

Emma ran her hand over the back of her neck. It was suddenly sweaty. Her heart was pounding really fast, too. "I'm just a little freaked out," she admitted.

"Why?"

They turned another corner and walked through the lobby, sidestepping a group of kids break-dancing by the ceramics display case. "Let's just say I'm tempted to blow off school for the rest of the year and hide in a cave somewhere."

"Is this about the Nisha prank?" Ethan asked. "Two

girls ahead of me in the coffee line were talking about it," he went on. One of his shoulders rose in a sheepish shrug. "It sounded . . . crazy."

Emma sank down on a lobby bench. "Yeah. My friends kind of went . . . too far."

Ethan sat down next to her, picking up a flyer that said FALL HARVEST DANCE! GET YOUR TICKETS NOW! and twisting it in his hands. One corner of his mouth pulled up into a sarcastic smile. "Isn't that kind of how it works? Don't you guys always go too far?"

A knot formed in Emma's stomach. Charlotte's words spun in her head like clothes in a dryer: *Like you haven't done worse? Was* that how it worked?

She swallowed hard, staring blankly across the room at a large display case next to the auditorium. A gold-lettered poster said IN MEMORIAM. Black-and-white yearbook portraits of dead students marched up and down the page, along with their names and death dates. *Sutton should be on that board,* Emma thought. She wondered if whoever had killed her passed this lobby all the time.

Two guys played tag down the hall, their footsteps ringing out on the hard floor. Emma blinked hard. Before she could say anything more, the bell rang. Ethan gave Emma a parting smile. "If you're sick of the pranks, you should tell your friends you want to stop. Just walk away from it, y'know? Everyone would thank you for it." He tossed the coffee cup in the trash. "See you around."

Emma watched him disappear down the hall. Her palms felt sweaty. She knew she needed to stand up, but her legs wouldn't work. The dead faces on the IN MEMORIAM poster watched her with eerie, knowing smiles. And then what she needed to do zinged through her body like a dart. "I have to get out of here," she whispered.

She'd never felt so sure of something in her life. Whatever Sutton was involved in, whatever the Lying Game was, it was scary and dangerous and way too intense. Just sitting here in the school hall made her feel like a target in a rifle range.

And maybe, I thought with a shudder, someone was already taking aim.

Laurel's Jetta made a screeching noise as Emma wheeled it into the parking lot of the downtown Tucson Greyhound station. She hit the brake just before ramming into a cinderblock parking divider. Turning off the ignition, she looked cautiously around.

The air was oven-hot and the blacktop shimmered. Two old men outside the station gave Emma a squinty look. Across the street, three scruffy college kids shuffling into Hotel Congress turned and stared right at her, too. Even the sex kittens in the S&M window seemed to be watching. Emma slipped on Sutton's big D&G sunglasses, but she still felt exposed.

It was later that afternoon, and Emma was supposed to be at tennis practice. She'd racked her brain all day for how she could get out of town—and where she'd go. Emma didn't want to use Sutton's ATM or credit cards to fund her escape—it would be too easy for the killer to track her.

And then she'd realized: the locker in Vegas. She'd stashed her two-thousand-dollar nest egg there, afraid to bring such a huge wad of cash to Tucson. The locker required a numerical combination, which Emma had set to Becky's birthday, March tenth. If Emma could just get back to the money, she'd be okay for a while. She could take a cheap bus to the East Coast, where no one would find her. Maybe, if she got out of the way, people would realize Sutton was gone and start searching for her.

And maybe I'd finally figure out why—and how—I'd died. Or would I? If Emma left, would I go with her—to live her new, anonymous life in New York or New England? Constantly following her while she moved on? Or would I disappear forever once she left my life? What would happen to me then?

Emma had swiftly stolen Laurel's keys from her tennis locker. *Please forgive me, Laurel*, she'd silently beseeched as she'd gingerly plucked the keys from the bag and slipped them into her pocket. Not a minute later, she was pulling out of the parking lot, stabbing *Greyhound Bus Station* into Laurel's GPS.

Emma entered the bus station and stood in line behind a thin balding man with square-framed glasses and a frizzy-haired woman with a giant rolling suitcase. The shifty-eyed ticket attendant glanced up and stared straight at her, then went back to ringing up a sale. A sign over the woman's head gave a bus schedule for Las Vegas. The bus left in fifteen minutes. Perfect.

The thin balding man leaned forward on his elbows at the ticket counter and made small talk about the weather. The overhead light made an anxious, high-pitched squeal. Every time the wind gusted, the door blew open and shut, making Emma jump. The hair on her arms stood on end. If only this line would move a little faster.

A Paramore song suddenly exploded from Emma's bag. She pulled out Sutton's ringing iPhone. LAUREL, said the Caller ID. Emma instantly hit SILENT.

The MISSED CALL message flashed on the screen, but then Laurel called right back. Emma muffled Paramore once again. Why wasn't Laurel on the tennis court? Emma thought she had at least an hour before Laurel would notice her car missing. After another MISSED CALL message flashed, a new text appeared. Emma opened it. 911, Laurel wrote. DID YOU TAKE MY CAR? ARE YOU OKAY? IF

YOU DON'T CALL BACK IN FIVE MINUTES I'M SENDING OUT A SEARCH PARTY.

The frizzy-haired woman in front of Emma peered at her curiously. The ticket attendant leered as she licked a finger to count out dollar bills. Emma tried to swallow the lump that had formed in her throat. All at once, her escape plan felt foolish. Laurel was probably freaking out about the missing car at tennis right now.

And even if Emma *did* get on the bus for Vegas, the police would find Laurel's car in the parking lot in no time. With no Emma inside, everyone would assume the girl they thought was Sutton had just run away. And then Shifty Eyes the ticket attendant would identify Emma as the girl who'd bought a ticket to Vegas . . . and the cops would be looking for Emma *there*, not for Sutton's body *here*.

Laurel called again just as Emma stepped out of the ticket line. Emma pressed the green answer button and said hello. "There you are, flake." Laurel sounded annoyed. Her voice was hollow, like the phone was on speaker. "Did you steal my car?"

"Just get your own car out of the impound lot already!" Charlotte's voice called from the background. "We'll all pool our money!"

"I'm sorry," Emma blurted. "I just . . . needed to do something. Something important." She walked to the window and gazed across the street at the girls in the shop window. What could be so important down here? Sex toys? Seeing an emo show at Hotel Congress?

"I'm taking Laurel home from tennis, so no worries," Charlotte said. "But finish up your little errand before our sleepover, okay? It won't be complete without the executive committee."

"Don't forget Lili and Gabby," Laurel piped up.

"Yeah, but they don't count," Charlotte countered.

The loudspeaker in the station crackled, making Emma jump. "Now departing in Stall Three, Greyhound 459 to Las Vegas," the ticket taker's bored, nasal voice boomed. "Las Vegas, now boarding."

Emma scrambled to muffle the iPhone, but it was too late. There was a pause on the other end. "Did they just say Greyhound?" Laurel sounded confused.

"Are you going to Vegas?" Charlotte asked.

Emma pushed the creaky door out of the station and walked as fast as she could to Laurel's car, afraid the blaring announcement might sound again. "I-I was just passing by the bus station. The window's down. But I'm on my way back home now, okay?"

The already hot upholstery in Laurel's car burned Emma's shoulders and the backs of her legs as she climbed in and hung up the phone. Her fingers shook as she pushed the key into the ignition. A motor growled, and she looked up. A bus chugged under the porte cochere, a big sign that said LAS VEGAS on the windshield. People threw their luggage in the lower compartment and climbed aboard.

Then a small clicking sound made her stiffen and turn. The backs of her ears burned. It felt like someone was staring at her. She looked around. The old men on the bench had vanished. On the street, traffic had come to a standstill. A neon green Prius that said DISCOUNT CAB honked. A red hatchback with a big dent in the fender idled behind it, and a black pickup revved its engine impatiently behind that. In front of them all, a silver Mercedes crept slowly past the bus station. Emma stared hard at its gleaming hood ornament. Through the tinted windows, Emma could just make out that the driver was looking at something in the bus station parking lot. *Her.*

I squinted hard to see who it was, but I couldn't make out a face.

The green cab honked once more, and the Mercedes driver faced forward again and rolled through the light. Emma watched the car until it vanished over the hill. Only after it had disappeared from view could she exhale. But her jittery paranoia was for good reason.

After all, whoever killed me was watching her every move.

~ 17 ~

NEVER HAVE I EVER

Later that evening, Laurel drove one-handed while twisting her long blond hair into a messy bun at the nape of her neck. She steered the car up a steep, undulating road toward Charlotte's house, a hidden estate tucked away on a high road halfway up the mountain, nestled into the desert rock.

Emma took it all in as Laurel pressed the intercom button outside the gates of Charlotte's house and waited. A voice buzzed through the speaker a few seconds later. "It's Laurel and Sutton!" Laurel called into the microphone. A latch clicked, and the gate slowly swung open.

A slate-paved path unfurled before them. A lush green

lawn surrounded them on either side, complete with sag-uaro cacti, flowering trumpet bushes, and creosote plants. In the middle of the circular driveway was a stone foun-tain filled with naked stone cherubs. Beyond that stood the house itself, a massive adobe mansion of floor-to-ceiling windows and skylights. A brass bell hung from a tower over the massive front door. Several horses grazed behind a split-rail fence to the left, and a shiny silver Porsche waited outside a five-car garage.

Laurel glanced at Emma as she shifted into PARK at the end of the long circular drive. "Thanks, for, like, not being weird about me coming tonight."

Emma brushed her hair out of her face. "It's cool."

Laurel leaned on the steering wheel. Dark lashes framed her eyes. "You've been a little . . . *different* this week. Are you on a new diet or something?"

"I'm not different," Emma said quickly.

"Don't get me wrong, it's not a bad thing." Laurel pulled the keys out of the ignition. "Except for your crazy-ass car theft. And how you took off in the park-ing lot the first morning of school." She shot Emma a crooked smile. "And, okay, one or two other things, too."

"I like to keep everyone guessing," Emma mumbled, ducking her head. While she didn't want Laurel to give her the third-degree about her odd behavior, it *was* kind of nice that Laurel had noticed that her sister wasn't exactly acting like herself.

The girls walked up a shiny path that led to the front door and rang the bell. Two deep strikes of a gong sounded, and a woman with a bright smile greeted them. She wore gray ultra-skinny jeans that left nothing to the imagination, a long striped shirt Emma had seen in the window of Urban Outfitters, and silver heels with cutouts at the toes. A pair of white Ray-Ban Wayfarers perched on her head and diamonds the size of chickpeas glittered in her ears. She had golden, lineless skin, rich blond hair, and bright eyes the color of the Caribbean. Emma looked at Laurel, wondering who this person was. *An older sister home from college?*

"Hi, Sutton," the girl said. "Hey, Laurel." She nodded appreciatively at Laurel's striped Madewell duffel. "*Love* the bag."

"Thanks, Mrs. Chamberlain," Laurel chirped.

Emma almost swallowed her gum. *Mrs.* Chamberlain?

I was pretty astonished, too. I couldn't remember her at all.

"Guys!" Charlotte called from the top of the stairs. Laurel and Emma gave Mrs. Chamberlain parting smiles— she had an expectant look on her face, almost like she wanted to be invited up to hang out with them—and climbed the winding double-staircase lined with splashy, Jackson Pollock–style paintings.

Charlotte pushed through two double doors to a bedroom twice the size of Sutton's—and a gazillion times the size of anything Emma had ever lived in. Madeline and the Twitter Twins already sat on a striped rug in the center of the room, munching from a bowl of pretzels and sipping Coke Zeroes.

"We were just telling Lili and Gabby about the Nisha prank." Madeline pulled up her off-the-shoulder blouse so that it wasn't showing half her bra.

"Not that we hadn't already heard, of course," Lili piped up, flicking a piece of lint off one of her Avril Lavigne–like fingerless gloves.

"Maybe one of these days you'll let *us* help you with one of your pranks," Gabby added, readjusting the grosgrain-lined headband that held back her long blond hair. "We have tons of killer ideas."

Charlotte sat down and grabbed a handful of pretzels. "Sorry. The Lying Game is limited to only four members. Isn't that right, Sutton?" Again she looked to Emma, as though Emma made the final decisions.

A shiver danced up Emma's spine. *The Lying Game.* Just the name turned her blood vessels to icicles. "Right," she said after a pause.

Gabby made a face. "So it's okay for us to be part of the club when the joke's on us, but not the other way around?" She nudged Lili, and she nodded, too. Their eyes blazed.

There was a long pause. Madeline exchanged a look with Charlotte. "That was different."

"Yeah, *really* different." Charlotte turned and stared pointedly at Emma. Emma fiddled with the ankle strap on her shoe, wishing she knew what they meant.

Charlotte cleared her throat, breaking the awkward tension. "Well. There's one game we can all play. . . ." She flung open the double doors of a large wooden wardrobe at the far end of the room. "Since we're all here, we can start." She unveiled a bottle of Absolut Citron from behind her back. "It's not a new school season without a round of Never Have I Ever."

She poured the clear liquid into round glasses and passed them around. "Just to review, you name something you've never done before. For instance, never have I ever French-kissed Mr. Howe."

"Ew!" Lili squealed.

"And then anyone who *has* kissed Mr. Howe has to drink," Charlotte concluded.

"Except they have to be *real* things," Madeline said, rolling her eyes. "Not stuff none of us would do."

"*Sutton* might kiss Mr. Howe." Charlotte shot Emma a coy look. "You never know."

Everyone giggled nervously. "I'll go first," Madeline volunteered. She looked around at all of them. "Never have I ever . . . skipped four days of school in a row."

She sat back on her haunches, not drinking. Gabriella and Lilianna also held their glasses in their laps. Emma didn't move either. Madeline flicked Emma's knee with her thumb and forefinger. "Hello? What about that time you ran off to San Diego for the long weekend?"

"The *really* long weekend," Charlotte giggled. "I thought you were dead!" Then she nudged her chin at Emma's glass. "Bottoms up, buttercup!"

Emma didn't know what else to do but take a sip. She nearly gagged. It tasted like sucking on the nozzle at the gas pump and eating a slightly rotten lemon at the same time.

Charlotte was next. She drummed her nails on the edge of the glass, thinking. "Let's see. Never have I ever . . . stolen someone's boyfriend."

Everyone sat very still once more. Madeline glanced at Laurel. Charlotte turned and stared at Emma, making a little *ahem* under her breath. Emma suddenly realized what Charlotte was getting at. Tentatively she lifted her glass to her mouth again. "Good," Charlotte said quietly. Emma bit down hard on the inside of her cheek. Who knew a drinking game would lead to such a gold mine of information about her sister?

Watching them, I was transfixed. Already I had learned two things about my past. I wanted them to play all night.

"Never have I ever gone skinny-dipping in the hot

springs," Laurel said next. Everyone drank except for Laurel and Charlotte. Figuring Sutton was probably ballsy enough to do something like that, Emma swallowed another sip.

"Never have I ever cheated on a test," Charlotte announced. Madeline and Lili glanced at her and drank a shot. "What would we do without you, Char?" Madeline said. Emma supposed she should drink, too.

"Never have I ever written a fake love note to Principal Larson," Gabriella said next. Charlotte and Madeline glanced at Emma and giggled, so again, down the hatch. Emma no longer gagged with each swallow; she was starting to get used to the taste. Her limbs relaxed. Her jaw softened from its clenched position.

Laurel volunteered next. "Never have I ever made out with a college guy." She leaned back and surveyed the crowd.

Madeline pointed at Emma and grinned. "Remember that guy at Plush? You thought he was our age but he was actually twenty-two?"

"Whoa!" the Twitter Twins squealed in unison, impressed.

Charlotte raised an eyebrow. "When was *this*?"

Madeline frowned. "July?"

The tip of Charlotte's nose turned red. "What did Garrett think about that?"

Madeline pressed her hand over her mouth. Gabriella coughed. Emma rolled the cup between her palms. *Great, so Sutton's a boyfriend-stealer and a boyfriend-cheater, too.*

I groped for a memory to explain it, but my mind was static fuzz. I'd cheated on Garrett? Why would I do that?

"Maybe I have my dates mixed up," Madeline blurted. "It was before Sutton started dating Garrett."

"Yeah, it was," Emma agreed, hoping it was true, but somehow doubting it. Charlotte fiddled with something on her iPhone and didn't answer.

Then it was Emma's turn. She looked around at Sutton's friends. All of them listed a little to the side. There was a goofy smile on Madeline's face. The room had begun to smell strongly of booze. "Okay," she said, taking a deep breath, trying to think how to phrase the question she most wanted to ask. "Never have I ever . . . pulled a prank for the Lying Game."

The Twitter Twins exchanged a bitter glance, but Charlotte, Laurel, and Madeline rolled their eyes. *"Duh,"* Charlotte groaned, tilting the glass at her mouth. "Hello, Nisha? *Today?"*

"No, something other than Nisha," Emma revised. "A really . . . *awful* prank. Something you felt terrible about when it was over." *Something that would prompt someone to get revenge,* she wished she could add. *Something that would drive someone to drag Sutton out into a field and choke her.*

The Lying Game members paused, looking a little caught off guard. Gabriella and Lilianna obviously refrained, but Laurel grabbed her drink, glanced nervously at Emma, and took a guilty sip. And then at the same moment, Charlotte and Madeline did, too. Charlotte nudged her chin toward Emma's glass. "I think you should be drinking too, sweetie."

Emma swallowed the rest of the vodka, the liquid searing the lining of her stomach. If she swallowed a match right now, she'd probably explode.

"Honestly, I thought you were going to pull the first prank of the year." Charlotte poured more Absolut into everyone's glasses. "What happened to that *great* thing you bragged about all summer? The ultimate *Gotcha*?"

"Yeah!" Madeline raised her glass into the air. Some of the liquid sloshed over the sides. "You said it was going to be huge. I've been on edge for weeks."

A bitter taste filled Emma's mouth. So the Lying Game wasn't just about tricking other people around school . . . it was about pranking people within the group, too. All of a sudden, the snuff film crackled in her mind. She thought of how Sutton had gone limp after the necklace had cut off her breathing. How she'd remained motionless until someone pulled the blindfold off her head and checked on her. What if she hadn't been as hurt as she seemed? How far would she go for a good joke?

Suddenly, like a row of dominos, the synapses of Emma's brain began making connections one after another. She thought of the note Laurel had found on her windshield. She pictured Sutton's phone and wallet sitting on her desk; there was practically an X-marks-the-spot over them for Emma to find. Then there was the matter of Emma's own ID going missing so that she had no way of proving who she was.

Her heart started to race. *Oh my God,* she thought. *What if the ultimate prank was happening right now?* What if *Emma* was the main attraction?

The alcohol burned in her stomach. She leapt to her feet, ran toward the nearest doorway, and flung it open. Inside was a whole wall of shoes and bags. She slammed the door again and fumbled in the opposite direction.

Charlotte stood and ratcheted Emma's shoulders to the left. "Bathroom's that way, sweetie." She gave Emma a gentle nudge toward a white door on the other side of the room. "Don't vomit in the tub like last time!"

"I'm totally tweeting this," Gabriella giggled.

"No, *I* am," Lilianna whined.

Emma staggered into the bathroom and slammed the door. She leaned over the enormous marble sink, the full weight of what was happening taking hold of her and squeezing hard. Sutton wasn't dead at all. She'd orchestrated the whole thing. She'd found out about Emma somehow and posted that snuff film online so her long-lost twin would find her. She summoned Emma to Sabino Canyon knowing full well that Madeline would see her on their way to Nisha's. Sutton had tricked all of them into thinking Emma was her . . . and she'd tricked Emma, too.

Emma's suspicions crashed into my own. *Did* I know about her before I died? Had I somehow lured her here, and then fallen victim to my own prank? The girl I'd learned about tonight, the Sutton everyone here knew so well, definitely seemed capable of it. But as I searched my faint memories and watched Emma, unable to help her at all, it didn't feel true. I didn't want it to be true.

Emma grabbed a spare toilet paper roll from the shelf and threw it across the room. It bounced off the tiled wall and fell into the tub. Then she sank to the woolly mat on the bathroom floor. The room was enormous, with a mini sauna and a vanity containing enough cosmetics to outfit Sephora. Photographs of Charlotte and the rest of the crowd were plastered all over the walls, some of them in frames, some of them pinned up with tacks, others crammed into the corners of the mirrors. Madeline stood in fifth position over the toilet. A shirtless Garrett grinned at her from next to the shower stall.

Most of the pictures were of Sutton. She stared, smiled, smirked, and blew kisses from every angle. She curtsied and cackled, spun with her arms outstretched, and *Vogue*-posed in fancy dresses, the missing silver locket dangling around her neck. Emma suddenly despised the sight of her sister. She glowered at the photo closest to her, a candid of Sutton, Charlotte, and Madeline standing in front of In-N-Out burger, shoving Double Doubles into their open mouths. Before she could stop herself, she grabbed an eyeliner pencil from the sink and drew a pig's nose over Sutton's face. After a moment, she added devil horns and a tail. *There.* It made her feel a tiny bit better.

She heard the girls snicker in the bedroom. Emma stood up, glared at her wild-animal expression in the mirror, and splashed cold water on her face. There was only one thing she could do: ruin Sutton's stupid prank before she could leap out from wherever she was hiding and scream, "Gotcha!" There was no way she was going to let Sutton win.

"Emma . . ." I wished so badly that she could see my flickering body and understand this wasn't a joke. That I was dead, really and truly. It was one thing when she rolled her eyes at my life and wrinkled her nose at my boyfriend, but I didn't want her to think I was the kind of person who would use her own long-lost sister that way. I didn't want to *be* that kind of person.

And then, all at once, the fluorescent light on the ceiling burnt out.

"Hello?" Emma called. She fumbled for the doorknob but couldn't find it anywhere. Her foot hit the metal trash can with a *clang*. Something crashed on the other side of the door. Charlotte screamed.

"Sutton? Was that you?" Laurel called. An alarm sounded from downstairs. There were footsteps . . . and then a siren. Emma trembled.

All of a sudden, the darkness sparked something in my mind. Spots appeared in front of my eyes. I heard a whooshing sound in my ears. And then I was back in that creek bed behind the resort again, calling Laurel's name, a hand over my eyes, a knife against my neck. *Scream and you're dead.* And just like that, I saw what happened next. . . .

18

WHO'S LAUGHING NOW?

"Scream and you're dead," the voice hisses in my ear, the knife still at my throat. Someone restrains my arms behind my back and ties a scarf so tightly around my eyes that the fabric presses into my eye sockets. Next they pull a gag around my mouth, the cotton digging into my cheeks. Hands shove me forward. Sandy gravel crunches under my feet and brambles scratch my legs. I hear footsteps next to me. Keys jingle.

I am pushed up a small hill. My toe hits a jutting rock, and cold pain streaks up my spine. I cry out, but then someone behind me pinches my arm. "What part of 'Scream and you're dead' don't you understand?" The blade digs deeper into my skin.

After a minute of walking, we halt abruptly. A sharp beep

punctuates the air, a car door unlocking. I hear the hydraulic hiss of a trunk opening wide. "Get in." Someone shoves me from behind, and I fall forward. My cheek hits what feels like the spare tire at the back. My legs bend awkwardly to fit the space. Thump. The trunk slams shut again, and all is quiet.

I smile to myself in the darkness. Let the next round of the Lying Game begin.

My friends had me going for a couple of minutes, but they can't fool me for long. I can't wait until they lift the trunk again, probably hoping to take a picture of me paralyzed with fright. Lame! I'll scream, scaring them instead. Could you have been any more obvious? "Scream and you're dead" was my line—I used it on Madeline when I sneaked into her bedroom last spring while pretending to be a burglar. Laurel probably said it, knockoff that she is. They're going to pay for this though. Maybe in the form of a 150-minute massage at La Paloma tomorrow. I'll need one to undo all the kinks in my back from squeezing into this tiny space.

Then the engine growls. The car backs up and pivots to the right, shifting me into an even more uncomfortable, Twister-like position. I frown. We're going somewhere? What's the point of that? I roll again when the car lurches into DRIVE, *banging my knee against the underside of the hood. "Mmmm," I moan through the gag. Can't they be a little gentler on me? Keep this up and I'll be sidelined from tennis this year. I wriggle my hands to see if I can free them to remove the scarf from my eyes, but whoever bound* them must have taken an advanced Boy Scout class in knot tying. Probably Laurel again. More than likely Thayer had taught her. The two of them always used to do queer Outward Bound shit like that.

Gravel crackles beneath the tires, then gives way to the smooth, even sound of freshly tarred pavement. The highway. Where are we going? I strain to listen for conversation inside the car, but it's dead silent. No pounding radio. No high-pitched giggles. Not even a low murmur. I try to move my knee, but it's wedged against the spare tire. "Mmm!" I call again, louder this time. "Mmm?" I kick the carpeted side of the trunk that borders the backseat. Hopefully I'm kicking someone's back.

The car doesn't stop. The tires buh-bump over the concrete highway. The gag around my mouth cuts into my skin. My back aches. My fingers begin to lose feeling from the tight bind. I thrash some more, but it makes no difference. The car keeps going.

And then a nervous thought sears my brain: Maybe this isn't a prank at all. Maybe I've been kidnapped.

Amusement gives way to white-hot fear. I scream as loud as I can. I press my wrists against the rough rope, the scratchy fibers cutting my skin. My friends and I do crazy things to one another, but we know when to stop. We've never sent anyone to the hospital. No one ever gets hurt—not physically anyway. I think of that voice in my ear. It had sounded like Charlotte's attempt at a gruff baritone . . . but maybe it wasn't. I kick at the back of the trunk. I shift as best I can and kick at the ceiling above me, hoping the trunk will pop open. I kick again and again, the flip-flops sliding off my feet. It feels like we've driven far by now, maybe into the desert. No one will know where to find me. No one will even know where to look. "Mmm!" I scream, again and again.

The car finally lurches to a stop. I catapult forward and hit my chin against the interior wall. A door slams. Footsteps crunch in the dirt. I freeze, hot tears in my eyes. There's another sharp bleep, and then the trunk latch pops. I roll onto my back, straining to see through the scarf over my eyes. I can just make out a corona of a streetlight above and a zigzagging blur of passing headlights to the left. A broad-shouldered shape looms above me, backlit by the streetlight. I can just make out what looks like deep reddish hair through my gauzy blindfold. "Mmm," I cry out desperately.

But then, just like that, everything goes dark again.

19

LEAVING IS NOT AN OPTION

Back in Charlotte's bathroom, I watched Emma fumbling through the darkness. After the memory I'd just seen, I had to admit I felt a little relieved. Whatever had happened wasn't a prank gone wrong that I'd orchestrated myself. I hadn't lured Emma here. I hadn't toyed with her emotions just to one-up my friends. It made me feel a little bit better about everything. I might have been a lot of things, but at least I didn't use my long-lost twin as frivolously and expendably as a lipstick-blotting Kleenex at Sephora.

Emma finally managed to find the doorknob. Twisting it, she emerged into Charlotte's bedroom. Five phones glowed in the middle of the carpet, throwing long shadows onto my friends' faces.

"What happened?" Emma whispered.

"We lost power." Charlotte sipped the last of her drink. She sounded annoyed.

There was a knock at the door, and everyone yelped. Charlotte quickly stuffed the vodka bottle and glasses under the bed. Moments later, Mrs. Chamberlain shone a flashlight into the room. "You girls okay?"

"Is the power out at the neighbors', too?" Charlotte asked. Emma noticed she was trying to enunciate very precisely, which just made her sound even drunker.

Mrs. Chamberlain walked to the window and looked out. Golden light spilled from the windows of the house nearest to them. "Guess not. Spooky, huh?"

Emma shifted from foot to foot. *Yes.*

"Oh, don't worry, girls," Mrs. Chamberlain said. "It's just a power outage. If you light candles, blow them out before you go to sleep."

She shut the door again. Everyone turned back to the center of the circle and exchanged wide-eyed glances. Suddenly there was a whirring sound, and the lights snapped back on. The stereo, which had been playing an iPod mix before the power went out, blared, making everyone jump. Charlotte's printer in the corner groaned, warming back up. All the girls rubbed their eyes. After a beat, the Twitter Twins simultaneously grabbed their phones and started typing.

Charlotte reached into the bowl of chips in the center of the room and took a greedy handful. "Okay, Sutton. Tell us how you did it."

"Did what?" Emma blinked. The girls looked at her hard. "The power?" Emma squeaked, suddenly realizing what they meant. "I had nothing to do with that!"

"Yeah, right." Madeline leaned on a large striped bolster pillow. "Good timing, though. Just when we were grilling you about losing your touch, you make the lights go out. I don't know how you did it, Sutton."

"She's a regular enchantress," Charlotte said wryly. "Broomstick and all."

"I didn't do it," Emma protested. "I swear."

"Cross your heart, hope to die?" Madeline demanded.

Emma paused, confused. Madeline had said it quickly, like a chant. "Yes," she answered. "Absolutely."

But then she remembered what she'd been thinking in the bathroom before the lights went out: it was possible her sister was close—*really* close. Which meant this craziness might come to an end very, very soon. The animosity that had soared through her veins instantly yielded to anticipation. Was she finally going to meet Sutton, the evil pranking genius, face-to-face? Would she be strong enough to stand up for herself and scold Sutton about how she'd sent her emotions on a wild roller-coaster ride, all for a prank . . . or would she buckle as soon as she saw her twin, filled with relief that Sutton wasn't dead, brimming with gratitude that she finally had someone to call family?

Emma glanced out the window. The backyard was empty. A pool glistened, the solar lights on the path glowed. Then she covertly lifted the dust ruffle on Charlotte's bed with her foot and peeked underneath. The only thing she saw was an old copy of *Vogue* and a sports portrait of Garrett, a soccer ball wedged under his arm. She even looked in the bathroom again, thinking maybe Sutton would pop out of the sauna, a big grin on her face. But the only Sutton in there was the many versions of her on the walls.

Everyone agreed they were too tipsy to continue Never Have I Ever. Charlotte refilled the bowl of pretzels and stuck the first season of *The Hills* into the DVD player. Everyone settled in on the couches, in sleeping bags, or on Charlotte's bed. It was like the power outage had had a sedative effect on everyone but her. Emma felt more awake and sober than she had before. *Is Sutton in the house? Is she close?* Every tiny sound, every movement, Emma glanced at the door, certain Sutton was going to cartwheel into the room.

She was so convinced, I half expected it to happen myself.

One by one, the girls' heads went limp and their eyes closed. Charlotte snuggled into her bed. Madeline snored softly on the trundle. Lilianna burrowed into a black sleeping bag, and Gabriella climbed into a pink one. Laurel had curled up on the couch next to Emma; her fingers slowly and sleepily twitched. Emma watched the DVD until the last episode aired and the credits rolled. She tried to close her eyes, but she wasn't sleepy. *Come out, come out, Sutton.* What would her life be like once Sutton returned? Once again she pictured their first meeting. *Your life is so crazy!* Emma might say to Sutton. Surely after putting Emma through so much turmoil, she'd let Emma stay with her for a while. After all, if this was some sort of demented test, Emma had passed with flying colors, hadn't she? She envisioned the Mercers' slack-jawed expressions when they found out Emma was telling the truth that first morning at breakfast. Perhaps they'd let her sleep in a guest room. Set a place for her at the table. Was it too much to hope for?

I didn't think it was. Not that it could ever come true.

Emma's mouth felt cottony from all the vodka. She groped for her water glass, but she couldn't find it. She slid from the couch as quietly as she could and tiptoed out the door and down the stairs toward the kitchen. The marble floors in the foyer felt like ice cubes on the soles of her feet. An angular coat rack by the front door resembled a giant tarantula. Emma sucked in her breath and stepped toward a glowing light down the hall.

The digital clocks above the microwave and stove shone a stoic green. A metal chandelier hung over the center island. Emma's skin prickled in a mix of fear and excitement. She cocked her head and listened for sounds of Sutton sneaking up on her. Breathing. Giggling. Waiting.

But there was nothing. Emma grabbed a water glass from the cabinet and tried the faucet. The water dribbled noisily into the sink. Just as she swallowed the last of the water and turned for the stairs again, she heard a creak. She halted and peered around. Her heart thudded. The clocks ticked from 2:06 to 2:07 in perfect synchronicity.

Another creak rang out. "Is someone there?" Emma whispered. Her vision blurred in the darkness. And then, all of a sudden, there was a loud crashing sound. Pain shot through Emma's hip. She started to turn, but someone pushed her harder against the island and pressed a hand over Emma's mouth. The water glass slipped out of Emma's hand and clattered to the floor. Fear streaked through her, hot and messy. *"Mmm!"* she cried out.

The person didn't pull away. A body pressed up against her, warm and close. "Don't you dare yell out," said a voice in her ear. It was raspy and indecipherable, a mere whisper. "What were you thinking? I told you to play along. I told you not to leave."

Emma tried to whip around to see who it was, but the figure shoved her forward and pressed her cheek to the kitchen island. "Sutton's dead," the voice insisted. "Keep being her until I tell you different. And don't try and skip town again or you're next."

Emma whimpered. The hand squeezed her wrist so hard she thought her bones might break. Then something cold and metallic encircled her neck. It grew tighter and tighter around her throat until Emma's windpipe began to collapse. Her eyes bulged. She flailed her arms, but the wire just constricted her throat even more. Emma fought for breath, but she couldn't inhale, couldn't swallow. As she thrashed up and down, her feet began to tingle.

I stared in horror. My vision was clouded, just like Emma's; all I could tell was that the strangler had broad shoulders. I thought of the dark shadow hovering over me in the trunk from the memory I'd just been given. That voice sounded a lot like this one.

But then the stranglehold around Emma's neck loosened. Whoever it was pulled Emma back up to standing. Bright spots danced in front of her eyes. Air rushed into her lungs. She leaned over and coughed.

"Now keep your head down and count to one hundred," the strangler went on. "Don't look up until you're done. Or else."

Trembling, Emma pressed her forehead to the island

countertop and started to count. "One . . . two . . ."

Footsteps rang out behind her. I strained to see who it was, but the figure was a dark shadow.

"Ten . . . eleven . . ." Emma counted. A door slammed. Emma cautiously raised her head. The kitchen was as silent and unassuming as it had been five minutes ago. She tiptoed to the front door and peered out, but the strangler was gone.

She bent over her knees for a moment, wheezing. As she stood up again, something knocked heavily against her collarbone. She cautiously groped her skin. Dangling from a chain around her throat was a round locket—*Sutton's* round locket. The one she'd looked for in Sutton's jewelry box but couldn't find. The one Sutton had been wearing in the snuff film. The chain fit perfectly in the red, freshly strangled indentations on Emma's neck.

Emma's world turned upside down all over again. Sutton really *was* dead. There was no doubt about it now. Hot, wet tears dotted her eyes. Her shaky hand flew to her mouth and muffled a sob.

She did a full 180, peering frantically into the kitchen doorway, the bookcase-filled study, the double staircase, the majestic front entrance. Her gaze locked on a shining, uninterrupted red beam above the doorway. Next to it was a security system keypad, a green light illuminated over the word ARMED. Emma tiptoed to the device. She'd lived briefly with a foster family in Reno who had this same alarm system—they had a cabinet full of valuable antique Wedgwood china, and yet they made four foster kids sleep in the same cramped bedroom—and Emma's foster brother had showed her how to use it. She hit the down arrow, and a list of times when the alarm had been armed and disarmed appeared. The last entry said ARMED, 8:12 PM. It was from when Mrs. Chamberlain had shut the door after letting in Emma and Laurel. There was no record that the power outage had disabled the alarm after that, though. Nor did the log indicate that Mrs. Chamberlain had had to rearm the alarm system after the power snapped back on. There was also no record that someone had tripped it, which would've happened if the strangler had gotten in through the doors or the windows. So . . . how had he gotten in? How had he gotten out?

Emma raised her head, a cold, slippery feeling passing through her. Maybe there was no need to get past the alarms. Maybe the strangler had been inside the house to start with. She thought about the voice in her ear. *I told you to play along. I told you not to leave.* And then she thought about the call with Charlotte and Laurel today. *Are you at the Greyhound station?* Laurel had asked. Could it *be*?

I was pretty sure it *could* be. I thought about the memory

I'd just had. The broad-shouldered figure pulling me out of the trunk. The shock of red hair when she stepped into the light. Whoever had strangled Emma was indeed someone inside the house: one of my very best friends.

20

DEAR DIARY, TODAY I DIED

As soon as Laurel pulled into the Mercers' driveway on Saturday morning, Emma shot out of the car, flung open the door, and started up the stairs. She almost knocked over Mrs. Mercer, who was crossing the foyer with a pile of laundry in her arms. "Sutton?"

"I just . . ." Emma muttered, then trailed off. She reached Sutton's bedroom, slammed the door shut, and locked it fast. The first thing she saw was a large stack of pink envelopes sitting on Sutton's bed. RSVP said the one on top. Emma stared at an unfamiliar girl's name written in pink pen at the top of the card. *Can't wait!* the girl had added. She turned it over. SUTTON MERCER'S

BIRTHDAY BASH, FRIDAY SEPT 10. GIFT OPTIONAL, FABULOUS-NESS REQUIRED. There were at least fifty RSVP cards in the pile.

Emma collapsed on the bed, jostling a few of the RSVP cards to the floor. Her head felt like it had been crushed in a vise. Every time she closed her eyes, she felt the strangler press up against her, that voice in her ear.

Keep being Sutton, or you're next.

She'd lain awake all night in Charlotte's bedroom, armed with the new information and petrified from the assault in the kitchen. The home screen of *The Hills* had played over and over. Someone had killed Sutton—and it was one of her very best friends.

How could one of my best friends or my sister do such a thing? But then I thought about how nasty I'd been to all of them that night at the hot springs. What if I was like that all the time? What if, sometimes, I was *worse*?

Emma flopped down on the bed and stared at the pink paper lantern that hung by the window, trying to think things through. The killer must have taken the video down from the site because she knew Emma would show it to the cops immediately. The killer also knew, obviously, that Emma wasn't Sutton. Emma tried to piece together the timing of everything. Had Sutton received the note from Emma, written her back, and then coincidentally died that very night? Had Emma's arrival been a surprise—but a *good* surprise—for the killer? After all, there was an Insta-Sutton in Tucson again. No missing girl meant no crazed search, no hunt for a dead body, no crime.

Then Emma's eyes widened, hitting on an even scarier idea. What if Sutton hadn't received Emma's note at all? What if the *killer* had been the one to lure Emma to Tucson, not Sutton? One of Sutton's friends could have easily hacked into her Facebook account. She could have seen Emma's note and sent one back immediately, knowing she had a naive girl to manipulate and put in Sutton's place.

A tiny spider crawled along the upper corner of Sutton's bedroom, pulling behind it a thin, gossamer thread. Emma stood, rolled back her shoulders, and marched over to the filing cabinet under her sister's desk. THE L GAME, it said. Aka the *Lying Game*.

She held the heavy padlock in her palm. There had to be a way to unlock it. Pulling open Sutton's drawers, she searched once more for the missing key, feeling for secret compartments built into the back, looking in every single empty jewelry box and CD case, and even spilling a nearly full pack of Camel Lights onto the carpet. Tobacco flaked onto her hands.

"Get it open!" I shouted to her uselessly. Screw feeling protective of my stuff. I was dead, and we both needed to know why.

Then something came to Emma in a flash. *Travis*. That YouTube video he'd watched about how to open a padlock with a beer can. During the brief time they'd been friendly, Travis had made Emma watch it, too. It hadn't looked hard.

She leapt up and found an empty Diet Coke can on Sutton's windowsill. Grabbing a pair of scissors, she drew out the design for the shim that would be used to break the lock and started to cut. In moments, she'd made an M-shaped shim, just like the criminal-in-training had made in the YouTube video. As soon as she wiggled the shim down the left shackle, the ball released and the lock snapped open. Emma couldn't help but grin. "Thanks, Travis," she murmured. She never thought she'd say *that*.

The lock clunked to the floor. The drawer made a grating *screech* as it opened. Emma peered inside. Sitting in the bottom was a thick spiral-bound notebook. That was all.

Emma pulled it out and held it in her lap. There was nothing written on the front cover—no names or doodles, just a shiny piece of blue card stock. The wire spirals were perfectly coiled and even, without a hint of bending or rust. She turned to the first page. There was Sutton's handwriting, round and neat and eerily similar to Emma's own. *January 10,* she'd written.

Emma sucked in her stomach. Did she really want to read her sister's diary? When she lived in Carson City, she'd sneaked into a bedroom that belonged to Daria, a pretty, mysterious older foster sister who paid no attention to her. She'd read every page of Daria's diary, which was mostly about boys and how she thought her legs and arms were too fat. Emma had also searched through the pockets of Daria's jeans. She'd stolen a pair of headphones out of Daria's room, purely because they were hers. She'd taken little things every time she went in after that: a rap CD, a black jelly bracelet, a department-store sample of Chanel No. 5. After she'd moved on to another home, Emma felt ashamed about what she'd done. She'd put all of Daria's pilfered things in a manila envelope, wrote Daria's name on the top, and sent them back to social services, vowing she'd never do something like that again.

It's nice that she was being all moral, but I just wanted her to read the damn diary.

Sighing, as though she'd actually heard my thoughts, Emma looked down at the first page again and started to read.

Each entry was short and sweet, more like quick Twitter entries and scattered thoughts. Sometimes Sutton wrote things like *Elizabeth & James clogs* or *B-day party on Mount Lemmon?* Sometimes she wrote exclamations like

I hate history! or *Mom can kiss my ass!* The entries that seemed like they might be about something deeper were even more baffling though. *C has been so bitchy lately,* Sutton had penned on February 10. *She just needs to get over it.* On March 1: *I had an unexpected visitor after school today. He's such a cute little puppy dog, following me everywhere.* On March 9: *M outdid herself today. Sometimes I think C is right about her.*

Emma leafed through the pages, trying to extrapolate meaning from the entries. There were a lot about *L,* who she could only assume was Laurel. *L came downstairs this morning in an identical outfit to mine.* And, *Playing an awesome prank on L this afternoon. Maybe she'll be sorry she wanted in so badly!* And then on May 17, *L is still ruined over T. Pull yourself together, bitch. He's just a guy.* Emma's gaze landed on an entry from August 20, just a week and a half ago: *If L brings up that night one more time, I'm going to kill her.*

What *night?* Emma wanted to yell. Why was Sutton so ridiculously vague? It was like she was keeping a journal for the CIA.

I was just as frustrated as she was.

Then a small construction-paper square fell out of the notebook and fluttered to the floor. Emma picked it up, gazed at the bold writing on the front, and gasped: THE LYING GAME MEMBERSHIP CARD. Below that was Sutton's name, the title EXECUTIVE PRESIDENT AND DIVA, and then a date in May more than five years ago.

On the other side of the card was a list of rules:

1. Don't tell ANYONE. Telling will be punishable by expulsion!

2. Only three people allowed in the club at one time. (But someone had crossed out three and written four above it.)

3. Every new prank must be better than the last. Those who outdo one another earn a special badge!

4. If we're really in trouble, if it's not a prank, we will say the sacred code words: "Cross my heart, hope to die." This means 9-1-1!

Beneath that was a sub-list of pranks that were off-limits. It mostly contained things like hurting animals or little children, damaging stuff that was irreplaceable or really expensive (Charlotte's dad's Porsche was the example), or doing something that would have the government after them (someone had written a *ha!* after that). In different-colored blue ink at the very bottom, someone had added *No more sexting,* underlining it three times.

I stared at the membership card, too, my brain buzzing. I had a flash of Madeline, Charlotte, and me cutting out the cards and presenting them to one another ceremoniously, like we were receiving Oscar statuettes. But then, just like that, the memory was yanked away.

Emma read and reread the membership card several times over, feeling affirmed. At least she had a clear picture of what the Lying Game was now: Girl Scouts for psychopaths. She thought again about the snuff film. Perhaps it had started out as a prank, too. But maybe one of Sutton's friends took it too far. . . .

She placed the membership card aside and went back to the journal. On the very next page, she noticed an entry from August 22: *Sometimes I think all my friends hate me. Every last one.* Nothing more, nothing less. Below it Sutton had written down what looked like a Jamba Juice order: *bananas, blueberries, Splenda, wheatgrass detox shot.*

Okaaay, Emma thought.

The next page was full of drawings of girls in dresses and skirts, titled "ideal summer outfits." Sutton's last entry was on August 29, two days before Travis showed Emma the video. *I feel like someone is watching me*, she'd written in shaky, hurried handwriting. *And I think I know who it is.* Emma read the entry again and again, feeling like someone had reached into her heart and squeezed.

I concentrated hard, but nothing came to me.

Emma placed the journal on Sutton's desk next to her computer. She moved the mouse on the sky blue pad, and the screen flickered to life. She opened Safari and clicked on Facebook. Sutton's page loaded automatically. As Emma scrolled through the posts and notes, patterns began to emerge. In August, Sutton had written, *I see you* on Laurel's Wall. In July, she'd told Madeline, *You're such a naughty spy.* She wrote Charlotte a private message in June: *You're after me, aren't you?* She'd even written something similar on the Twitter Twins' pages: *Will you two stop plotting against me?*

"What're you doing?"

Emma jumped and whirled around. Laurel leaned against the doorway, iPhone in her hand. Her blond hair was pulled up into a ponytail, and she'd changed into a pink terry beach cover-up and black flip-flops. Ray-Ban sunglasses obscured her eyes, but there was a broad smile on her face.

"Just checking email," Emma said in the airiest voice she could muster.

The iPhone in Laurel's hand bleeped, but she didn't look at the screen. She kept her eyes fixed on Emma, turning a silver ring around her finger. Then her gaze fell to the open padlock on the bed. The journal in Emma's lap. The Lying Game membership card on the desk. Emma's heartbeat pulsed in her fingertips.

Finally Laurel shrugged. "I'm going out to the pool if you want to join me." She shut the door behind her as she left.

Emma opened to a page in Sutton's journal again: *Sometimes I think my friends hate me. Every last one.* Emma gritted her teeth. Emma had never known her father. She'd been abandoned by her mother. And now her sister had been taken from her, too, before she'd ever had the chance to meet her. Emma wasn't even sure she would have liked Sutton, but now she'd never know. And Sutton's friends—or sister— weren't going to get away with it. Not if she had anything to do with it. She was going to find out what they did to Sutton. She'd do whatever it took to prove they'd hurt her sister. She just had to get close enough to find out more.

She swiveled to the computer, clicked the mouse on Sutton's Facebook status update window, and began to type: *Game on, bitches.*

Three responses to the status pinged onto the screen almost immediately. The first comment was from Charlotte: *A game? Do tell. I'm in!* Then Madeline: *Me too!* And Laurel added: *Me three! It's a secret, right?*

Kind of, Emma typed in answer. Except now the prank was on them. And this time it was a matter of life and death.

21

UNREQUITED SPYING

"So where do you want to go for dinner?" Garrett asked Emma, guiding his Jeep Wrangler down a hill.

"Um, I don't know." Emma bit her pinkie. "Why don't you pick somewhere?"

Garrett looked shocked. *"Me?"*

"Why not?"

A glassy, indecisive look swept across Garrett's face. He reminded Emma of the malfunctioning Tickle Me Elmo doll she had inherited from an older girl her first year in foster care; sometimes the Elmo stared into space and didn't know what to do next. "But we always go somewhere *you* like," Garrett said.

Emma pressed her nails into her palm. If only she could just tell him she couldn't pick a damn restaurant because she didn't *know* any around here. Then she spotted a Trader Joe's out the Jeep window. "Why don't we buy some cheese and stuff and have a picnic on the mountain?"

"Great." Garrett swerved across three lanes of traffic to get to the grocery store parking lot.

It was Saturday night just past 7 P.M., and the sun hung on the horizon. Garrett had shown up at the Mercers' door a half hour earlier with a bouquet of flowers in his hands and a bouquet of different fragrances on his body—colognes, body sprays, hair gel, the works. There was such a hopeful, eager expression on his face that Emma couldn't bring herself to call off the date, even though every cell in her body was dying to. She didn't want to deal with Garrett right now; she wanted to be searching for Sutton's killer.

After standing in line behind an old lady who insisted on paying with a check, Emma and Garrett finally arrived at Catalina State Park, a shopping bag full of sparkling cider, black olives, crackers, grapes, trail mix, fancy Australian licorice, and a wedge of Brie swinging from the crook of Garrett's elbow. The air was cool and crisp and smelled like sunscreen. Other hikers bounded up the path. After another few twists and switchbacks, they reached the vista and settled on a big boulder. Emma could see all the way

down the mountain. Garrett's car looked like a toy ı
up here.

"It's so nice out tonight," Garrett murmured, running his hand through his blond hair. He removed his
long-sleeved shirt and spread it on the ground as a picnic
blanket. His tanned biceps bulged. He twisted the cider
bottle open with a satisfying *psst*.

"Uh-huh," Emma replied. She stared blankly ahead.
There were tumbleweeds in her mind where conversation topics should have been. What did Garrett and Sutton
used to talk about? Did they have inside jokes? What
brought them together? If only Sutton's journal had been
normal, Emma might've actually learned something useful like this.

Sighing, she pulled the crackers, olives, trail mix, and
licorice out of the bag. She absentmindedly placed a cracker
on the napkin and added two olives for eyes, a trail-mix
peanut for a nose, and a piece of licorice for a smile. Thinking
of Ethan, she poked Garrett. "Like my new friend?"

Garrett glanced at it for a moment and nodded. "Cute."

"You want to make a face, too?"

Garrett shrugged. "I can hardly draw a circle in art
class."

Emma popped one of the olive eyes into her mouth. *So
much for common ground.*

But I was kind of glad she didn't like Garrett. I couldn't

remember exactly why I loved him. I couldn't recall what it was that made me think of him as damaged, I just knew that I did. And even in death, I wanted him all to myself.

Emma sat back and stared at the horizon, absently touching the scratches on her throat from last night. Tiny red marks lacerated her skin. Her windpipe still ached from the pull of the necklace. She'd taken a bunch of Advils and covered up the scrapes with the Dior foundation she'd found in Sutton's bathroom, hoping Garrett wouldn't notice anything amiss. She could still feel the assailant's hot, stale breath on her neck. She shut her eyes and winced.

"You okay?" Garrett asked.

Emma nodded. "Yeah. I'm just tired."

"Fun sleepover last night?"

Emma paused. "Actually, *sleep*over is inaccurate. I didn't get any."

"Is that a good thing or a bad thing?"

Emma fiddled with Sutton's locket, saying nothing. It still felt foreign around her neck.

"C'mon." Garrett poked her side. "You can tell me what happens at your crazy sleepovers. I wish you told me more."

Emma reached for another cracker, suddenly getting an idea. Actually, Garrett might be useful to this investigation after all.

"Well, I'm not sure 'fun' is the word I'd use," she said slowly. "More like . . . intense. Sometimes I think my friends hate me. I think they'd stab me in the back if they could." It felt weird to recite the words she'd found in Sutton's journal.

A couple of college kids smelling strongly of pot emerged from behind the curve. The air shifted and suddenly reeked of smelly armpit. Garrett bit down on a grape; some of the juice dribbled down his chin. "Are you talking about that night?"

Emma jolted up. "What night?"

Garrett slowly chewed a cracker. "The night you won't tell me about?"

Emma's eyes widened. *What did he mean?*

"Or do you mean Charlotte?" Garrett asked when Emma didn't answer.

Emma lowered her eyes. *Charlotte?* "Um, yeah," she said, hoping this led somewhere. "I just don't know what her problem is."

Garrett pressed the edge of his sneaker into a scrubby patch of desert grass. "You're going to have to give her some time, Sutton. Try to see it from her perspective. I dumped her . . . to go out with you. A lot of girls would have a tough time with that."

Emma pushed another piece of Brie into her mouth to hide her shock. Charlotte and Garrett . . . *dated*? She certainly hadn't learned anything like *that* from Sutton's journal.

But it made sense. It explained the death stare Charlotte had given Emma last night when boyfriend-stealing came up in Never Have I Ever. There was that picture of Garrett's naked torso hanging outside the shower in Charlotte's bathroom, too. And the picture of him that had been abandoned under her bed.

"She's clearly not over it," Emma agreed. "Actually, I don't think she's over *you*."

Garrett sighed and wrapped his arms around his knees. "I wish it never happened. I thought she understood my position. We were friends, and when we tried being more, there wasn't any romance. I didn't think she felt a spark either." He broke off a piece of cracker and held it in his palm. "She's actually called me a couple of times. Sometimes she just hangs up."

Emma sat up straighter. "Like . . . prank calls?"

Garrett frowned. "I don't think so. She just doesn't know what to say. I feel bad for her. I mean, she's so tough, but it's got to be hard on her. And I still see her all the time with you. I want her to be my friend—I want *all* of us to be friends. Besides, Charlotte was there for me during everything that happened with Louisa." His voice cracked on *Louisa*. A pained look crossed his face. "We share a lot of history together."

The words rushed over Emma. She felt dazed as she tried to process all Garrett had said. Then he grabbed her hand. "I don't want it to be anything *more* than that with her though. I'm with you now. I *want* to be with you."

He moved a little closer to her and draped his arm around Emma's shoulders. "That reminds me though . . . of what we talked about this summer. Our . . . plans?"

Emma searched his way-too-close face, trying hard not to pull away. Garrett looked so serious all of a sudden. "Uh-huh," she lied, hoping he'd elaborate.

"Well, I was thinking of making that happen for your birthday." He shot her a bashful smile as he traced a squiggle on her arm. "What do you think?"

Emma shrugged. "Um, sure," she said.

Garrett snuggled toward her and leaned his face close to hers. Emma braced herself as he touched his lips to hers, but he tasted like sweet grapes and fizzy cider, and his lips felt warm and soft. She relaxed a tiny bit into the kiss.

A twig snapped close by. Emma pulled back and sat up straight, instantly on edge. "Did you hear that?"

There was another snapping sound. "Yeah." Garrett frowned and looked around, too. Someone emerged from a dirt path off the main trail. It was a girl with pale skin and bright red hair. Emma drew in a breath.

"Oh!" Charlotte stopped short and pulled a pair of iPod earbuds from her ears. Her gaze darted from Garrett to Emma, then to their entwined hands. What was Charlotte doing up here? *Had she been watching?*

Garrett tugged nervously at the collar of his shirt. "Uh, hi, Char. What's up?"

Charlotte fiddled with a rope bracelet around her wrist. "Oh, just getting a hike in."

"Cool," Garrett said.

"Nice night for it," Emma added stupidly.

A hawk screamed ominously from a nearby ledge. When Charlotte raised her head again, her expression was placid. Her mouth no longer trembled. "Anyway," she said. "See you lovebirds later."

"L-Later," Emma stammered.

Charlotte slipped the earbuds back in. Garrett waved weakly. Emma did, too. Just as Charlotte made the turn, darkness crept over her face. She glanced over her shoulder, and met Emma's gaze.

All at once, Emma felt the hands at her neck and heard the raspy voice from last night in her ear. *Sutton's dead.* Could it have been Charlotte?

I recalled the broad-shouldered shape standing over me in the trunk and wondered the same thing. Could it have been Charlotte staring angrily, finally getting her revenge?

Then Charlotte whipped her head around, red ponytail bouncing. She shook her hips to the song on her iPod. As she rounded the next rock, her footsteps didn't make a sound, almost like she'd never been there at all.

22

DIRTY SECRETS

On Tuesday afternoon, when Mr. Garrison the gym teacher dispatched the class to either take a walk or play floor hockey—*bleh*—Emma strode along the hedged-in path past the tennis courts toward the empty running track. The afternoon was breezy but warm, smelling faintly of ground coffee beans from the cafeteria's espresso bar. Bits of dried grass turned tumbleweeds blew across the eight yellow-outlined lanes and nestled in the long jump pit. Red-and-white-striped hurdles were stacked neatly in the middle of the field, and an abandoned gray sweatshirt lay next to them, along with a half-drained bottle of Gatorade. The only sounds were the crows cawing in the far-off trees.

Emma pulled out Sutton's iPhone and composed a text to Madeline: SPA AFTER TENNIS PRACTICE?

She hit SEND. Emma had been dying to talk to Madeline alone ever since her strange encounter with Charlotte on the trail on Saturday, but Madeline had been at a ballet workshop in Phoenix all weekend. And Emma had just found out that Charlotte had a doctor's appointment after tennis—"the gynecologist," Charlotte had covertly whispered to Emma at lunch, giving her a loaded look—which meant Emma and Madeline could have some time alone.

She desperately needed to find out Charlotte's state of mind. This weekend, she'd pored over Sutton's journals, searching for clues about just how angry Charlotte was. But there was only the entry that said, *C has been so bitchy lately. She just needs to get over it.* And, of course, *Sometimes I think all my friends hate me. Every last one.* Was that enough? Perhaps Charlotte had been furious at Sutton for stealing Garrett away . . . angry enough to strangle her. Angry enough to kill her. It would've been easy for her to sneak downstairs in her own house, too, strangle Emma in the same way, and slip back upstairs unnoticed. Maybe there was a secret staircase in that crazy-big house.

Emma's theory terrified me. How many times had I picked on Charlotte like I had at the hot springs? How many times did I put her down? Had stealing Garrett made her snap . . . or had it been something else?

"Sutton," a voice called.

Emma turned to see a figure looming between the hedges. Whoever was there was backlit by the sun, and at first Emma couldn't quite make out who it was. All kinds of things flashed through her mind in an instant. Her gut knotted with nerves.

Then Ethan stepped into the light. Emma's muscles relaxed. "Hey," Emma said gratefully. Ethan walked out to the track and fell into step with her. "I didn't know you had gym right now."

"I don't," Ethan said. "I'm supposed to be in calculus. But I'm so lost about functions it's not even worth it to go."

Their footsteps were nearly silent on the spongy all-weather track. The odor of bus exhaust wafted from the front of the school. A hummingbird darted to a tube-shaped feeder one of the groundskeepers had hung near the field house, its wings flapping lightning fast. "So did you do it?" Ethan asked after they'd made a lap. "Did you have a big no-more-pranks intervention with your friends?"

"Not exactly." Emma attempted a laugh. "I'm still working on it."

"Still think they're evil?"

"Kinda." *More than you know*, Emma wanted to say. Then her gaze fell to handwriting on Ethan's arm: HOW

FRAIL THE HUMAN HEART MUST BE—A MIRRORED POOL OF THOUGHT. She recognized it instantly. "You like Sylvia Plath?"

A bloom of red appeared on Ethan's cheeks. "You caught me. I read depressing girls' poetry."

"It's better than *writing* depressing girls' poetry." Emma laughed. "I have a whole notebook full of it." A notebook that was stuffed into the pocket of a missing duffel bag. Emma felt a longing pang. She'd probably never see it again. "Have you read *The Bell Jar*?" she asked Ethan.

He nodded. "Loved it."

"I read it three times this summer," Emma said excitedly.

"Sutton Mercer read *The Bell Jar*?" Ethan shot her a quick surprised look. "And has a notebook full of depressing poetry? You're a complex creature."

Mr. Garrison blew the whistle, signaling for Emma's class to return to the gym. Emma turned back to the hedge-lined path. "See ya." She smiled at Ethan, heat rising in her cheeks. She whirled around and crunched back to the gym door, a smile on her face.

Beep.

It was the iPhone. Emma pulled it out and checked the text. I'D LOVE A SPA NITE, Madeline wrote back. LA PALOMA AT 7?

SOUNDS GREAT, Emma texted back. Maybe she'd finally start getting some answers.

"Miss Vega and Miss Mercer?" A freshly scrubbed, freckled woman in a lab coat stood at the door of the La Paloma waiting area. "Your room is ready."

"Sweet." Madeline minimized the gossip site she and Emma had been perusing on her iPhone. They'd been playing "punch-drunk"—the object was to punch one another first whenever they saw a picture of a drunk-looking celebrity. Double punches if the celebrity had a boob hanging out.

The aesthetician, whose name tag said SOFIA, opened a glass door and let the girls pass into a long, narrow hall. A male spa worker walked toward them, giving Madeline and Emma an appreciative once-over. Madeline met his gaze and giggled. As he passed, she quickly slapped his butt. The guy swiveled around, but Madeline sauntered on, her long hair swishing.

Sofia opened yet another glass door and revealed a large porcelain tub. A soft yellow haze shone down from recessed lights in the ceiling. Rain forest noises played softly through the speakers. "I'll let you get settled," Sofia trilled, shutting the door.

Madeline instantly dropped her robe to the floor, adjusted the ties of her black string bikini, and climbed the mini plastic stairs to enter the tub. "Coming in?" she called to Emma over her shoulder.

Emma undid the belt of her robe and carefully stepped into the tub. The mud was thick and grainy. It was like sitting in a big bowl of oatmeal. Madeline rested her head, a blissed-out expression on her face. Sofia appeared again and placed cucumber slices over the girls' eyes. "Enjoy," she lilted, turning down the lights, turning up the rain forest music, and shutting the door.

The mud tub burbled. Emma tried to enjoy the moment. The cucumber slices smelled fresh next to her nose, but the jungle music blared through the speakers so loudly that it was hard to relax. The sound of heavy rain morphed into tribal drums, followed by a buzzing insect. Birds tweeted and cawed. An African flute tooted. When a monkey let out a loud screech, Emma started to giggle. She heard a snort from across the tub and pulled the cucumbers from her eyes. Madeline's lips were pressed tightly together, as if she were trying very hard not to laugh, which only made Emma's shoulders shake harder. Then two monkeys started hooting together. Emma burst out laughing, and Madeline did, too. Emma covered her mouth, smearing mud all over her face. A cucumber fell from one of Madeline's eyes and plopped into the murky liquid.

"Dude," Madeline said between giggles. "I think the monkeys are doing it."

"It's definitely monkey mating calls," Emma agreed, flicking a glop of mud at Madeline.

They settled back into the mud, every once in a while letting out another giggle or snort. Then Madeline took a long sip from the glass of lemon water near her head and sighed. "So what's been with you this past week? You've seemed kind of . . . sedate. Like someone upped your meds."

At least *someone* noticed there was something different about me.

"I'm okay," Emma answered. "Just tired. School always makes me want to hibernate."

"Well, wake up, baby bear." Madeline pointed at her mock-accusingly. "Your public will be very disappointed in you if you're not a rock star for your birthday. And by your public, I mean me."

"I'll try not to disappoint," Emma giggled.

Steam billowed into their faces, smelling vaguely sulfuric. Someone's shadowy head passed by the frosted-glass doors. Then Emma took a deep breath. *Here goes.* "If anyone's been acting like they've had a med change, it's Charlotte. Don't you think?"

Madeline shook a stray piece of hair from her eyes. "She's been no weirder than usual."

Emma's hip started to itch, but she didn't want to reach into the mud to scratch it. "Do you know where she was the night before Nisha's party?"

Madeline shrugged. "Do you honestly expect me to remember something that happened over a week ago? My brain's too fried from a week of school." But Emma noticed that she wouldn't make eye contact with her. She fiddled nervously with a bracelet around her wrist.

"Char and I had plans that night, and she ditched me," Emma lied, thinking quickly. "Sometimes I think she's really pissed at me. She keeps making these little remarks to me about Garrett. I think I caught her spying on us on Saturday."

And perhaps plotting to kill me, *too*, she silently added. *Just like she killed Sutton.*

A muscle next to Madeline's right eye twitched. Steam swirled around her face. "I don't think she's pissed at you. She's probably just worried about Garrett."

"Worried? Why?"

The mud sloshed as Madeline shifted positions. "Come on, Sutton. You're not exactly gentle on guys. You kind of destroy every boy you touch."

"No I don't." Emma's voice cracked.

But Madeline's words shook me. I wanted Madeline to be wrong, only . . . maybe she wasn't. I didn't know what to believe about myself anymore.

Madeline sniffed indignantly. "Look at all those guys last year. You practically forced Brandon Crawford to break up with Sienna at Homecoming, and then you didn't return his calls. You acted like you were dying to go out with Owen Haas, and then you treated him like crap. Look at Thayer," she added.

Thayer? Was Sutton why he left?

I racked my brain to remember, to feel something. Nothing surfaced.

Madeline met Emma's gaze without blinking. The room suddenly felt very small and close. Emma lowered her eyes and stared at the four slices of cucumbers floating on the surface of the mud.

Suddenly Madeline climbed out of the tub. Brown goop dripped from her stomach and legs.

"What are you doing?" Emma said, half rising.

"I totally forgot." Madeline pressed a towel to her head. "I was supposed to be at my dad's house right now. Can Laurel pick you up?" She turned her body away from Emma as she spoke. There were thick brown smudges on the towel from where she'd dried her arms.

"Wait, Mads—what's going on?" Emma groped through the mud toward the stairs. It was just like the anxiety dream she sometimes had where she kept trying to run, only to realize the road was a backward-moving sidewalk.

Madeline had already stuffed her arms through the bathrobe sleeves. "I'll talk to you in school tomorrow, okay?" she mumbled in a rush and slipped into the hall, leaving muddy footprints all over the tiled floor.

The door whooshed shut again. The only sounds in the room were the occasional burps from the mud tub; even the rainforest music had stopped. Emma climbed out of the tub and pressed a towel to her face. What the hell just happened? And what had Sutton done to Thayer?

Just as she was grabbing a second towel from the table, something on the floor caught her eye. It was an iPhone. She turned it over and inspected the back. There was a glittery sticker of a girl with devil horns doing a pirouette. SWAN LAKE MAFIA. Madeline's iPhone.

Emma glanced at Madeline's muddy footprints, then at the door, then back at the phone again. She rinsed her hands at the sink on the counter and took a deep breath. Should she do this?

"Yes!" I yelled at her as loudly as I could.

Emma slid the bar on the iPhone screen to unlock it. With shaking hands, she pressed on the little thought bubble icon to open Madeline's texts. First on the list was one she'd written herself, inviting Madeline to the spa today. There were a bunch of texts about the prank on Nisha: Laurel writing to say she'd found the perfect actress to play the cop, Charlotte asking Madeline if she could pick up fake blood at the Halloween store in the mall. Emma scrolled backward through earlier messages. There were a few texts discussing travel plans to Nisha's party the week before, though nothing about a fake kidnapping.

Footsteps sounded on the other side of the door, and Emma froze. Whoever it was whistled softly as he passed. Emma gripped the phone hard. Next she tapped the screen to view Madeline's photos. A shot of an electric guitar popped up. Emma pulled the screen to the left. There was a photo of two ballet dancers on a stage, one of them Madeline. A shot of the jewelry display case at Anthropologie. A picture of Madeline and Sutton on chaise longues.

She flipped through more and more photos: A self-portrait of Madeline in a full-length mirror. A shot of Sutton, Madeline, and Charlotte by some kind of outdoor hot tub. Sutton and Madeline wore skimpy bikinis, but Charlotte wore a terry-cloth cover-up.

I leaned in closer, recognizing it immediately. My body flickered before me, as if it was shuddering. This was the photo I'd taken of everyone at the hot springs. My words clanged in my ears. *Picture time!* And when Laurel whined that she wasn't in the photo, I'd smirked and said *I planned it that way.*

Emma kept eyeing the door, her fingers trembling. She flipped to the next photo. It was a shot of the same dark location, showing Sutton running after Laurel down a dark path.

Laurel! I'd called out. *I'll buy you a new necklace, okay?*

Just seconds later, that knife had pressed to my throat.

When the next photo appeared on the screen, Emma frowned. It was a close-up of Laurel sitting on a big red rock, the sun rising behind her. A round pendant on a silver chain hung around her neck. With shaking hands, Emma pulled the chain around her throat and examined the locket. It looked exactly the same as the one in the picture.

"Oh my God," Emma and I whispered at the same time.

Emma wondered what Laurel was doing wearing Sutton's locket—the locket someone had strangled her with. Could it be . . . ?

It could. After all, I'd thrown hers deep into the woods. The only thing that didn't make sense now was, well, *why*? Why would my own sister want to kill me? I obviously hadn't been the best sister in life—but how bad could I have been?

The doorknob jiggled. Emma dropped the iPhone. It landed in a heap of towels just as Madeline flung open the door. She'd changed into her skinny jeans, slumpy striped tunic, and wide belt. "I was just looking for . . . oh." Her gaze dropped to her iPhone on the floor.

"Yeah." Emma tried to smile, even though her insides were screaming. "I just noticed that, too. I was going to come after you."

Madeline scooped up the phone and stuck it in her

pocket. "Thanks." She stared at Emma. Emma held her breath.

But then Madeline whipped around and opened the door. "See you in school tomorrow." She waltzed through the door again, her long hair swinging. Emma leaned against the side of the tub and rolled Sutton's round locket between her fingers.

I felt more dazed than ever before. Whatever was going on here was just like a mud bath. The deeper my sister plunged, the darker and dirtier it got.

23

SOMEONE WAS A VERY, VERY BAD GIRL . . .

"So you see, Medea *had* to kill her children," Mrs. Frost explained to the class on Wednesday. She paced around the room like she was some big-time defense lawyer pleading for an innocent victim's life. "It was the only way Medea could get back at her husband, Jason, for his betrayal."

Everyone in the class scribbled notes. Suddenly Emma felt a buzz inside her bag. She inched her fingers into the purse until she felt the iPhone's smooth sides. Anything would be a welcome distraction from Mrs. Frost's obsessive retelling of *Medea*. Something about the forcefulness of the English teacher's literary interpretations made Emma wonder if Mrs. Frost had had a less than faithful husband.

"Miss Mercer?" a voice snapped. Emma looked up and saw Mrs. Frost standing right over her desk. She waved her tattered copy at Emma. "Drop the phone right now, or I take it for the rest of the year."

Emma raised both empty palms in the air. "I surrender." Everyone giggled.

Fortunately the bell rang right then, and English was the last class of the day. Emma fled into the hall, checking the iPhone screen for who had called. Even after all this time, even knowing what she knew, she still carried around a tiny seedling of hope that the incoming message might be from Sutton.

But it was just an email from Sutton's mom. FINAL BIRTHDAY PARTY MENU was the subject. Emma scanned the list of crudités, appetizers, and desserts. LOOKS FINE, she began to write back, but then she noticed carrot cake cupcakes on the list. Carrot cake had always grossed her out—the raisins in the cake mix made her think of gerbil poop. MAKE THEM RED VELVET INSTEAD, she tapped on the screen.

The halls swarmed with students emptying out their lockers and kids in sports uniforms rushing to games. A knot of girls Emma didn't recognize stood in the corner near the trophy case, whispering. Emma glanced quickly around the hall, her heart jumping whenever she saw blond hair that looked like Laurel's or a willowy frame like

Madeline's. She'd avoided Sutton's friends and her sister all day, claiming she had a photography project to work on at lunch—"Photoshopping unibrows on yearbook portraits again, Sutton?" Charlotte had joked—and ignoring their snarky texts and IMs. The idea of facing them right now made her skin itch. Why would Laurel have been wearing Sutton's locket? And how come Madeline had taken that picture? Was it like some kind of trophy?

Emma ducked into the girls' bathroom to splash some water on her face. Just as she reached for a paper towel, a hand touched her shoulder. Emma yelped and turned around.

"God." Nisha stood next to her at the sink, shielding her face with her hand. "Jumpy much?"

Emma turned back and shakily twisted on the tap. "Oh. What's up?"

Nisha raised a piece of hair behind her ear. "Did you forget already?"

"Forget what?"

Nisha placed her hands on her hips. She stared at Emma with disdain. "Decorating the lockers? The thing all captains do at the start of every year?"

Emma blinked. How was she supposed to know *that*?

"Uch." Nisha made a frustrated noise at the back of her throat. "You know, some of us can't do all of the work by ourselves. Some of us have college applications to fill out."

Emma shot up. *Whoa.* "I want to go to college," she said indignantly. "I want to go to USC."

Nisha paused for a moment, as if waiting for the punch line. Then she burst out laughing. "That's the funniest thing I've heard all day."

She shoved open the bathroom door and started down the hall toward the sports locker room. Emma followed. Nisha walked briskly. Her ponytail swished back and forth, and her hands were clenched into tight fists. They darted down the stairs and whizzed past Jason and Kendra, the pimply couple who were always making out in the little alcove under the risers. As they passed, Emma noticed that Jason's hand had disappeared up Kendra's shirt.

Nisha strode into the sports locker room, marching past the girls changing into swimsuits, fencing uniforms, and cheerleading skirts and heading straight into a small private office. Stacks of construction paper, Crayola markers, brightly colored sand, and stickers occupied most of a wide, dented table. A pot of red glitter had tipped over, spilling tiny sparkly shards all over the floor. It made Emma think of fairy blood.

Twenty-five individual name tags, one for each girl on the tennis team, had been laid out in the middle of the table. Brooklyn Killoran's name was in pink bubble letters and surrounded by shooting-star stickers. A black piece of construction paper displayed Isabella McSweeny's name in glow-in-the-dark paint. Nisha had drawn flow-ers sprouting out of each of the letters in Laurel's name and a loopy scribble around the border. And then Emma noticed Sutton's tag, her name written in plain font on a white square. There was no glitter or puff paint or stickers that said YOU GO, GIRL or ACE! It could've been a name tag on a jail cell.

"I'm basically done." Nisha picked up the name tag closest to her, one for a girl named Amanda Pfeiffer. "But you can help hang these on the lockers, if you think you can handle that."

"When did you make them?" Emma asked.

"Over the weekend." Nisha flicked a piece of glitter off her wrist.

"Why didn't you ask me to help?"

Nisha stared at Emma for a moment, and then let out a shrill witch laugh. "As if I would ask *you* to help me with anything." She yanked a name tag off the table, sending a few crayons to the floor. As Nisha walked down the tennis aisle, Emma noticed that tiny specks of red fake blood from last week's prank still covered the walls, lock-ers, and floor. Nisha stood squarely on top of one patch as she pinned her own name tag—drawn out of interlocking tennis rackets—on her locker door.

Emma bit her lip. "I'm sorry about what we did last week."

Nisha moved calmly to the next locker and hung up Bethany Howard's name tag. "Whatever," she said airily.

"You didn't deserve it," Emma went on. She wanted to add that perhaps she didn't deserve Nisha sticking her with a child-sized tennis uniform last week, but maybe that was pushing it.

Nisha ripped off a new piece of masking tape, then whipped around to face Emma again. Her eyes were wild. "Your stupid fake blood ruined my favorite tennis fleece." She pointed hard at Emma's chest. "It was my mom's fleece. I had to throw it away because of you."

Emma took a step away, flattening someone's mouth guard with her shoe. But as Nisha stood there, seething, Emma realized there wasn't just anger in her voice. There was pain.

With her shoulders hunched and her mouth puckered, Nisha looked small and young. Emma wondered how Nisha's mom had died. It was the kind of question Old Emma would have asked. So many foster kids had lost parents. And even though she could never be sure what had become of Becky, sometimes Emma felt as though she was one of those kids. Sometimes, although it made her feel guilty to admit it even to herself, she wished Becky had died, because that would have meant she hadn't chosen to leave Emma.

I felt my own guilty pang, for all that I obviously had

in my life but seemed to have taken for granted. There had been loss all around, but death hadn't seemed like something that could touch a girl like me. How wrong I was.

Sighing, Emma picked up Sutton's drab name tag and taped it to her outer locker door. It looked pathetic next to the other bright, cheery name tags on either side. After a moment, she pulled the handle and looked at the contents of Sutton's tennis locker again. The shiny varsity jacket hung from a hook. An empty bottle of Propel water lay crumpled at the bottom. There was a balled-up pair of gym socks on the upper shelf, crusted over with sweat. Emma wished she could tell Nisha she'd lost her mom, too.

Nisha ripped off more tape and silently hung up more signs. Emma went to shut the locker, but then she paused. Something bulged in the front pocket of the varsity jacket. After a moment, she reached in and pulled out a large folded paper napkin. On the inside was a note written in sloppy, boyish handwriting: *Hi Laurel!* And then there was a drawing of a smiley face with googly drunk eyes and a lolling tongue holding a frothy mug of beer. It was signed *Thayer.*

"What's that?"

Emma whirled around. Nisha stood right beside her, her Altoid breath icy on Emma's neck. Emma moved to fold up the napkin before Nisha could see it, but Nisha's eyes had already narrowed, reading the words. "So you steal your sister's mail, too?"

Emma blinked hard. "I . . ."

Nisha shook her finger at Emma. "I heard Laurel was ready to kill you for what you did."

"Kill me?" Emma repeated. She thought of the picture of Laurel wearing Sutton's necklace on Madeline's iPhone.

Nisha watched her carefully. A tiny sparkle stuck to her cheek glinted in the overhead light. "Don't play dumb, Sutton. You knew Laurel had a thing for him."

Emma blinked. But before she could say anything more, Nisha spun on her heel and walked back to the office, leaving a trail of red glitter in her wake.

And leaving Emma and me reeling, desperate to know more.

24

DOESN'T EVERY GIRL THINK
HER SISTER WANTS TO KILL HER?

On Thursday, after yet another terrible tennis practice, Emma sat on Sutton's bed with a notebook and pencil on her lap. *Top story,* she wrote. *Sister Tries to Track Down Twin's Murderer. Too Intense for Words.*

She dropped the pencil on the mattress and shut her eyes. She'd hoped writing this out like a news headline might put it in perspective, make it seem more normal. Nothing about this was normal though. Instead she wrote another list about Sutton's friends and the potential motives each of them had to kill her. She'd probably composed ten versions of the same list so far, scrawled on notebooks, crumpled in trash cans, written in shorthand on Sutton's iPhone, which was somehow the most ironic of all. The problem was, every single member of the Lying Game had motives—Charlotte because Sutton had stolen Garrett. Laurel because Sutton . . . well, she'd done *something* to Thayer. Had that same something pissed off Madeline, too?

Emma's old cell phone bleeped from its hiding spot under the bed. She set the notebook aside and reached down to retrieve it. After using a new iPhone, her BlackBerry struck her as old and banged-up. It was like seeing a stray mutt on the street after spending time only with shiny show dogs.

Alex had sent her a text: EVERYTHING OKAY IN SISTER LAND?

SURE, Emma replied. She didn't even itch from lying anymore. She and Alex had texted a few more times during the week, and Emma hadn't revealed a single thing about what was really happening. As far as Alex knew, Emma was staying with the Mercers while she and Sutton got to know each other, just like a fairy tale.

A note pinged back into Emma's inbox immediately: WHAT ABOUT THE STUFF YOU STASHED IN THE STORAGE LOCKER? YOU GOING TO GET IT, OR DO YOU WANT ME TO SHIP IT TO YOU?

Emma flopped back on the bed and scrunched up her

face. She had no idea what to do with that stuff in the locker—especially the money. CAN LEAVE IT THERE FOR NOW, she wrote back.

Just then, the bedroom door slowly opened. Emma wheeled back on the bed, shoving the BlackBerry under a pillow. Laurel appeared in the doorway. Mrs. Mercer stood behind her, a laundry basket in her arms.

"Whatcha doin'?" Laurel asked, walking into the room.

Heat rose to Emma's cheeks. "Have you ever heard of *knocking*?"

Laurel's face fell. "Sorry."

"Be nice, Sutton," Mrs. Mercer scolded. She marched over to Sutton's chest of drawers and dropped a stack of clothes next to the TV. Among them was Emma's striped dress. Emma wanted to thank her—she hadn't had anyone wash clothes for her in years—but she had a feeling this was probably something Mrs. Mercer did for Sutton all the time.

Laurel remained after Mrs. Mercer padded out of the room. Emma smoothed her hair behind her ears. Adrenaline coursed through her veins, and her hands began to tremble. All she could think of was that picture of Laurel wearing Sutton's necklace. "What do you want?" she asked.

"I wanted to know if you were ready to get mani-pedis at Mr. Pinky." Laurel clasped her hands at her waist. "If you still want to go, that is."

Emma gazed blankly at the white-and-pink egg chair in the corner. It was still covered with the bikinis and socks Sutton had left there before she died; Emma hadn't had the heart to move any of it. After Nisha's elusive comment last night, she'd logged into Sutton's Facebook account and searched Laurel's page once more. Emma had figured Laurel and Thayer were friends, but she hadn't guessed that Laurel had a crush on him. As she looked back at the pictures though, it was obvious. In all the group shots, Laurel stood next to Thayer. In a shot where Thayer laughed at something with Charlotte, Laurel lurked in the background looking at Thayer. A YouTube link showed Thayer and Laurel dancing a tango at a school formal. When Thayer dipped Laurel low, Laurel had a delighted, enchanted smile on her face. It was a smile of someone who wanted something more than just friendship. But in May, a month before Thayer allegedly ran away, the Wall messages between the two of them abruptly stopped. There were no more pictures of Laurel and Thayer together. It was as though something—or someone—had forced them apart.

Don't play dumb, Sutton, Nisha had said. *You knew she had a thing for him.* And there was the entry in Sutton's journal from May 17: *L is still ruined over T. Pull yourself together, bitch. He's just a guy. T* obviously stood for *Thayer.* There were no easy answers, though. It wasn't as if anyone had written what exactly had happened.

And it certainly wasn't like I remembered. I hoped I hadn't done something to hurt my little sister, but I really didn't know.

Emma watched Laurel as she picked up a bottle of perfume from Sutton's dresser and sniffed the top. She smiled pleasantly, as if she didn't have a mean cell in her body. Then Emma thought about the crane Laurel had placed at Emma's plate last week. Maybe she was jumping to conclusions. Just because Nisha *said* Laurel would kill her didn't mean she actually had. It's just something people say. And maybe there was a good reason Laurel was wearing Sutton's locket in that picture on Madeline's phone. The same locket that now hung around Emma's neck.

"Let me put on jeans," Emma decided.

Laurel smiled. "Meet you downstairs." Just as she was halfway across the room to the door, Laurel paused and widened her eyes at something on the bed. "What's *that?*"

Emma followed her gaze and panicked. Her notebook lay face-up on the mattress. Scrawled across the top sheet were the words *Girl Strangled in Mansion. Thinks Friends to Blame.* She grabbed for the notebook and covered it with her hand. "Just a project for school."

Laurel paused for a moment. "You don't do projects for school!" She shook her head and walked out of the room. But before she stepped down the stairs, she cast one more glance at Emma.

From where I watched it was hard to tell if it was questioning . . . or something more.

Mr. Pinky was a small salon tucked into the foothills, in a complex that also contained an organic yogurt shop, a holistic cat daycare, and a place that advertised ULTRA-CLEANSE COLONICS! LOSE FIVE POUNDS IN MINUTES! in the front window. At least Laurel hadn't dragged her *there*.

The salon was part upscale spa, part *Star Trek*. All the nail technicians wore formfitting jumpsuits that were supposedly trendy, but Emma thought they looked ready to board a starship and fly the whole salon to the Crab Nebula.

Emma and Laurel plopped down on a sleek gray couch to wait. "So are you ready for your party?" Laurel pulled ChapStick out of her bag and smeared it over her lips.

"I guess," Emma lied. More RSVP cards had been waiting in Sutton's bedroom when she came home from tennis today. All of them said things like *Can't wait!* and *The party of the year!*

"You'd better be." Laurel nudged her in the ribs. "You've been planning it for long enough! So has Garrett told you what he's getting you yet?"

Emma shook her head. "Why? Has he told you?"

Laurel's smile broadened knowingly. "Nah. But I've heard rumors. . . ."

Emma pinched a handful of fabric on the couch. What was the big deal with Garrett's present?

Nail dryers hummed across the room. The smell of polish remover and aloe hand lotion filled the air. Emma reached into her bag and touched the napkin from Thayer. Her stomach streaked with nerves. She'd intended to bring it up at the end of the manicures, but she couldn't wait any longer. "Laurel?"

Laurel looked up and smiled. Emma placed the napkin on the empty cushion between them. "I found this in my tennis locker."

A wrinkle formed between Laurel's eyes as she gazed at Thayer's drunk smiley face. Her fingers worked a tiny hole in her jeans. There was a sharp rip, and the hole suddenly, forcefully, split open. "Oh," she whispered.

"I'm really sorry." Emma's voice shook. "I don't know how it got there." It wasn't technically a lie.

Laurel balled the note in her hands and stared blankly at the rainbow-colored bottles of nail polish on the shelf. Emma gripped the arm of the couch hard. Would Laurel explode? Scream? Come after her with nail scissors?

"No biggie," Laurel finally said. "It's not like I don't have a million notes exactly like that from Thayer in my room."

Then she calmly pulled out her iPhone and checked her email.

"Do you miss him?" Emma blurted.

Laurel continued to tap her iPhone. "Of course." Her voice didn't rise or dip. It was as though they were talking about the differences between creamy peanut butter and crunchy. Then she nodded at the Snapple bottle Emma had taken from the Mercer fridge. "Mind if I have some?"

Emma shrugged, and Laurel took a long sip. As soon as she set the bottle back on the coffee table, her shoulders began to convulse. Her head jerked back, and she tipped over on the couch. She clutched her throat and stared at Emma with frightened, bulging eyes. "I . . . can't . . ."

Emma shot to her feet. "Laurel?" Laurel made a choking sound, flopped once, and went limp. Her blond hair fanned out on the couch cushion. Her right hand spasmed.

"Laurel?" Emma shouted. "Laurel?" She shook her shoulders.

Laurel's eyes were glued closed. Her mouth hung open limply. The iPhone she'd been holding slowly released from her grip and clonked to the carpet.

"Help!" Emma called out. She bent down and listened for breathing. No sounds escaped from Laurel's lips. She pressed her fingers to Laurel's wrist. It felt like there was a pulse. "Wake up," she urged, shaking her. Laurel's head bobbed like a rag doll. Her chunky silver bracelets jangled together.

Emma leapt to her feet and looked around. A black

girl stared at them from a pedicure chair across the room, *Vogue* in her lap. A small Spanish woman rushed over. "What's the matter with her?"

"I don't know," Emma said frantically.

"Is she pregnant?" the woman suggested.

"I don't think so. . . ."

"Hey." The Spanish woman jostled Laurel's arm. "*Hey!*" she yelled in her face, slapping her cheek. Emma put her ear to Laurel's mouth again. The mouth-to-mouth unit of the babysitter training class she'd taken in sixth grade rushed to her mind. *Did you pinch the nose* then *breathe into the mouth, or the other way around?*

Then something cold and wet touched her earlobe. Emma pulled back in alarm. Was that . . . a *tongue?* She stared at Laurel's face. And then, suddenly, Laurel's eyes popped open. "Boo!"

Emma screamed. Laurel exploded with giggles. "I totally had you! You thought I was dead!"

The lady made a *tsk* sound with her tongue. "You had all of us! What's wrong with you?" She stormed away, shaking her head.

Emma sat back up. Her heart felt like a flag flapping crazily in the wind.

Laurel adjusted her T-shirt, color rising to her cheeks. "You've taught me well, sis. But I never thought I'd get you with something so easy!" And then she stood, slid her purse over her shoulder, and cruised to the wall of nail polishes to choose the color for her manicure.

Emma stared at Laurel's straight, slender back, her head spinning. That *certainly was an innovative way to change the subject from Thayer.* But something unsettled her, too. A girl whose older sister did something to ruin her chances with her crush didn't just shrug it off with a laugh and a prank. If someone had done that to Emma, she'd tell them off. Fight back. Retaliate.

And then Emma raised her head. The hot lights above scorched her scalp. She could think of one reason Laurel might not be angry anymore.

I thought it at the exact same time, too: Maybe Laurel had already gotten her revenge.

25

A LATE ADDITION TO THE GUEST LIST

"I'd like to solve the puzzle, Pat," a constantly smiling soccer mom said on TV. The screen switched to a shot of the *Wheel of Fortune* board. All of the letters of THING had been filled in except for one. "Picking fresh flowers?"

Triumphant music played as Vanna turned the final letter. Soccer mom jumped up and down, ecstatic that she'd won nine hundred dollars. It was late Thursday evening, and Emma was watching a *Wheel* rerun on the Game Show Network from Sutton's bed. *Wheel of Fortune* usually calmed her down. It reminded her of watching it with Becky on the tattered La-Z-Boy—she could almost smell the Burger King takeout and hear Becky calling out the answers and critiquing Vanna's sequined ball gown.

But now all Emma could think of when she saw that wheel on the screen was how it seemed like a metaphor for her life—a wheel of chance. Risk or reward. One twin getting the good life, one twin getting the bad. One twin dying, the other twin living. The living twin choosing either to go after the person she was almost certain had killed her sister . . . or slip quietly away.

Laurel killed Sutton.

The thought flashed into her mind every couple of seconds, giving her a fresh scare each and every time. She felt positive it was true. All signs had pointed to Charlotte before, but now Laurel seemed like the only answer. When she got home from the nail salon, she'd searched for more clues, and too much connected: Sutton's Facebook account was on Autofill, which meant Laurel could've sneaked into Sutton's room, logged in, found the message from Emma, and written an eager note back, summoning Emma here. And then there was the SUTTON'S DEAD note Laurel had found on her car. Besides the bit of pollen on the corner, the paper didn't have any creases, folds, or dirt marks like it should have if Laurel had really dug it out from under a windshield wiper. And Emma hadn't actually *seen* the note on Laurel's car—who was to say Laurel hadn't lied about someone leaving it there? She just as easily could have pulled it out of her bag.

Laurel had been at Charlotte's sleepover, too. She'd slept next to Emma in Charlotte's cavernous bedroom, which would've made it easiest for her to see when Emma had gotten up for a drink. She could've crept downstairs and strangled Emma with Sutton's locket. And *speaking* of that locket, there was the photo of Laurel wearing the locket on Madeline's phone. It looked identical to the one that now hung around Emma's neck.

They looked identical to me, too. I thought about the memories I now possessed. How I had flown off the handle so quickly and thrown her copycat necklace into the darkness. Laurel's shattered expression. Then I thought about those hands grabbing me and shoving me into the car. The trunk had been tiny and cramped, probably about the size of Laurel's Jetta.

But I kept returning to the flickering memory of Laurel and me giggling together at the La Paloma pool. Holding hands. *Friends.* What had driven us apart? Why hadn't I tried to rekindle that relationship? I didn't want to believe Laurel could've murdered me. And what about the shock of red hair I'd seen through my blindfold when the assailant pulled me from the trunk? Had my eyes been playing tricks on me?

Emma rose from the bed and started pacing around the room. She didn't have any solid proof yet, but the snuff film *had* to be from the night Sutton died. It made sense. Maybe when Laurel pulled the blindfold off Sutton's head and discovered she wasn't dead, she'd wrapped the necklace back around her sister's neck and finished the job. Maybe the actual murder happened after the video ended. . . . If *only* the video were still online—it would be enough to make the police believe that what Emma was telling them was true. And how had that video gotten online anyway? Why would the killer post something that would seal her own doom?

Unless of course Laurel posted it online to attract Emma. Maybe she somehow knew that her adopted sister had a twin. And maybe she knew the video would reach Emma . . . and Emma would reach out. It had worked.

Emma placed her palms against the smooth white walls. Muffled music sounded from Laurel's bedroom next door. For all Emma knew, Laurel could be inside her room right now plotting what to do next. She walked over to the TV and shut it off. All of a sudden, it felt dangerous to linger so close to the killer. She felt like a prisoner in this room—a prisoner in her dead sister's life. She yanked the door open and started down the stairs. Just as she was about to pull open the front door, someone cleared his throat behind her. "Where are you going?"

Emma turned. Mr. Mercer sat in the office off the foyer, tapping away on a netbook. There was a Bluetooth earpiece in his ear. "Uh, out for a walk," Emma said.

Mr. Mercer peered at Emma over his glasses. "It's after nine. I don't like you wandering around outside alone in the dark."

The corners of Emma's mouth jerked into a smile. Foster parents never cared when she came and went. They never worried about her safety. Even Becky let Emma walk around at night—if they were staying in a motel, she sent little Emma out to the vending machines to get her Mountain Dew and goldfish crackers.

Then again, he wasn't worried about Emma's safety. He was worried about his daughter, *Sutton*. Emma couldn't bear to meet his eyes, knowing that his daughter was far from safe, and it might all be due to his other daughter. Emma *had* to get the hell out of there. She spied Sutton's tennis racket leaning against the hall closet and grabbed it. "I need to practice my serve."

"Fine." Mr. Mercer turned back to the computer screen. "But I want you back home in an hour. We still need to discuss the ground rules for your party."

"Okay," Emma called out. She slammed the door and jogged down the center of the street. Everyone had dragged their large green trash cans to the curb, and the air smelled like rotting vegetables and dirty diapers. The farther she got from Sutton's house, the better—safer— she felt. She stopped at the park, noticing the faintest outline of a familiar figure lying in an X on the tennis courts. Her heart lifted.

"Ethan?" Emma called out. Ethan shot up at the sound of his name. "It's Sutton!"

"Fancy meeting you here." It was too dark to see Ethan's face, but Emma detected happiness in his voice. She suddenly felt happier, too.

"Can I join you?" she asked.

"Sure."

She opened the chain-link gate without jamming quarters into the meter to turn on the lights. The door slammed shut with a bang. She felt Ethan's gaze on her as she walked to the net and lay down next to him. The court was still warm from the heat of the day and smelled faintly of baked asphalt and spilled Gatorade. The stars above glinted like bits of quartz in a sidewalk. The Mom, Dad, and Emma stars pulsed just below the moon. It was frustrating that even after so much had changed, the stars were in exactly the same place they'd always been, laughing at Emma's futile struggles on earth.

Tears welled in Emma's eyes. *Futile struggles* was right. All the fantasies she'd concocted in her mind on the bus ride here. All the fun she thought she and Sutton would have as sisters.

"You okay, Sylvia Plath?" Ethan teased.

The air had grown colder, and Emma pulled her arms closely into her sides for warmth. "Not really."

"What's up?"

Emma ran her tongue over her teeth. "God, whenever I see you I'm a complete mental case."

"It's cool. I don't mind mental cases."

But Emma shook her head. She couldn't tell him what was really going on, no matter how much she wanted to. "It's my birthday tomorrow," she said instead. "I'm having a party."

"Really?" Ethan propped himself up on one hand. "Well, happy birthday."

"Thanks." Emma smiled in the darkness.

She tracked a slow-moving jet as it sliced across the night sky. In some ways, this would probably be the best birthday she'd ever had. Most of Emma's birthdays had been nonevents—she'd spent her sixteenth in the social worker's office waiting to get reassigned to a new foster home, and she'd spent her eleventh as a runaway with the kids at the campsite. The only real birthday celebration she'd had was when Becky had taken her to a Renaissance fair near where they lived. Emma had ridden Ye Olde Donkey in a slow circle, eaten a giant turkey leg, and made a construction-paper coat of arms in neon green and turquoise, her favorite colors at the time. On their way to the parking lot at the end of the day, Emma had asked if they could do this for her birthday again the next year. But by her next birthday, Becky was gone.

Emma stared at the sky. A cloud passed over the moon, obscuring it for a moment. "Will you come?"

"To what?"

"To my party. I mean, if you're not busy. And if you want to." Emma bit her thumbnail. Her heart kicked in her chest. Asking him suddenly felt like a big deal.

The moon illuminated Ethan's angular profile. Emma waited patiently for him to decide. *If he says no, don't get upset*, she told herself. *Don't take it personally.*

"Okay," Ethan said.

Emma's stomach swooped. "Really?"

"Yeah. Sure. I'll come."

"Great!" Emma grinned. "You'll be the only normal person there."

"I don't know about that." By the way he said it, Emma could tell Ethan was smiling. "I don't think any of us are normal, do you? I think we all have crazy secrets."

"Oh yeah? What's yours?"

Ethan paused a moment. "I have a huge crush on Frau Fenstermacher."

Emma snickered. "That's totally understandable. She's *so* sexy."

"Yeah. I'm super-hot for her."

"Well, good luck with that," Emma said. "I hope you two lovebirds find true happiness."

"Thanks." Ethan shifted positions to lie back down, and his hand bumped hers. Emma stared at their two hands together, the fingers just touching. After a moment, Ethan curled his pointer finger around hers and squeezed once before pulling away.

Suddenly, in the safe, close darkness, Emma's insane, dangerous world felt as far away as the stars.

26

A FACE FROM THE PAST

Plink. Plink. Plink.

Hours later, Emma woke from a dreamless sleep and looked around. What was that?

Plink. She whipped around to the window that faced the front yard. A tiny pebble ricocheted off the glass and plummeted to the ground below. Emma ran to the window and looked down. A figure stood under the large floodlight by the front porch. Emma rubbed her eyes hard.

"Mom?" she cried.

She barely felt the stairs on her feet as she whipped down them. The door creaked when she flung it open and stepped into the night. Becky stood in the middle of the driveway next to Laurel's car.

I gawked at the woman on the driveway. This was the first time I'd ever seen our mother. She had chin-length, silky dark hair and blue-green eyes. Her body was thin—almost *too* thin—and she wore baggy jeans with a hole in the knee and a faded T-shirt that said THE CASUAL CLAM RESTAURANT. She would've been someone I'd just pass by on the street. I felt no connection to her, no instant bond. It didn't feel real.

But when Emma got to Becky, her arms went right through her body. She stepped back, blinking hard. "Mom?" she cried again. She tried to touch Becky, but it was as though she was made of vapor. Emma touched her own face to make sure she was still real. "What's going on?"

"It's not what you think, honey," Becky said in her gravelly smoker's voice. "You have to be careful," Becky added. "You have to be quiet. Things are about to get very dangerous."

"W-What do you mean?" Emma asked.

"Shh."

"But—"

Then Becky stepped forward and pressed her hand over Emma's mouth. It felt like a real hand to Emma, solid and stable. "You need to do this for me."

Suddenly a vision flashed in my brain. I heard that same voice say, *You need to do this for me*, loud and clear. At least I *thought* it was the same voice. I wasn't sure if the voice was speaking to me . . . or to someone else. But just as I was grappling to see this memory, it dissolved.

All at once, Emma's eyes popped open.

She was in Sutton's dark bedroom once more. The curtains fluttered in the breeze. The glass of water she'd filled before she went to sleep sat on the nightstand. The dream still pounded in her head. She sat up, and her vision cleared. There was a figure standing over her.

Becky? Emma thought immediately. But this person's hair was blond, not brown. Her nose turned up at the end, and freckles splashed across her cheeks. Emma stared straight into Laurel's tourmaline-green eyes. Laurel's hand clapped tightly over Emma's mouth.

"Scream!" I yelled frantically at Emma.

That was just what Emma did. She kicked the sheets off and whacked her hands at Laurel's arms. Laurel backed away, an astonished expression on her face. In seconds, the bedroom door opened and the Mercer parents burst inside. Mr. Mercer didn't have a shirt on. Mrs. Mercer wore plaid pajama pants and a lacy tank top. Drake bounded in, too, emitting a few short, low barks.

"What's going on?" Mr. Mercer demanded.

"Laurel's trying to kill me!" Emma screamed.

"*What?*" Laurel backed away from the bed as though it were on fire.

Emma shuffled back until she was pressed against the headboard. Her chest heaved with sobs. "She was trying to suffocate me."

Laurel let out an indignant squeak. "No, I wasn't!" She gestured to the digital clock next to the bed. The red numbers flashed 12:01. "I came in here because I wanted to be the very first one to wish you a happy birthday."

"Don't deny it." Emma held the sheets to her chest. "I saw you!"

"Sutton, honey, Laurel wouldn't do something like that," Mr. Mercer said gently.

"You probably just had a nightmare." Mrs. Mercer rubbed her eyes. "Are you worried about your birthday party?"

"Why would I be worried about a *birthday party*?" Emma snapped. She whipped a finger in Laurel's direction. "She. Tried. To. Kill. Me!"

But when she looked at the Mercers again, sleepy skepticism was obvious in both of their faces. "Honey, why don't you go downstairs and have a glass of milk?" Mrs. Mercer suggested.

And then, yawning, they turned for the door. Drake and Laurel followed. But before Laurel turned in the hall, she wheeled around and met Emma's gaze. Her eyes narrowed. The corners of her mouth arced down. Fire shot through Emma's veins. The words Becky had said in the dream flashed into her mind once more. *Things are about to get very dangerous.*

The words swirled in my mind, too. Talk about a dream come true.

27

HAPPY BIRTHDAY, NOW DIE

"There's the birthday girl!" Madeline cried, tottering across the patio in bright blue stilettos, a silver party dress, and a foil crown. She plopped an almost identical crown on Emma's head, which said 18 in pink numbers.

"Smile!" Charlotte darted up to them, dressed in a short striped dress and espadrilles. She smushed close to Emma and held a digital camera out from their bodies. Just as the flash went off, Laurel leapt into the picture, throwing her arm around Emma and grinning broadly.

"Cheese!" Laurel said overenthusiastically, her smile as white as the gauzy tunic she wore over black leggings.

Emma tried her best to smile, but she had a feeling she just looked scared.

Sutton's friends broke from the hug and launched into another round of "Happy Birthday." Charlotte belted it out at the top of her lungs. Madeline sang it like Marilyn Monroe when she serenaded JFK. And Laurel sang sweetly, innocently. Emma took a slight step away from her.

It was 9 P.M., and Sutton's birthday party was in full swing. A DJ spun records on the patio table near the grill. Throngs of kids swayed and twirled on the dance floor. Girls from the tennis team held plates of canapés. Mrs. Mercer had strung tiny pink Christmas lights all around the patio and filled punch bowls with virgin sangria. At least twenty-five cheapo digital cameras were strewn around the patio. Three laptops sat on a table near the door; each had USB cords to upload photos to Facebook and Twitter. The Mercer parents had mapped out a radio-controlled car obstacle course in the desert-dust part of the backyard. The air smelled like a mélange of everyone's perfume and hair products, with a slight undertone of booze. A large card table near the door held a pile of wrapped birthday presents, more than Emma had ever seen in her life.

Not that Emma was able to enjoy any of it. She might have been dressed up in the pale-pink minidress that she'd found hanging in Sutton's closet with the word *birthday* written on the hanger; she might've spent an hour in the salon getting her hair curled just so; and she might've been wearing high-heeled booties that probably cost more than her entire year's clothing budget. But it didn't mean she felt particularly festive. Every time a flash went off, she winced and wheeled around. Every time someone touched her to say hi, she stiffened. Every firework Mr. Mercer and some of the boys set off at the end of the yard made her flinch. They sounded like gunshots. It felt like any minute might be her last.

I hoped she was wrong.

After they finished Happy Birthday–ing, Madeline, Charlotte and Laurel surveyed the picture on the preview screen. "Madeline looks drunk," Charlotte said.

"And I look drugged." Laurel sidled up to Emma and showed her the camera. "You're the only one who looks normal. If you put this on Facebook, you have to Photoshop all of us out of it."

Emma slowly inched away from Laurel's muscular frame; being this close to her made her tingly with nerves. All night, she'd watched Laurel. She'd been on the dance floor for most of the party, requesting fast, edgy songs that got everyone moving. An hour ago, she'd cornered Emma by the pool and presented her with a birthday gift, two tickets to a revival of *Les Misérables* the following week. "You can take anyone you want, but I'd love to go," Laurel said bashfully. "Remember how we used to act out the scenes when we were little? You always insisted on being Cosette."

I remember, I wanted to shout out. Not that I did exactly, but I *wished* I could. Something seemed so wrong about this. How had Laurel and I gone from playing *Les Miz* to hating each other? How could my sister have killed me?

But Emma was convinced Laurel had done it—the memory of Laurel trying to suffocate her this morning burned brightly in her brain. What she couldn't figure out was why. Wouldn't she want to keep Emma alive so that no one would know Sutton was missing? Maybe Emma wasn't playing Sutton well enough. Maybe Emma was asking too many questions, poking around too many places.

Something across the patio caught Emma's eye. A tall guy with shorn hair and dressed in a slim-cut black button-down and jeans pushed through the back gate. There was a box of Godiva chocolates under his arm and a tense scowl on his face. He looked around the crowd as if searching for someone. Emma's heart did a flip. *Ethan.*

Emma handed the digital camera back to Madeline. "I'll be right back."

"But, Sutton," Charlotte whined. "We haven't given you *our* gift yet."

"In a minute," Emma called over her shoulder.

As she pushed through the mob of kids, she heard Charlotte sigh. "What's *with* her?"

Everyone was either packed around the food table or writhing on the dance floor. The strong scent of rum tickled Emma's nostrils as she wove through the mass of kids, keeping tabs on Ethan's head. He was having a hard time getting past the gate. Gabriella noticed him and snickered at the Godiva. "Looks like someone still has a burning crush on the birthday girl, huh?" She nudged Emma in the ribs.

Emma ignored her, standing on tiptoes. Ethan was wedged between Jennifer and Julia, the only outed—and popular—lesbian couple at school, and three soccer players seemingly reenacting a play from a recent game. Emma could see his patience quickly dwindling away, like battery power on a cell phone.

Emma zigzagged around the girls at the makeover table. And finally, there he was, setting down the chocolate on an empty spot on the gifts table and pivoting back toward the gate. She grabbed his wrist. Ethan's shoulders tensed, but when he saw it was her, he smiled.

"You made it!" Emma exclaimed.

Ethan shrugged nonchalantly. "I was driving by. I can't stay long."

"Oh." Emma's shoulders sagged.

Ethan's long-lashed eyes darted around the rest of the party. Then he touched the Godiva box. "Anyway, these are for you. Happy birthday. I hope you have a great one."

He leaned in closer. "I hear all the great poetesses have a chocolate obsession."

"Thank you." Emma ran her fingers along the top of the square-shaped gold box. Ethan had selected a dark chocolate mix, her favorite. "I'm really glad you came."

A smile flashed across Ethan's face, too. But then, just as quickly, his expression wilted at something behind her. Emma turned just in time to see Garrett pushing past a crowd of kids. He grabbed Emma, wrapped his arms around her waist, spun her around, and gave her a long, seductive kiss.

Emma flailed helplessly, balking at the feel of Garrett's lips against hers. Her cheeks burned. She could feel everyone's eyes on her. "Whoo!" a girl called near her. "Yeah!" one of the soccer players said. "Get a room!" Madeline whooped nearby.

Finally, Garrett pulled away and released her. Emma searched for Ethan . . . only, he'd disappeared.

28

SEDUCTION AND MURDER ALWAYS GO HAND IN HAND

Garrett had pulled Emma all the way into the house before she refused to go any farther. "That was really rude of you back there. You can't just tear me away from a conversation like that. I'm supposed to be the hostess."

Garrett turned and grabbed her hand. "I was rescuing you, Sutton. Landry had you trapped."

Emma scoffed. "No, he *didn't*!"

"Yeah, he did." There was a chivalrous but also slightly condescending tone to Garrett's voice. As if he knew what was best.

Emma's mouth hung open for a long beat. The music

pulsed outside. There was a *thwonng* of the springs on the diving board as someone jumped off. "I'm not your damsel in distress," she finally said, her cheeks burning.

A confused look registered on Garrett's face. "I'm sorry." He grabbed Emma's hands. "Shit. I just wanted some alone time with you. I haven't seen you all night."

Emma leaned against the grandfather clock, remembering the bashful look on Ethan's face when he'd given her the chocolates.

"Once I give you your present, you'll forgive the intrusion," Garrett said confidently. "I promise." At that, he grabbed Emma's hand and pulled her up the stairs.

Emma followed, stepping over a stack of folded T-shirts Mrs. Mercer had left on one of the risers. What was Garrett giving her that he couldn't show her downstairs?

"Here we go," Garrett said in a hushed voice. He pushed open the door to Sutton's bedroom. Candles flickered from every possible surface. The smell of lavender essential oils assaulted Emma's nostrils. The faint sounds of Billie Holiday tinkled out of stereo speakers. Garrett had drawn the curtains tight and sprinkled rose petals all over the floor and on the bed. There was a box of Valrhona chocolates on the pillow and two glasses of champagne on the nightstand.

Emma's mouth dropped open. The conversation on the mountain trail flooded back to her. *Remember what we talked about this summer? Our plans? I was thinking about making that happen for your birthday.* "Oh my God," she mouthed.

The Billie Holiday song morphed into an acoustic love song by Jack Johnson. Garrett smiled earnestly at Emma. Then, as though he were in a stripping race, he tore off his T-shirt and threw it to the floor. He kicked off his shoes next and unbuckled his belt.

"Oh my God, stop!" Emma cried.

Garrett froze, his cheeks flushing bright red, and his hands trembling a little. The candles flickered against the wall.

"Um . . ." Emma started to nervously giggle. Something about it seemed so ridiculously . . . *ridiculous.* She'd known Garrett for what, two weeks? And now she was supposed to *be* with him?

"I'm sorry, I can't do"—Emma gestured to the bed—"*this.*"

Garrett sat tentatively on the edge of the bed, staring at Emma as if her skin had turned purple. "But . . . we've been talking about it all summer."

Emma's mouth fell open.

"I mean, I thought about it," Garrett went on, running his hands over his spiky hair. "And I realized you were right: There's no reason to wait. I want my first time to be with you. Don't you want it to be with me, Sutton?"

Emma looked everywhere in the room except at the big strip of boxer shorts peeking out of the top of Garrett's jeans. *I'm not Sutton*, she wanted to scream. "I-I guess I've changed my mind," she said instead.

"Changed your *mind*?" Garrett searched her face desperately. Then he placed his palms flat on the petal-strewn mattress. "Wait a minute," he said in a low, shaky voice. "Were all of our sex talks just some big prank? Is this what you did to Thayer?"

"No, of course not!" Emma shook her head fast, wondering what Sutton had done to Thayer. "It's just . . . I can't . . ."

She took a big step back. The essential oil smell was starting to make her woozy. "I'm sorry," she said again. Then she flung the door open and fumbled clumsily into the hall. Instead of galloping down the stairs to the party, she turned the other direction and dove into a room one door down.

She shut the door just as Garrett stepped into the hall. "Sutton?" he called. Emma crouched next to the door. She heard him spinning around, his footsteps soft on the carpet. "Sutton?" he called again.

Emma didn't move, forcing herself to breathe quietly and praying he wouldn't come in.

After a moment, Garrett groaned. A door slammed, and a few seconds later opened again. Emma heard his footsteps down the staircase, then stomping through the foyer.

She turned and slumped against the door, sighing in relief. The room she was in had two diamond-shaped night-lights that illuminated a bed with a black-and-white striped bedspread. A white-and-pink egg chair sat in the corner. An avant-garde mobile hung by the window and millions of photos of girls lined the walls. Emma blinked hard at the three-way mirror on the wall by the closet. She frowned at the MacBook Air on the desk and the flat-screen TV on the low bureau. This looked exactly like Sutton's room, but in reverse. So this was . . . Laurel's room?

Emma's knees cracked as she slowly rose to her feet. She'd never seen inside Laurel's room before—Laurel always kept the door closed. Emma flipped on a light at Laurel's desk and peered at the photos on the bulletin board. The picture of Sutton and her friends in front of the monkey house at the zoo looked oddly familiar. So did the one of Sutton, Madeline, and Charlotte waving cookie-batter spoons at one another. They were exactly the same photos from Sutton's room—Laurel wasn't even *in* most of them.

There was something eerie about Laurel's room being such a precise knockoff of her sister's. *Almost like she's studying Sutton*, she thought. *Preparing to become her.*

Emma tiptoed to Laurel's bed and stuck her head under

the dust ruffle. Besides an extra tennis racket, there were only balled-up socks and a couple of hair ties. She peeked into the closet. A slight smell of perfume and brand-new denim wafted out. While everything in Sutton's closet had its place, Laurel's blouses and dresses hung messily on their hangers, straps and sleeves dangling halfway off, jeans and T-shirts piled in the corner. Shoes lay scattered on the floor.

Emma closed the closet again and rubbed her temples. There *had* to be something here. Some kind of proof of what Laurel had done.

I hoped there wasn't. I hoped she hadn't done it.

A single blue light on Laurel's computer monitor glowed across the room. Swallowing hard, Emma paced to the desk and sat down. The screen saver was a montage of Sutton, Laurel, and the rest of the crowd at dances, restaurants, and sleepovers. It quickly dissolved when Emma touched the mouse, showing a dark desktop jammed with icons and files. Most of them were labeled things like SHAKESPEARE PAPER or C'S PARTY.

A creak sounded outside the door. Emma froze and cocked her head. A shout emerged from the party downstairs. Someone's cell phone rang. She strained for any sounds that were close, every nerve ending tingling. Slowly she breathed out.

Turning back to the computer, she pulled up the Finder

and hurriedly typed *Lying Game* into the search field. The little rainbow wheel whirled. One folder popped up, buried deep within a temporary drive. Emma clicked on it several times. The computer made a sharp barking sound.

The folder listed a series of videos. Emma clicked on the first one, and a short clip of Madeline pretending to drown in a pool appeared. It was the same video Emma had seen on Facebook. Another video showed Sutton, Charlotte, and Madeline on a green golf course at night, spray-painting a rock. "A thousand bucks says Laurel doesn't show," Sutton said. It was another video from Sutton's Facebook page.

She clicked on more videos: one of Sutton calling the police and telling them she'd heard a baby crying in a Dumpster. One of Madeline stealing Mrs. Mercer's car while she shopped at AJ's Market, the rest of the girls hiding in the bushes with the camera and giggling when Mrs. Mercer came out of the store and panicked. One of the girls turning the desks in a classroom backward and hanging the American flag upside down on its pole. On and on it went. Prank after prank. It never seemed to end.

I watched, too, feeling sicker and sicker. Every prank we'd pulled was cunning—and cruel. We'd hurt a lot of people. Maybe not everyone found it funny.

Emma clicked on the very last video, a file at the bottom of the list titled THE QUEEN GOES DOWN. A dark screen appeared. For a few seconds, the camera bucked, shooting trees and bushes and the moon and then swirling back to the ground. Someone breathed close to the microphone. There was a sharp snap, and the camera became level and still, as if it had been fastened to a tripod. It focused on a close-up of a chair in the middle of an empty field. Then, with a whoosh of sound, a figure landed on the chair as if she'd been pushed. She had a black blindfold over her face. A round silver locket bounced at her throat. Emma clapped her hand over her mouth, filled with both terror and relief.

This was the video that had started it all for Emma. The video that had brought her here. This was her *proof.*

A figure appeared on the screen. Emma gasped as the person leaned into the camera and adjusted the lens. Moonlight from above made an eerie halo around her head. The lighting features adjusted, and her face came into focus. Emma pressed her hands to her mouth. She felt like she was on a roller coaster that had just plunged down a hill. *Laurel.*

I gasped silently, too. So it was . . . true?

Laurel's empty green eyes stared blankly into the lens. There was a sinister smile on her face. Very faintly in the background, Emma could hear Sutton whimpering. Emma's eyes widened as she realized that this version of the video had sound. Her hands trembled. Her heart rocketed. Her whole body screamed at her to *run*, but she couldn't tear her eyes away from the screen.

"*Shhh*," a voice said from behind the camera. Sutton turned her head toward the direction of the noise. Suddenly Charlotte appeared on the screen. She walked over to Sutton and straightened the blindfold on her head. And then *Madeline* emerged in the frame, dragging Charlotte back out of view.

Emma's heart beat so fast she could feel it churning away behind her ribs. This couldn't be happening. They'd *all* been there that night?

Laurel appeared in the frame once more and pulled a ski mask over her head. She waited as the camera tilted right and left. After a moment, someone whispered "Go!" from behind the lens. Then Laurel nodded and approached the back of Sutton's chair. Calmly, she pulled the locket hard against Sutton's throat, the video finally synching with the version Emma had seen nearly two weeks before. Sutton kicked blindly. Her shoulders rolled right and left, trying to fight Laurel off. Laurel pulled and pulled.

I watched, horrified. How could they *all* do that to me? How could all my friends band together to kill me?

"Harder!" Emma heard a voice whisper off-screen. It sounded like Madeline. Laurel yanked with more force. "A little higher up!" Charlotte whispered next.

It went on for an agonizing twenty seconds. The girls

off the camera hooted and giggled, and Sutton continued to claw and thrash. And then Sutton went limp, and her head slumped forward. Emma pressed her hand to her mouth.

The camera whipped to Laurel. She stood a few steps away from Sutton, staring at her in horror. She reached out to touch her sister, then nervously drew her hands away. "You guys . . ." Her voice cracked.

"What the hell?" Madeline sounded on the verge of panic. "What did you do, Laurel?"

"What are you talking about?" Laurel's chin trembled. "I did exactly what you told me to do!"

Charlotte's footsteps crunched through the dead grass. "Sutton? You'd better not be fucking with us." When Sutton didn't answer, Charlotte let out a shrill combination of a whimper and a shriek. "*Shit*, guys. Shit."

And then, close by, someone let out a loud scream. The video camera lost picture for a moment. After a clonk it was on the ground, the image of Sutton now on its side. Footsteps scuffled through the grass, growing softer and softer until they were inaudible.

Another figure appeared on the screen almost instantly. Whoever it was pulled the blindfold off Sutton's head and the gag from her mouth. Her hair was matted and sweaty, and her face drained of color. After a moment, Sutton opened her eyes and looked blearily into the camera lens. Emma searched her sister's barely conscious face.

Then the monitor went dark. Emma sat rigid in the chair. "They were all there," she said, her voice quavering. "They all did it."

Suddenly the past two weeks snapped into sickening focus. The reason no one had noticed Emma wasn't actually Sutton was because they all *knew* she wasn't—they were all in on it. Madeline had kidnapped Emma at Sabino and taken her to Nisha's party. Charlotte had brought Emma home to Sutton's after Nisha's party, and she'd walked her to tennis practice the next day. Laurel had driven Emma to and from school. They'd all been at the sleepover, and Laurel and Charlotte had figured out Emma was in the bus station so they knew they had to stop her from leaving.

They needed Emma to be Sutton. After all, no body, no crime.

"Sutton?" someone called from the hall.

Emma jumped, banging her knee on the bottom of the desk. It was Charlotte's voice.

"Sutton?" Charlotte called again.

Emma searched the desktop frantically for Safari so she could open her Gmail. She had to send this video to herself. But her vision was blurry. All the icons looked like hieroglyphs.

"Hello?" Charlotte called again. And then, more softly, to someone behind her: "Maybe she's in here?"

"Sutton?" a second voice called. Garrett. He knocked on Laurel's door.

Emma darted frantically away from the computer, tipping over the desk chair in the process. She wheeled in the center of Laurel's room for a moment, trying to figure out where to go. *Under the bed? In the closet?* She dashed to the window and pressed her back to the wall.

Another knock. "Sutton?" Garrett called. The doorknob began to turn. She inched over to the window and looked out. Laurel's bedroom faced a long line of hedges in the backyard. Kids raged at the party just a few feet away.

Trembling, she touched the window sash and lifted it up. Cool night air wafted in.

"Sutton?" Charlotte's voice called. "You here?"

Emma glanced over her shoulder. The strip of light under the door began to widen. Emma caught sight of Garrett's blond hair in the doorway. *Here goes*, she thought. She turned back to the window and took a deep breath.

"Sutton?" a voice sounded from inside Laurel's room. But by that time, Emma had already hit the ground.

29

THE GREAT ESCAPE

Emma's fall landed her square in a hedge and tore a big hole in the hem of her dress. Her hand scraped against a rock and her high-heeled ankle twisted on the hard dirt. Letting out a groan, she ripped off her shoes and stashed them under a cactus.

She peered through the hedge. The guys continued to play Speed Racer with the RC cars. Girls giggled and passed around a chrome flask. Gabriella and Lilianna stood just a few feet away, their backs to her, heatedly whispering, frustrated looks on their faces.

The sliding glass door opened. Garrett and Charlotte emerged from the house. Garrett went one way, but

Charlotte found Madeline and Laurel and all three huddled in a knot near the bushes. Emma crouched down close by. She didn't dare move a muscle.

Madeline's voice floated over the other sounds of the party. "Was she up there?"

"I even checked Laurel's room," Charlotte said. "She's gone."

"She can't be *gone*." Madeline made a face.

The girls turned for the gate. Emma crouched down and crawled to the next bush, then the next. Her bare knees dug into the gravel. When she reached the wall surrounding the house, she hoisted herself up and over. The rough surface scraped her arms and the top of her thighs.

Her bare feet crunched to the gravel on the other side. She looked around wildly. She had no money, no phone. No shoes. Where could she go?

A wall of parked cars stood in front of her, blocking her passage to the street. A Jeep Cherokee stood closest to her, a Toyota was to her left, and a crookedly parked Subaru Impreza pinned her in on the right. Then Emma spied a narrow escape corridor on the other side of the Subaru along the block-wall fence that separated the Mercers' yard from the neighbors'. All she had to do was get around the Subaru and she was free. Sucking in her stomach, she squeezed past the car's side mirror, praying that the car didn't have one of those car alarms that blared as soon as someone touched it.

A clang made her stop halfway. Three figures stood at the back gate. One was tall and angular, with dark hair and golden skin. Another was shorter and thicker, with pale skin that shone luminously in the moonlight. The third girl had a familiar blond ponytail. All of them looked around. Laurel had a flashlight. Emma quivered, momentarily paralyzed.

"Sutton?" Madeline shouted, her voice cold and unfriendly.

Then Laurel gasped. "There she is!" She shone the flashlight across the yard to where Emma stood. They ran toward her, tramping through the flowerbeds and past the porch. Emma took off down the narrow corridor, her heart drumming in her ears.

"Sutton!" Charlotte, Madeline, and Laurel wove around the cars. "Come back here!"

Emma sprinted, her feet screaming, her gaze on the street just a few yards away. Just as she reached the end of the driveway, her foot landed on something sharp and hot. She yelled out and flew to her knees.

"Get *up*!" I screamed uselessly at her. "Get up!"

Emma scrambled to her feet. The girls had squeezed past the Subaru, too, and started down the corridor. Emma locked eyes with Laurel. Her shoulders were hunched angrily. Emma let out a whimper and staggered into the street.

And then the automatic light timer on the garage clicked off, bathing the driveway and the street in total darkness. Emma froze, her heart jumping to her throat. She groped for the edge of the block wall that surrounded the Mercer house, then ducked around it, out of their view.

"Sutton?" the girls called. Their high-heeled shoes clicked on the asphalt. They were moving closer and closer in the darkness. For all she knew, they were right next to her.

A hand shot out and grabbed her wrist. Emma jumped and cried out. She was yanked to her knees and dragged farther into the neighbors' yard. Her palms hit hard, sharp gravel. Tears came to her eyes. Her foot throbbed in pain. Her nose twitched with the sharp smell of a cigarette. She stared at the dark figure in front of her, expecting to see Charlotte's angry face or Laurel's searing gaze. "What are you *doing*?" a guy's voice asked instead.

Emma blinked hard. "Ethan?" she whispered, her eyes adjusting. She could just make out Ethan's shorn head and angular jaw. He held a cigarette between his fingers, the red tip glowing eerily in the darkness.

Ethan stubbed out his cigarette in the gravel and stared at Emma's sweaty, harried face, her torn dress, her lack of shoes. "What the hell's going on?"

"Sutton?" Madeline called out at the same time. She

was right next to them, separated only by the block wall. "Where are you?"

Emma grasped Ethan's hand hard. "Can you get me out of here? Now?"

"What?"

"Please," Emma whispered desperately, clasping Ethan's hands. "Can you help me or not?"

He stared at her. A look Emma couldn't quite discern flashed over his eyes. He nodded. "My car's a couple houses down." Hand in hand, they slipped into the darkness.

I only hoped he could get her away before they caught her.

30

SOMEONE KNOWS . . .

Ethan led Emma to an old red Honda Civic hatchback with a gray door and a crack in the windshield. The inside smelled like McDonald's and old shoes, and the passenger seat was littered with textbooks and papers. Emma swept them aside and belted herself in. Ethan swung behind the wheel. Swiveling around, Emma saw Laurel standing at the edge of the driveway, looking right and left.

The stereo blared as soon as Ethan turned the ignition. It was a fast, raging song, and Ethan dove quickly for the dial and snapped it off. The wheel squeaked as he maneuvered into the street and drove away. Emma's nails pressed hard into her thighs. She watched the Mercer house grow smaller and smaller in the side mirror until it was no longer visible.

"What's this all about?" Ethan's low voice pierced the silence.

"It's hard to explain," Emma answered.

They passed the park where she and Ethan had played tennis. Big floodlights illuminated one of the courts, but no one was there. Next they drove past the complex that contained the nail salon where she and Laurel had gotten manicures. Then La Encantada, where she and Madeline had shopped. The road for Hollier curved to the left; a big one-armed cactus pointed the way.

"Where are we going?" Ethan asked.

Emma slumped down in the seat. Where *could* she go? What about the police? Would they believe her now? Could she get them to search Laurel's room and find the video?

Then she took a deep breath. "The bus station downtown."

Ethan's eyebrows did a quick lift-and-drop. "The one near Hotel Congress?"

"Yep."

"You taking a trip?"

Emma hugged her chest. "Something like that."

He nodded toward her feet. "Without shoes?"

"I'll figure it out."

Ethan gave her a strange look, then took a left turn at the next intersection and merged onto the highway. It was sparse at this time of night, the concrete lanes empty far into the distance. Neon signs for highway businesses peppered the drive. GREAT DANE TRUCKING. MOTEL SIX. A tall cowboy hat for Arby's. Lights glittered on the mountain. A helicopter zoomed overhead.

"Can I ask why you're fleeing your own party?" Ethan asked as he veered off the highway at an exit.

Emma leaned her head against the seat. "I just need to . . . go. It's too crazy to explain."

The light turned green, and he made a left at an intersection. They drove in silence for a while on a dark, hilly road. For a few minutes, there wasn't a single light anywhere. No cars passed them going the other direction. No houses loomed at the curbs. Emma frowned and glanced at the receding highway behind her. The city lights were all in the other direction. "I think you took a wrong turn."

"No, I didn't."

Emma continued to watch the city fade in the rearview mirror. The street rose and dipped. Ethan took another turn, but this road was even more desolate than the last. Dusty gravel crunched under the tires. Tall cacti passed within an inch of the car. Emma's heart suddenly started to thump. "Ethan, this is the wrong way," she insisted.

Ethan didn't answer her. He maneuvered the car up a

small slope. Lights twinkled in the distance, as far away as the stars. Emma felt the scratches on her neck from the near-strangulation last weekend. Her mouth immediately felt dry. She peeked at Ethan's profile. His eyes were narrowed. His jaw jutted out. His hands gripped the steering wheel hard.

"Emma . . ." I cried weakly. Something about this suddenly seemed really wrong.

Emma's stomach turned over. Slowly, carefully, she reached for the door handle and started to pull.

Click. The tiny knob that locked the door depressed all on its own. Emma hit the button to unlock the door, but it wouldn't budge. "Stop the car!" she shrieked, suddenly reeling with fear. "Stop the car now!"

Ethan hit the brake so hard that Emma shot forward, ramming her arm against the glove box. The car lurched back again. The engine idled loudly. She squinted in the flinty darkness. As far as she could tell, they were in the middle of a barren, empty desert. This wasn't even a *road*.

"What?" Ethan asked. "What's the matter?"

She turned to Ethan, trembling. The tears flowed freely and easily down her cheeks. "I want out. Please unlock the door. *Please*."

"Settle down," Ethan said gently. He unbuckled his seat belt and turned so that he was facing her. Then he grabbed Emma's wrist. Not tightly exactly, but not very loosely either. "I just wanted to get us far away from where anyone could see or hear us."

"Why?" Emma wailed. All kinds of awful possibilities flashed through her mind.

"There's something I think I know," Ethan's voice dropped a half octave. "Something I don't think you want anyone else to know."

"What are you talking about?"

Ethan's Adam's apple bobbed as he swallowed. "You're not who you say you are."

Emma blinked hard. "I-I'm sorry?"

"You're not Sutton. You can't be."

The words sliced through Emma's brain. She opened her mouth, but no sounds came out. *How could he know that?* Slowly, she felt the door handle with her free hand. It still didn't open. "Of course I'm Sutton," she said, her voice shaking. Her heart pounded.

"You're acting nothing like her."

Emma swallowed awkwardly. She was beginning to feel woozy. "H-How would you know?"

Ethan leaned forward a little. "For a while I thought Sutton had changed—ever since that night you showed up in my driveway. But tonight you're totally different. You're someone else," Ethan said in a lonely, sad voice. "It's freaking me out. So you'd better tell me what's going on."

Emma stared at him, her body stricken with fear. But as Ethan talked, things started to whirl in my head. Ethan's lost, haunting smile. The smell of the desert plants, the dust. The feel of someone pulling something soft over my head and squeezing something thin and sharp around my neck. A giggle.

All of a sudden, a chain reaction went off in my head. Lights sparking other lights. Images rolling into new images. And just like that, a new, lucid memory unfurled before me, like a red carpet unrolled for a queen. All I could do was watch helplessly. . . .

❦ 31 ❧

NOT FUNNY, BITCHES

The blurry, shadowed figure grabs my shoulders and pulls me out of the trunk. I bang my knee on the side of the car and twist my ankle on the hard ground. Hands press against my shoulder blades and shove me forward. I pitch my head down, trying to get a look at the ground beneath me, but it's too dark. I can smell a desert fire somewhere in the distance, but I have no idea where I am. I could be in Tucson. I could be on the moon.

The same hands push me to sitting. The bones in my butt dig into what feels like a wooden folding chair. I make a couple of muffled cries, the gag in my mouth sopping wet from my saliva. "Shut up," someone hisses.

I try to kick whoever is near me, but my feet grope in thin air.

There's more crunching through gravel, and then a tiny electronic ping. Through the blindfold, I see a small LED beam staring at me. I bite down hard on the gag.

"Go," a voice whispers. A girl. More crunching footsteps. And then someone's hands grab my neck. The chain of the locket I always wear pulls against my throat. My head jerks back. I wriggle my hands in their binds, but I can't free them. My bare feet thrash, hitting the cold, rough ground.

"Harder," I hear a voice whisper. "A little higher," says another. The chain digs into my throat. I try to breathe, but my airway can't expand. My lungs scream for air. My whole body starts to burn. I thrash my head forward and see the little red light still watching me. Two shapes hover behind the light, too. I can see whites of teeth, glitters of jewelry. I'm dying, I think. They're killing me.

My vision starts to turn gray. Spots appear in front of my eyes. My head throbs, my brain desperate for oxygen. I want to fight, but all at once I'm too weak to kick or wriggle. My lungs shudder, wanting to give up. Maybe it would be easier to give up. One by one, each muscle surrenders. It's like a delicious reprieve, like falling into bed after a long tennis match. All sounds around me dribble away. My vision narrows until it's a tunnel of light. Even the chain collapsing my windpipe doesn't hurt so much anymore. I feel my head flop forward, my neck no longer rigid. Darkness envelops me. I see no visions. I'm still afraid, but the fear feels muffled now. It's too much effort to fight.

From far within my head, I hear sharp whispers. Someone calls my name. Then there's a muffled scream, and then more footsteps. Something heavy hits the ground with a muted thud. Seconds later, my skin vaguely registers the sensation of someone pulling the blindfold from my head and the gag from my mouth.

"Sutton?" a soft voice calls. A guy's voice. Wind whips across my face. I feel my hair tickle my forehead. "Sutton?" the same voice calls again.

Consciousness begins to dribble back to me. The tips of my fingers tingle. My lungs expand. A spot appears in front of my eyes, and then another. One of my eyelids flutters. I stare groggily around, feeling just like I had when I'd woken up from the anesthesia after I'd gotten my tonsils out. Where am I?

My vision clears and I see an empty tripod in front of me. A video camera lays tipped over on the grass, the red LED power button now flashing. I'm in a clearing of some sort, though I don't see any cars or lights. The air smells a little like a cigarette. Then I notice someone crouching right next to me. I jump and stiffen.

"Are you okay?" whoever it is cries. He touches the rope on my hands. "Jesus," he says under his breath.

I take him in, still so disoriented. He has close-cropped hair, startling blue eyes, and is wearing a black T-shirt, green cargo shorts, and black Converse sneakers. The blindfold that had just been covering my face is in his left hand. For a moment I wonder if he is the one who did this to me, but the look on his face is such a mix of disgust and concern that I immediately dismiss the idea.

"I can't really see that well," I say in a hoarse, scratchy voice. "Who's there?"

"It's Ethan," he says. "Ethan Landry."

I blink hard. Ethan Landry. My brain feels like it's slogging through mud. I can't quite think who he is for a minute. I remember a brooding boy roaming the halls. A hopeful face watching me from across a parking lot. "W-What happened?" I ask faintly.

"I don't know." Ethan reaches down to untie my hands. "I saw someone strangling you. I ran into the clearing and they took off."

"They threw me in a trunk," I murmur. "Someone dragged me here."

"Did you see who?"

I shake my head. Then I gaze at Ethan, trying to figure out what I know about him. Why I don't like him. Maybe it's just one of those things—we haven't liked him for so long we forgot what started it. But it suddenly feels like he's my only friend in the world.

Crack. Twigs snap behind me, and I turn. Three figures emerge from the trees and scamper toward me. "Gotcha!" Charlotte cries, stepping into the light. Madeline follows. And then Laurel appears, a ski mask in her hand. She looks like she might cry.

Ethan gapes at them. "This was a joke?"

"Uh, duh." Madeline scoops up the video camera from the ground. "Sutton knew it all along."

Ethan stands in front of me protectively. "You almost killed her."

The girls pause and exchange a glance. Laurel licks her lips. Madeline slips the camera into her bag. Finally, Charlotte sniffs and tosses her hair over her shoulder. "What were you doing following us anyway? Stalker."

Ethan looks at me for a moment. I turn away, feeling both vulnerable and humiliated. He waves his hand dismissively and backs away toward the brush. But as Madeline bends down to cut through the knots around my hands, I catch his eye again. Thank you, I covertly mouth, my heart banging steadily but firmly in my chest. Ethan nods, resigned. You're welcome, he mouths back.

And then, just like that, everything fades out once more. My memory has hit yet another dead end.

32

THE BITTER TRUTH

In the car, Ethan was still gazing intently at Emma. "What's going on?" he asked again.

"I'm Sutton," Emma answered, trembling. "I swear."

"You're *not*." A sad smile appeared on Ethan's face. "Just tell me the truth."

Emma stared at his glowing teeth in the darkness. She glanced around at the dark desert before them. A terrible thought crackled through her head like a lightning bolt: He sounded so sure. But how could he be positive, unless . . . "Did . . . did *you* kill her? Is that how you know?"

Ethan jolted back. He triple blinked, his face turning gray. "*Kill* her? Sutton's . . . dead?"

Emma bit hard on her lip. Ethan looked shattered. "She was murdered," she admitted in a tiny voice. "I think someone strangled her. Someone she knows. I saw it on a video."

Ethan frowned. "Strangled?"

"With this necklace." She lifted the locket from under her dress to show him. "In the woods. Her friends caught it all on tape. They even posted it online."

Ethan's gaze shifted to the right. A horrified look of understanding swept over his face. "Oh. *Oh*."

"What?"

Ethan sank back into the seat and covered his face with his hands. "Was she blindfolded in this video?"

"Yes . . ."

Ethan took a deep breath and looked at her again. "I was there that night."

Emma blinked hard. "You were *there*?"

"I was riding my bike when I saw this familiar car whip past," he explained. "I recognized it by the SWAN LAKE MAFIA sticker on the back window—Madeline and I had assigned parking spots next to each other last year. It stuck in my head."

Emma gulped.

"I don't know why, but something made me follow them down this hill into a clearing," Ethan went on. "By the time I got there, the camera had been set up and they'd just started strangling Sutton. I didn't know what was going on or why they were doing it, but it seriously looked like they'd killed her."

Emma sat completely still as Ethan explained what had happened: Just as Sutton had lost consciousness, he'd run into the clearing. The girls screamed and hid, knocking the camera off its tripod. He ran to Sutton and worked to untie her hands. "Sutton was still breathing," he told Emma. "She came around."

Emma stared out the dark windshield. "So . . . you were that person at the end of the video who took the blindfold off her? You saved her?"

Ethan shrugged. "I guess."

He cleared his throat and went on. "But see, after that night, I didn't hear anything from Sutton. Not that I thought she owed me anything, but it would've been nice to get . . . I don't know. A real thank-you, maybe. So when you approached me outside Nisha's party, I figured that's what was about to happen. Something seemed off that night though. Different. The way you talked about Bitch Stars . . . your sense of humor. And every time I saw you after that, I kept getting that same nagging feeling. You were . . . sweet. And funny. And interesting. And . . . remorseful. The Sutton I knew—*everyone* knew— wouldn't have felt bad about anything, ever. So I started to wonder if she had multiple personalities. Or had had, like, a spiritual awakening that made her not so . . . hard." He pressed his thumbs into his eye sockets. "Whatever happened, I started to kind of fall for her."

"That was me," Emma said quietly, staring at her lap. "I was that girl at Nisha's party. And every time after that. Not Sutton."

Ethan ran his tongue over his teeth, nodding slowly. "So . . . who *are* you?"

A firecracker boomed in the distance. After it finished crackling, Emma took a breath. "I'm Sutton's twin. Well, long-lost twin. We never knew each other. I didn't even get to meet her once."

Ethan stared at her without blinking. "Hold up. Long-lost twin? Like, for real?" He shook his head. "Start from the beginning."

And then the whole story exploded from inside Emma, desperate to get out. "I tried to leave," she explained when she got through explaining the SUTTON'S DEAD note. "I didn't want to be stuck in her life. But her killer saw me at the bus station, I guess. And they cornered me in Charlotte's house and said they'd kill me if I tried to leave again." She shut her eyes, the feeling of the locket against her neck was as fresh and vivid as though it had happened just moments ago. "Sutton's friends and her sister were the only people who knew I'd tried to leave. And Charlotte's house is locked up like a fortress. It must have been someone who was already inside—one of Sutton's friends. They tried to strangle me just like they strangled Sutton that night in the woods. The night they *killed* her."

Ethan shook his head vehemently. "I'm not saying her friends didn't kill Sutton, but if they did, it wasn't the night the video was made. That happened two weeks before you got here. And everyone left after I stopped it. Sutton included. She was fine."

"She *left* with them?" Emma asked, shocked.

A conflicted look crossed Ethan's face. "Sutton and her friends pull crap like that all the time."

"I know." Emma rubbed her temples. "I never realized they got that dangerous though."

All at once, it began to rain. The drops on the windshield sounded like tiny bombs going off. Emma looked at Ethan. "I have to get out of here."

Ethan frowned. "Where will you go?"

"Anywhere." Fresh, terrified tears cascaded down Emma's cheeks. "I'll get on the first bus that comes along. I can't stay. This is insane."

Ethan sat back in the seat, the leather making a crinkling noise. "Are you sure that's a good idea?"

"What do you mean?"

He turned toward her, biting hard on his thumb. "It's just . . . you tried to leave once already, and that didn't work out. Who's to say this time will go any better?"

"But . . ." Emma stared frantically out the window at the tall cacti silhouettes. "It's my only chance."

They were both silent for a moment. A police car whipped past on a road in the distance. Its blue and red lights punctuated the otherwise coal-black night. "But . . ." Ethan began, tentatively. "What if leaving is what the killer wants you to do?"

"No." Emma crossed her arms over her chest. "The killer wants me to stay here and be her."

"Hear me out. If Sutton's really . . . *dead*, maybe whoever did this is trying to frame you for her murder. They know you're a foster kid. They know your life was probably hard. It won't be rocket science to prove. If you leave, everyone will know Sutton is missing. Don't you think whoever did this will tip off the cops that *you've* been impersonating her for two weeks? And don't you think you'll be the person the cops will immediately suspect of killing Sutton?"

Emma let her hands fall limply to her lap. *Would they?*

"It's just, Sutton had a really charmed life," Ethan said quietly, gazing out the window at the crescent moon. "She's popular, she's well-off, she gets everything she wants. And from everything you've said . . . you're not. While Sutton got a nice house in Scottsdale, you ended up in foster care. It's seriously not fair, Emma. Lots of people in your position would do anything to switch places with their twin sister."

Emma's mouth fell open. "I'd never *kill* her!"

Ethan waved his hands in surrender. "I know you wouldn't. But . . . some people are awful. Some people automatically assume the worst. They might make judgments about you without looking into who you really are."

Emma blinked. The walls of the car began to close in on her. She certainly knew about the awful people in this world making judgments. Look at Clarice—she'd assumed Emma had stolen her money over her thuggish son, simply because she thought that was what foster kids always did.

"Oh my God," Emma whispered, covering her head with her arms. Ethan was right. He leaned in and, after a moment, pulled her into a hug. He squeezed hard and buried his head into the crook of her neck. Sobs shook Emma's body.

I watched as they stayed that way for minutes, clinging to each other. I wished I was Emma so badly. I wanted to hug someone—maybe Ethan—right now, too.

Then Ethan sat back and gazed at Emma. His light eyes crinkled with concern. The corners of his pink, kissable lips arced up in a compassionate smile. He had a sooty splotch on his cheek that Emma wanted to reach out and wipe away. "God," he whispered. "You look *exactly* like her."

"That's how it works with identical twins," Emma said softly. Her mouth wobbled into a smile, but then a new sob rushed in.

Ethan touched her chin. "Stay. If Sutton really was killed, we'll find who did it."

"I don't know," Emma murmured.

"You can't let whoever did this get away with it," Ethan insisted. "I'll help you. I promise. And when we have proof, we can go back to the cops and they'll have to believe you."

The rain abruptly stopped. Far in the distance, a coyote howled. Emma felt like she'd been holding her breath for hours.

She gazed into Ethan's endless blue eyes. "Okay," she whispered. "I'll stay."

"Good." Ethan leaned forward and squeezed her shoulder. Emma shut her eyes, the touch of his hands on her bare skin sending sparks down her back. She hoped this was the right decision. She hoped she hadn't just made an enormous mistake.

I hoped so, too.

33

LOOK OUT, SUTTON'S BACK

A while later, Ethan dropped Emma off at the foot of Sutton's driveway. Most of the lights in the house were still on, though all of the cars were gone. When Emma opened the door, Drake bounded over to her and licked her arm. The same fear didn't paralyze her muscles anymore. She supposed she was getting used to him.

"*There* you are!" Laurel ran in from the living room and threw her arms around Emma's neck. "We've been looking all over for you!" Then she stood back and looked Emma up and down. "Why did you run off like that? You took off from us like the driveway was on fire!"

"I just needed to be alone," Emma admitted, hoping

the lie she'd concocted in Ethan's car sounded believable. "I—something weird happened with Garrett."

Laurel's eyes were saucers. "What?"

Emma sank into the love seat and hugged a pillow into her chest. "It's a long story." She stared at the credenza across the room. Someone had brought all of the birthday presents in from the patio. She wondered if Sutton's room still looked like a honeymoon suite.

"Did you have fun tonight, otherwise?" Laurel asked. An apprehensive look crossed her face.

Emma looked away. "Oh yeah. Definitely," she lied. Informative, yes. Terrifying, definitely. But fun? Not even close.

"You weren't . . . mad about anything?" Laurel flicked the tassels on the pillow. "Charlotte said you might've gone into my room. And that you might've . . . *seen* something. And then you ran crazily from us in the driveway. . . ."

Emma leaned into the cushions. Even though she wanted to admit that she'd seen the video, even though she wanted to believe Laurel, Sutton's *sister*, was innocent in all this, trusting her was dangerous.

Emma's brain swirled with what she needed to do. According to Ethan, the snuff film had happened almost a month ago—not the day before Emma had arrived. That meant Sutton had been around for weeks after that video was made and before her death. For all Emma knew, the strangling incident, the snuff film, had blown over long ago. But what had happened in between?

Emma looked up and regarded Laurel coldly, her face drained of feeling. All at once she knew what she should do. "I did see something in your room," she said in a monotone.

Color drained from Laurel's face. "What?"

Emma rose to her feet and slowly advanced toward Laurel. Laurel gasped when Emma wrapped her hands around her neck. Her eyes bulged. "Sutton!" she whimpered.

Emma froze for a long moment, her hands lightly around Laurel's throat. Then she pulled away, rolled her eyes, and smacked Sutton's sister playfully on the cheek. "Gotcha, bitch."

It took a few seconds for relief to flood across Laurel's face. She sat back in the chair and ran her hands over her throat. "You are *so* evil."

"I know. But now we're even." Emma breezily returned to her seat. But her hands trembled as she moved a pillow out of the way. None of this was going to be easy. She was back to square one again—*everyone* was a suspect.

"There's our birthday girl!" Mrs. Mercer's voice rang out from the hall. She swept into the living room. Mr. Mercer followed with four cupcakes on a pink plate. A sparkler candle stuck out of the biggest one, which he positioned on the coffee table right in front of Emma. Red velvet. *Her* favorite.

Mrs. Mercer perched on the ottoman, lifting her hands as though conducting an orchestra. "Ready, everyone?"

They launched into a rousing version of "Happy Birthday," Mr. Mercer trilling the high notes, Laurel singing loudly and strongly off-key. This was the first time this many people had sung "Happy Birthday" to Emma all at the same time.

When the song was over, Mrs. Mercer wrapped her arms around Emma's shoulders. Mr. Mercer followed, then Laurel.

"Happy birthday, baby girl," Mrs. Mercer said. "We love you."

"Now make a wish," Mr. Mercer instructed.

The sparkler on the cupcake crackled and snapped. Emma leaned forward and closed her eyes. Her birthday wish had been the same ever since Becky vanished: for a family. And now, amazingly, backwardly, technically, it had finally come true. But there was something bigger Emma needed to wish for now, something that eclipsed all of that: to find who had murdered her twin sister, Sutton. Once and for all.

I leaned in close. That was what I wanted, too. Even dead girls deserved birthday wishes.

Emma repeated the wish once, twice, three times in

her head and exhaled strongly, like she was blowing away all her past. The sparkler flickered and went out. Everyone applauded and Emma smiled.

And so did I. My sister had blown out the candle in one breath. That meant our wishes were definitely going to come true.

EPILOGUE

I hung around my bedroom as she got ready to go to sleep that night, waiting, thinking. Staring at the items that used to be mine. Waiting for memories to come. They didn't.

The three flashbacks I'd been given back blazed through my head on a continuous loop: my friends' cruel giggles. The necklace pulling at my throat. The desperate look in Ethan's eyes as he waited for me to breathe again. But what had happened *after* that memory—and that video—ended? My friends might not have killed me that night, but someone got me later. It could have been Madeline or Charlotte or Laurel . . . but it also could have been someone else.

Whoever had pulled this off was doing quite an acting

job though. There were still so many possibilities and questions, too. What had I done to deserve such a horrible prank from my BFFs, anyway? The Lying Game was all about one-upmanship—so what had warranted my almost murder? And what about our poor Twitter Twins, excluded from the Lying Game's inner sanctum? They claimed they had a lot of killer prank ideas up their sleeves—*killer* being the operative word. And then there was the mysterious missing Thayer Vega. Would we ever hear from him again? Would we ever find out what I'd done? A guy disappearing shortly before a girl's murder seemed awfully suspicious . . .

I watched Emma as she floated toward sleep, her face untroubled and unsuspecting. I wished we could've had one day together, one *hour*. I wished I could whisper in her ear and tell her what I knew for sure: *Always sleep with one eye open. Never take anything for granted. Your best friends might just be your enemies.* Most important, she shouldn't trust a single thing she knew about me yet. I wasn't sure how I knew, but something deep inside, something I couldn't quite comprehend, told me I was the trickiest member of the Lying Game by far.

Sweet dreams, long-lost twin sister. I'll see you in the morning . . . even though you won't see me.

⌒〜 ACKNOWLEDGMENTS 〜⌒

Wow, starting a new series is hard! I've forgotten how difficult it is, and I absolutely could not have done it without the help of Lanie Davis, Sara Shandler, Josh Bank, Les Morgenstein at Alloy Entertainment, and Farrin Jacobs and Kari Sutherland at HarperTeen. All of you were so amazingly instrumental in making the first book in *The Lying Game* work, from fiddling with the voice and the structure to drilling down to the teensiest minutia that gives it polish and panache. I cannot overstate how very grateful I am for all your encouragement and support these past few months—especially Lanie, who probably had to edit this, what, six times? We are definitely a team, and I hope we will stick together for a long, long while.

Also a big thanks to Andy McNicol and Anais Borja at William Morris for their supervision and enthusiasm. To Kristin Marang at Alloy Entertainment for your creativity and spirit, and to Liz Dresner for designing the book's beautiful cover. To Joel, my husband, who read a late-late draft and told me, even though I didn't want him to because I didn't want to write another sentence, what wasn't working and what would make it better. To my good friend Andrew Zaeh, the quickest learner on a surfboard I have ever met—watch out for the scary Mini Marts! To my parents, Mindy and Shep—scary county fair carnival!—and my sister, Ali—owl!—and to Caron and Melissa Crooke, girls one should never walk into a Mexican restaurant with unless you're prepared to do shots. And a huge shout-out to all the readers I've met both this year and in past years for reaching out and telling me what you think. You guys rock, each and every one of you!

And because I love all of you too much to lose any of you, please don't try any of these Lying Game pranks at home. I hope you agree that what happens in *The Lying Game* stays in *The Lying Game* . . . and nowhere else.

Read on for a preview of
THE LYING GAME
book two

NEVER
HAVE I
EVER

PROLOGUE

LIFE AFTER DEATH

It's the little things you miss when you die. The feel of sliding into bed when you're exhausted, the clean scent in the Arizona air after a storm during monsoon season, the flutter in your stomach when you see your crush walking down the hall. My killer took all those things away from me just before my eighteenth birthday.

And because of fate—and a threat from my murderer—my long-lost twin sister, Emma Paxton, stepped into my life.

When I died two weeks ago, I popped into Emma's world, a world that was about as different from mine as you could get. From that very first moment I saw what

Emma saw, went where she went . . . and watched. I watched as Emma reached out to me on Facebook and as someone posing as me told her to visit. I watched as Emma traveled to Tucson, cautiously hopeful about our reunion. I watched as my friends tackled Emma, thinking she was me, and brought her to a party. I stood beside her when she got the note that said I was dead, warning her that if she didn't continue to pretend to be me, that if she told anyone who she really was, she'd be dead, too.

I watch today as Emma pulls on my favorite thin white tee and swipes my shimmery NARS blush onto her high cheekbones. I can say nothing as she slides into the skinny jeans I used to live in on weekends and sorts through my cherrywood jewelry box for my favorite silver locket, the one that sends rainbow prisms around the room when it catches the light. And I sit silently by as Emma sends a text confirming brunch plans with my best friends, Charlotte and Madeline, even though I would've worded it differently. Still, Emma has the basics of me down cold—almost no one has noticed she isn't me.

Emma puts my phone down, an uneasy look on her face. "Where are you, Sutton?" she asks aloud in a nervous whisper, as if she knows I'm close.

I wish I could send her a message from beyond the grave: *I'm here. And this is how I died.* Only when I died, my memory died, too. I have glimpses here and there of who

I used to be, but only a few solid, fleshed-out moments have bobbed to the surface. My death is as much a mystery to me as it is to Emma. All I know in my heart, in my *bones*, is that someone killed me. And that same someone is watching Emma as closely as I am.

Does this scare me? Yes. But through Emma, I've been given a chance to uncover what happened in those final moments before I took my last breath. And the more I discover about who I was and the secrets I kept, the more I realize how much danger surrounds my long-lost twin.

My enemies are everywhere. And sometimes, those we least suspect turn out to be our biggest threats.

A CHARMED LIFE

"This way to the terrace." A tanned, button-nosed hostess grabbed four leather-bound menus and marched through the dining room of La Paloma Country Club in Tucson, Arizona. Emma Paxton, Madeline Vega, Laurel Mercer, and Charlotte Chamberlain followed her, snaking around tables full of men in tan blazers and cowboy hats, women in tennis whites, and children munching on organic turkey sausage.

Emma dropped into a booth on the stucco veranda, staring at the tattoo on the back of the hostess's neck as she glided away—a Chinese character that probably meant something lame, like *faith* or *harmony*. The terrace had a view of the

Catalina Mountains, and every cactus and boulder was in sharp relief in the late-morning sun. A few feet away, golfers stood around a tee, contemplating their drives or checking their BlackBerrys. Before Emma had arrived in Tucson and assumed her twin sister's life, the closest she'd gotten to setting foot in a country club was working as an attendant at a mini-golf course outside Las Vegas.

I, however, knew this place like the back of my hand. As I sat, invisible, next to my twin, tethered to her always like a balloon tied to a little kid's wrist, I felt a tingle of memory. The last time I ate at this restaurant, my parents had brought me to celebrate getting straight Bs on my report card—a rarity for me. A whiff of peppers and eggs brought back my favorite meal—huevos rancheros, made with the best chorizo in all of Tucson. What I wouldn't give for just one bite.

"Four tomato juices with lime wedges," Madeline chirped to the waitress who'd appeared. When the waitress sauntered off, Madeline straightened her spine into her signature ballet-diva posture, whipped her obsidian black hair over her shoulder, and produced a silver flask from her fringed purse. Liquid sloshed as she shook the container back and forth. "We can make Bloody Marys," she said with a wink.

Charlotte tucked a piece of red-gold hair behind her freckled ear and grinned.

"A Bloody Mary might knock me out." Laurel pinched her thumb and forefinger on the bridge of her sun-kissed nose. "I'm still exhausted from last night."

"The party was definitely a success." Charlotte inspected her reflection in the back of a spoon. "What do you think, Sutton? Did we properly usher you into adulthood?"

"Like she'd know." Madeline nudged Emma. "You weren't even *there* half the time."

Emma swallowed. She still wasn't used to the taunting banter between Sutton's friends, the kind that grew out of years of friendship. Just sixteen and a half days ago, she'd been living as a foster child in Las Vegas, suffering silently with Travis, her vile foster brother, and Clarice, her celeb-obsessed foster mom. But then she discovered an online strangulation video of a girl who looked exactly like her, down to the oval shape of her face, high cheekbones, and blue-green eyes that changed colors depending on the light. After contacting Sutton, the mystery doppelganger, and discovering that they were long-lost identical twins, Emma took a road trip to Tucson, giddy and excited to meet her.

Fast-forward to the very next day when Emma learned that Sutton had been murdered—and that Emma would be next unless she took Sutton's place. Even though she felt anxious about living a lie, even though her skin prickled every time someone called her "Sutton," Emma didn't see any other option. But it didn't mean she was going to sit silently by and let her sister's body languish somewhere. She had to find out who killed Sutton—no matter what. Not only was it justice for her twin, but it was the only way for Emma to get her own life back and stand a chance of keeping her new family.

The waitress returned with four glasses of tomato juice, and as soon as her back was turned, Madeline unscrewed the cap of the stainless-steel flask and dumped clear liquid into each cup. Emma ran her tongue over her teeth, her journalism-obsessed mind producing a headline: *Underage Girls Caught Boozing at Local Country Club.* Sutton's friends . . . well, they lived on the edge. In more ways than one.

"Well, Sutton?" Madeline slid a glass of spiked tomato juice toward Emma. "Are you going to explain why you bailed on your own birthday party?"

Charlotte leaned in. "Or if you told us, would you have to kill us?"

Emma flinched at the word *kill.* Madeline, Charlotte, and Laurel were her number-one suspects in Sutton's murder. Someone had tried to strangle Emma with Sutton's locket during a sleepover at Charlotte's house last week, and whoever had done it was either capable of hacking the house's many alarms . . . or already inside. And last night, at Sutton's birthday party, Emma had discovered that her friends were behind Sutton's strangulation video. It was only a prank; Sutton's friends were part of a secret club called the Lying Game that prided itself on scaring the crap out of its members and the other kids at school. But what if Sutton's friends had meant to take things much, much further? They'd been interrupted by Ethan Landry, Emma's only real friend in Tucson, but maybe they'd finished Sutton off later.

To calm her nerves, Emma took a long sip of spiked tomato juice and summoned her inner Sutton, a girl she'd learned was snarky and sassy and didn't take shit from anyone. "Aww. Did you miss me? Or were you just nervous that someone dragged me away and left me for dead in the desert?" She glanced at the three faces staring back at her, trying to detect anything that looked like an admission of guilt. Madeline picked at her chipped peach nail polish. Charlotte coolly sipped her Bloody Mary. Laurel gazed out at the golf course as if she'd just spotted someone she recognized.

Then Sutton's iPhone chimed. Emma pulled it out of her bag and checked the screen. She had a text from Ethan. HOW ARE YOU AFTER LAST NIGHT? LET ME KNOW IF YOU NEED ANYTHING.

Emma shut her eyes and pictured Ethan's face, his raven hair and lake-blue eyes, and the way he'd looked at her, a way no boy had ever looked at her before. Her body flooded with desire and relief.

"Who's that from?" Charlotte leaned over the table, nearly impaling her boobs on the cactus arrangement. Emma covered the screen with her hand.

"You're blushing!" Laurel pointed a finger at Emma. "Is it a new boyfriend? Is that why you ran out on Garrett last night?"

"It's just Mom." Emma quickly deleted the text. Sutton's friends wouldn't understand why she'd left her birthday bash with Ethan, a mysterious boy who was more interested in stargazing than popularity. But Ethan was the sanest person Emma had met in Tucson so far—and the only person who knew who she really was and why she was here.

"So what exactly happened with Garrett?" Charlotte pursed her glossy, blackberry-tinted lips. From what Emma had gleaned in the past two weeks, Charlotte was the bossiest of their four-girl clique—and also the most insecure about her looks. She wore way too much makeup and talked too loudly, as though no one would listen to what she had to say otherwise.

Emma jabbed the ice at the bottom of her Bloody Mary with her straw. Garrett. Right. Garrett Austin was Sutton's boyfriend—or, more accurately, ex-boyfriend. Last night, his birthday gift to Sutton had been his naked, willing body and a pack of Trojans.

It had been painful to see the shattered look on my boyfriend's face when Emma rejected him. I could only guess at what our time together had been like, but I knew our relationship hadn't been a joke. Although now he probably thought that's what it had been to me.

Laurel's crystal-clear blue eyes narrowed as she took a sip of her drink. "Why did you run out on him? Does he look freaky naked? Does he have a third nipple?"

Emma shook her head. "None of that. It's my deal, not his."

Madeline pulled the wrapper off her straw and blew it in Emma's direction. "Well, you'd better find a rebound. Homecoming's in two weeks, and you need to snag a date before all the decent guys are spoken for."

Charlotte snorted. "As if *that's* ever stopped her?"

Emma flinched. Sutton had stolen Garrett from Charlotte last year.

It didn't make me the nicest friend, I admit. And from the doodles of Garrett's name on Charlotte's notebook and the pictures of him hidden under her bed, she was clearly still pining for him—which gave her a pretty solid reason to want me dead.

A shadow fell over the round table. A man with slicked-back hair and hazel eyes stood above Emma and the others. His blue polo was starched to a crisp and his khakis were perfectly pressed.

"Daddy!" Madeline exclaimed in a shaky voice, her controlled, cool-girl disposition instantly melting away. "I-I didn't know you were going to be here today!"

Mr. Vega gazed at their half-drunk glasses on the table. His nostrils twitched, as if he could smell the alcohol. The smile remained on his face, but it had a false edge that made Emma uneasy. He reminded her of Cliff, the foster father who sold used cars in a dusty lot near the Utah border and could swing from volatile dad to smarmy, ass-kissing salesman in four seconds flat.

Mr. Vega was silent a moment longer. Then he leaned forward and squeezed the top of Madeline's bare arm. She flinched slightly.

"Order anything you want, girls," he said in a low voice. "It's on me." He turned with military precision and started toward the brick-arched doorway to the golf course.

"Thanks, Daddy!" Madeline called after him, her voice trembling just slightly.

"That's sweet," Charlotte murmured hesitantly after he left, glancing sideways at Madeline.

"Yeah." Laurel traced her pointer finger around the scalloped edge of her plate, not making eye contact with Madeline.

Everyone looked like they wanted to say more, but no one did . . . or dared. Madeline's family was rife with secrets. Her brother, Thayer, had run away before Emma arrived in Tucson. Emma kept seeing his missing-person poster everywhere.

For just a moment, she felt a pang of nostalgia for her old life, her *safe* life—a feeling she'd never thought she'd have about her foster-care days. She'd come to Tucson thinking she'd find everything she'd always wished for: a sister, a family to make her whole. Instead, she'd found a family that was broken without even realizing it, a dead twin whose life seemed more complicated by the minute, and potential murderers lurking around every corner.

A flush rose on Emma's skin, the unspoken tension suddenly too much for her. With a loud scrape, she pushed her chair away from the table. "I'll be back," she said, fumbling through the French doors toward the bathroom.

She entered an empty lounge filled with mirrors, plush cognac-colored leather couches, and a wooden basket containing Nexxus hair spray, Tampax, and little bottles of Purell. Perfume lingered in the air, and classical music played through the stereo speakers.

Emma collapsed in a chair at one of the vanities and inspected her reflection in the mirror. Her oval face, framed by wavy sienna hair, and eyes that looked periwinkle in some lights, ocean-blue in others, stared back at her. They were the very same features as the girl whose image smiled happily from the family portraits in the

Mercers' foyer, the same girl whose clothes felt scratchy against Emma's skin, as if her body sensed Emma didn't belong in them.

And around Emma's neck was Sutton's silver locket—the same locket the killer used to strangle Emma in Charlotte's kitchen, the one Emma was sure Sutton had been wearing when she was murdered. Every time she touched the smooth silver surface or saw it glinting in the mirror, it reminded her that all of this, no matter how uncomfortable, was necessary to find her sister's killer.

The door swished open, and the sounds of the dining room rushed in. Emma whipped around as a blonde, college-age girl in a pink polo with the country club's logo on the boob crossed the Navajo-carpeted floor. "Uh, are you Sutton Mercer?"

Emma nodded.

The girl reached into the pocket of her khakis. "Someone left this for you." She proffered a Tiffany-blue ring-sized box. A small tag on the top read FOR SUTTON.

Emma stared, a little afraid to touch it. "Who's it from?"

The girl shrugged. "A messenger dropped it off at the front desk just now. Your friends said you were in here."

Emma took it hesitantly, and the girl turned and walked out the door. The lid lifted easily, revealing a velvet jewelry box. All kinds of possibilities flashed through Emma's mind. A small, hopeful part of her wondered if it was from Ethan. Or, more awkwardly, maybe it was from Garrett, trying to win her back.

The box opened with a creak. Inside was a gleaming silver charm in the shape of a locomotive engine.

Emma ran her fingers over it. A shard of paper poked up from the velvet pouch inside the lid. She pulled out a tiny rolled-up scroll to find a note written in block letters.

The others might not want to remember the train prank, but I'll be seized by the memory always. Thanks!

Emma jammed the note back into the box and shut it. *Train prank.* Last night, in Laurel's bedroom, she'd frantically skimmed through at least fifty Lying Game pranks. None of them had to do with a train.

The train charm etched itself in my mind and suddenly, a faint glimmer came to me. A train's whistle shrieking in the distance. A scream, and then whirling lights. Was it . . . were we . . . ?

But as quickly as it arrived, the memory sped away.

Photo by Daniel Snyder

SARA SHEPARD is the author of the #1 *New York Times* bestselling series Pretty Little Liars. She graduated from New York University and has an MFA in Creative Writing from Brooklyn College. Sara recently moved back to Philadelphia's Main Line from Arizona, where her new series, The Lying Game, is set.

For exclusive information
on your favorite authors and artists,
visit www.authortracker.com.

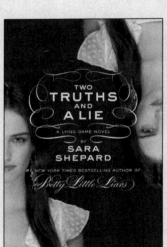

PRETTY GIRLS DON'T PLAY BY THE RULES...

THEY MAKE THEM.

DATE DUE

SEP 0 3 '13			
JAN 2 9 2015			
OCT 3 0 2015			
APR 1 0 2017			
SEP 1 4 2017			
OCT 2 2017			
OCT 2 3 2017			